OXFORD WORLD'S CLASSICS

THROUGH THE
LOOKING-GLASS

LEWIS CARROLL was the pseudonym of the Revd Charles Lutwidge Dodgson, born 27 January 1832 at Daresbury, Cheshire. He went to Christ Church, Oxford, in 1851, where he became a Senior Student, and lived there for the rest of his life. He was Mathematical Lecturer (1855–81) and was admitted as deacon in 1861, although he did not proceed to priest's orders. He was a noted photographer, especially of children, a prolific diarist, letter-writer, and pamphleteer; although in some ways reclusive, he had a wide range of acquaintances in literary and theatrical circles. His many mathematical publications include *Euclid and His Modern Rivals* (1879) and *Symbolic Logic* (1896). His two most famous books, *Alice's Adventures in Wonderland* (1865) and *Through the Looking-Glass, and What Alice Found There* (1872), were initially inspired by his friendship with Alice Liddell, the daughter of the Dean of Christ Church. He also published a facsimile of the original manuscript of *Alice's Adventures in Wonderland*, *Alice's Adventures Under Ground* (1886), and an adaptation for young children, *The Nursery Alice* (1890). *The Hunting of the Snark* (1876) is widely regarded as a surreal masterpiece, but his other works of fiction, *Sylvie and Bruno* (1889) and *Sylvie and Bruno Concluded* (1893), were not successful. He died at Guildford on 14 January 1898, and is buried there.

ZOE JAQUES is Professor of Children's Literature in the Faculty of Education, Cambridge University, and Dean of Homerton College. She has co-authored *Lewis Carroll's Alice's Adventures in Wonderland and Through the Looking-Glass: A Publishing History* (2013) and has written substantially about these books in *Children's Literature and the Posthuman* (2015). She runs an AHRC network on children's literature in US and UK archives and is co-general editor of the *Cambridge History of Children's Literature* in three volumes (2023).

OXFORD WORLD'S CLASSICS

*For over 100 years Oxford World's Classics have brought
readers closer to the world's great literature. Now with over 700
titles—from the 4,000-year-old myths of Mesopotamia to the
twentieth century's greatest novels—the series makes available
lesser-known as well as celebrated writing.*

*The pocket-sized hardbacks of the early years contained
introductions by Virginia Woolf, T. S. Eliot, Graham Greene,
and other literary figures which enriched the experience of reading.
Today the series is recognized for its fine scholarship and
reliability in texts that span world literature, drama and poetry,
religion, philosophy, and politics. Each edition includes perceptive
commentary and essential background information to meet the
changing needs of readers.*

OXFORD WORLD'S CLASSICS

——

LEWIS CARROLL

Through The Looking-Glass

——

Edited with an Introduction and Notes by
ZOE JAQUES

With illustrations by
JOHN TENNIEL

OXFORD
UNIVERSITY PRESS

OXFORD

UNIVERSITY PRESS

Great Clarendon Street, Oxford, OX2 6DP,
United Kingdom

Oxford University Press is a department of the University of Oxford.
It furthers the University's objective of excellence in research, scholarship,
and education by publishing worldwide. Oxford is a registered trade mark of
Oxford University Press in the UK and in certain other countries

Editorial material © Zoe Jaques 2022

The moral rights of the author have been asserted

First published as an Oxford World's Classics paperback 2022

Impression: 1

Published in the United States of America by Oxford University Press
198 Madison Avenue, New York, NY 10016, United States of America

British Library Cataloguing in Publication Data

Data available

Library of Congress Control Number: 2021951259

ISBN 978–0–19–886150–8

Printed and bound in Great Britain by
Clays Ltd, Elcograf S.p.A.

ACKNOWLEDGEMENTS

I AM extremely grateful for the extensive assistance of a number of people in the creation of this edition. Thanks are especially due to Peter Hunt, whose work for the previous Oxford University Press edition of *Wonderland* and *Looking-Glass* has provided the basis for this anniversary text. He has offered extensive advice throughout its preparation and has always been a generous supporter of my work. Selwyn Goodacre—guru of all things Alice—generously provided me with copies of his most recent work on the corrections to *Looking-Glass* and has been a long-time adviser on my scholarship. Thanks are also due to Jan Susina, with whom I have conversed extensively during the production of this text. Homerton College library, and Fellow Librarian Liz Osman in particular, have been incredibly generous with time and funds in sourcing reference materials—our ever-expanding collection of 'Alices' is quite the treasure trove. Doctoral scholar Lindsay Burton has tirelessly checked the text, helping to weed out those stubborn and peevish errors that threaten the sanctity of the work. Finally, thanks are owed to Eugene Giddens, who shares my love of Alice and provides gracious support of my research in untold ways.

CONTENTS

THROUGH THE LOOKING-GLASS

INTRODUCTION

Creating Alice's New Adventure

LEWIS CARROLL'S *Through the Looking-Glass, and What Alice Found There* is one of the best-loved tales from the golden age of children's literature. The period ushered in the rise of fantastical stories that celebrated childhood freedom, innocence, and play above moral and religious instruction. Lewis Carroll is often considered the herald of this age, especially in his ability to see the world through childhood wonder, empathizing thoroughly with a child's perspective. Although his *Wonderland*, published in 1865, is the iconic beginning of these attributes, *Through the Looking-Glass* not only sustains them, but introduces famous characters like Tweedledum and Tweedledee, Humpty Dumpty, and the Walrus and the Carpenter, alongside the enduring children's nonsense poem 'Jabberwocky'. *Looking-Glass* has never been out of print, and alongside its precursor it is one of the most famous works of British fiction, ranking with Dickens and Shakespeare in global recognition. It holds the rare status of being both canonical English literature and a children's perennial favourite, enjoyed by adults and children alike since its initial publication. This status means that few readers are likely to come to this edition without some knowledge of *Through the Looking-Glass*, whether through pop-cultural references in music or film, or through full-scale adaptations as found in the various Disney versions. This introduction, therefore, assumes familiarity with the text, so new readers should treat the following discussion as an afterword instead of a preface.

When *Through the Looking-Glass* was published late in 1871, Lewis Carroll had already enjoyed phenomenal reputational and sales success with *Alice's Adventures in Wonderland*, which by then had been printed to twenty-eight thousand copies. The second *Alice* was guaranteed to be a top-seller. Carroll's preparations for a follow-up Alice story began very soon after *Wonderland* was published in late 1865. On 24 August 1866, Carroll advised Macmillan, his 'Alice' publisher, that he was considering a sequel: 'It will probably be some time before I again indulge in paper and print. I have, however, a floating idea of writing a sort of sequel to *Alice*, and if it ever comes to anything,

I intend to consult you at the very outset, so as to have the thing properly managed from the beginning.'[1] Carroll alludes here to the fact that *Wonderland* was subject to extensive delays. Rumours around that time stirred excitement over a potential new adventure: 'Long before the publication of his second tale people had heard that Lewis Carroll was writing again, and the editor of a well-known magazine had offered him two guineas a page, which was a high rate of pay in those days, for the story, if he would allow it to appear in serial form.'[2] Carroll was, however, set on a book—one that would match in every way, from cover to illustrations, the style of *Wonderland*.

Carroll had started to write his continuation, still untitled, by early 1868. His diary of 16 January records him producing 'a few pages to the 2nd. volume of *Alice*'.[3] A year later, on 12 January 1869, he sent the first chapter to Macmillan of a story now called '*Behind the Looking-Glass, and what Alice saw there*'.[4] Even at this stage the exact name of the new book was unsettled, but it would be framed by Alice travelling through a mirror. A specimen title page was produced for *Looking-Glass House, and What Alice Saw There* in 1870.[5] Carroll remained uncertain about the title, writing for advice about it from Macmillan, with the publisher responding on 24 March 1870: 'as to the main title I decidedly prefer the first form of words: "Behind the Looking-Glass". "Looking-Glass World" is too specific.'[6] Later that same day, Carroll must have written to Macmillan about the final choice, with Macmillan responding: '"*Through*" is just the word—you'll never beat it.'[7] By 10 August 1870, the periodical press was advertising the new book. The *Derby Mercury* of that day notes that 'Mr Lewis Carroll, author of that most charming book, "Alice's Adventures in Wonderland," has in the press a new work about the same dear little lady, and called "Through the Looking Glass, and what Alice found

---

[1] M. N. Cohen and A. Gandolfo (eds), *Lewis Carroll and the House of Macmillan* (Cambridge: Cambridge University Press, 1987), 44.

[2] S. D. Collingwood, *The Life and Letters of Lewis Carroll* (London: Thomas Nelson, 1898), 110–11.

[3] *Lewis Carroll's Diaries: The Private Journals of Charles Lutwidge Dodgson*, ed. E. Wakeling, 10 vols, (Luton: Lewis Carroll Society, 1992–2007), v. 379.

[4] *Diaries*, vi. 76.

[5] S. H. Williams, F. Madan, and R. L. Green, *The Lewis Carroll Handbook* (1931; London: Oxford University Press, 1962), 59.

[6] Cohen and Gandolfo (eds), *House of Macmillan*, 85.

[7] Cohen and Gandolfo (eds) *House of Macmillan*, 85.

there." It will have forty-two illustrations, by John Tenniel.'[8] The book, however, would not be fully 'in the press' for over a year.

Carroll had been meticulous about the production of *Wonderland*. He famously rejected, at enormous personal cost, the entire print run of the first edition. That same carefulness shaped the construction of *Looking-Glass*: 'As to how many copies we sell I care absolutely nothing: the only thing I *do* care for is, that all the copies that *are* sold shall be artistically first-rate.'[9] The author scrutinized every aspect of the second book's production. He, for instance, complained to Macmillan on 15 April 1870 that his ideas for the title page were not being sufficiently accommodated:

the printer doesn't follow out my directions. I want the large capitals to have *more below the line than above*: nearly twice as much. [. . .] Secondly, the 'AND' ought to be half-way between the two lines [. . .]. Thirdly, the 3 lines of title ought to be closer together and not so close to the top of the page. Fourthly, the comma and full-stop ought to be set lower.[10]

This quotation is typical of the care Carroll took to make everything just right, and that thorough attention to the details of spacing, typography, and punctuation of the first edition gives weight to the idea that subsequent editions should be based upon it.

Carroll was especially keen to reflect the inversions of the Looking-Glass world typographically. He sought Macmillan's advice on this matter on 24 January 1868, 'Have you any means, or can you find any, for printing a page or two, in the next volume of *Alice*, in *reverse*?'[11] Not, apparently, having much success from the publisher, he mentioned the idea again exactly a year later: 'I think I told you that I want to have 2 pages of "reverse" printing in the new volume—such as you must hold up to the looking-glass to read. To cut the whole on wood, like a picture, would be a very expensive process.'[12] It did turn out to be too difficult to manage using letterpress or other techniques, so in the first printed edition only the first stanza of 'Jabberwocky' is reversed, having been beautifully carved into a woodblock. Interestingly the confusions over this reversal led to the most famous error in the first

---

[8] *Derby Mercury*, 10 Aug. 1870, n.p.
[9] Cohen and Gandolfo (eds), *House of Macmillan*, 97.
[10] Cohen and Gandolfo (eds), *House of Macmillan*, 84.
[11] Cohen and Gandolfo (eds), *House of Macmillan*, 59.
[12] Cohen and Gandolfo (eds), *House of Macmillan*, 76.

edition, a misprinting of 'wade' for 'wabe' in the 'Jabberwocky' poem, with a 'b' the woodcarvers have correctly reversed, but the typesetters have mistakenly 'corrected'. Carroll repeatedly had samples set in galley proofs, negotiated the placement and style of each illustration, and considered all components of the book from binding to title page to individual page design. Carroll records in his diary that 'The volume has cost me, I think, more trouble than the first, and *ought* to be equal to it in every way.'[13] Fastidiousness did not eliminate all errors, but it did ensure that the relationship between author and the first published text is unusually close.

As well as struggling with the printer over his textual and page-design wishes, Carroll faced particular problems in securing suitable illustrations. John Tenniel, the celebrated artist behind the forty-two *Wonderland* woodcuts, was not keen to contribute to *Looking-Glass*. Much later Tenniel expressed exasperation over working with Carroll at all: 'Dodgson is impossible! You will never put up with that conceited Don for more than a week!'[14] Certainly Carroll's fastidiousness did not suit Tenniel's considerably more relaxed working methods, and there is evidence that the illustrator refused to be employed by the author several times over the course of 1867 and 1868, when Carroll had to consider other artists, including Richard Doyle, Tenniel's fellow illustrator for *Punch*, and Sir Noël Paton, illustrator for Charles Kingsley's *The Water-Babies*. In June 1868, it seems that Tenniel's services were secured and a loose timetable was agreed: 'On the 18th I wrote to Tenniel, finally accepting his kind offer to do the pictures (at such spare times as he can find) for the 2nd volume of *Alice*. He thinks it *possible* (though not likely) that we might get it out by Christmas 1869.'[15] But something went awry again later that year, as Carroll in October requested the services of illustrator John Proctor, who worked as 'Puck'.[16] Finally, in November 1868 an unenthusiastic Tenniel agreed to produce illustrations during spare moments: 'The 2nd volume of *Alice* will after all be illustrated by Tenniel, who has reluctantly consented, as his hands are full.'[17]

---

[13] *Diaries*, vi. 140.
[14] Cited in M. P. Hearn, 'Alice's Other Parent: John Tenniel as Lewis Carroll's Illustrator', *American Book Collector*, 4/3 (1983), 11–20, at 13.
[15] *Diaries*, vi. 37.
[16] *Diaries*, vi. 59 n.
[17] *Diaries*, vi. 59.

Despite this reticence on the illustrator's part, Carroll and Tenniel were able to work closely together. They had carefully reviewed every picture for *Wonderland*, which of course was illustrated after the story had already been drafted. The collaboration on *Looking-Glass* differed from that of *Wonderland* because the text and illustrations were prepared at the same time, influencing one another and therefore existing in continual flux. The 1870 sample title page for *Looking-Glass House* reports only 'forty-two illustrations by John Tenniel', for instance. In 1992, Edward Wakeling discovered an illustration plan for *Through the Looking-Glass* in the archives of Christ Church, Oxford.[18] This plan discloses that the intended illustrations for the second *Alice* changed as author and illustrator worked together. It is also clear that Carroll did not develop a full conception of the contents of *Looking-Glass* himself until well into the period of illustration. The fifty illustrations of *Looking-Glass* would be two years in the making. The first ten or so sketches were completed in January 1870, and the final illustrations were not ready until the very end of 1871. It is difficult to ascribe all the blame for delays to Tenniel, as Carroll was very particular over the development of the illustrations, too. Special care was exercised over the Jabberwock illustration, for instance. It was meant to be the frontispiece, but Carroll was concerned that it would make too terrifying an opening to his story. His nephew, Stuart Dodgson Collingwood, records that 'On this point he sought the advice of about thirty of his married lady friends, whose experiences with their own children would make them trustworthy advisers; and in the end he chose the picture of the White Knight on horseback.'[19] The frightful Jabberwock became safely tucked away later in the first chapter and is replaced with a more romantic frontispiece.

Tenniel's work, or unwillingness to work, also shaped the textual contents of *Looking-Glass*. Carroll had drafted a section on 'The Wasp in the Wig' as a contribution to Chapter 8, but such a character, argued Tenniel, was 'altogether beyond the appliances of art'.[20] He wrote to Carroll on 1 June 1870: 'Don't think me brutal, but I am bound to say that the "*wasp*" chapter doesn't interest me in the least,

---

[18] E. Wakeling, 'The Illustration Plan for Through the Looking-Glass', *Jabberwocky*, 21 (1992), 27–35.

[19] Collingwood, *Life and Letters*, 118–19.

[20] Collingwood, *Life and Letters*, 123.

& I can't see my way to a picture. If you want to shorten the book, I can't help thinking–with all submission–that *there* is your opportunity.'[21] The episode was removed at a fairly late stage of the book's production, as it made it to galley-proof, and these proofs were rediscovered in 1974.[22] Before this discovery, the episode was known only through the Tenniel letters. The scene adopts the typical *Looking-Glass* pattern of Alice encountering a somewhat perplexed and perplexing older character. The Wasp is rendered particularly ill-humoured and peevish, while also having something of the White Knight and White Queen about him in being rather helpless. There has been some debate about the origins of those rediscovered galley-proofs, particularly about when they might have been set and the authenticity of marginal annotations to them.[23] As the provenance before 1974 has not been verified, unscrupulous interference is certainly a possibility. Others have objected to the piece being Carroll's at all on the grounds of its poor quality, but, as Martin Gardner points out, Carroll 'frequently had a book set in type long before he began to work in earnest on revisions', so the wasp episode might be a draft.[24] Whatever the status of this fragment, Carroll took up Tenniel's suggestion, and 'The Wasp in the Wig' was kept from the eyes of early readers, and therefore it is not included in this edition.

Tenniel also worked closely with Carroll on more minor shifts to the story and its illustrations. In the same letter that recommends removing the 'Wasp' fragment, Tenniel suggests that in the train carriage Alice should 'lay hold of the Goat's *beard* as being the object nearest to her hand—instead of the old lady's hair'.[25] In the final version of the text, the old lady is excised entirely. Several critics have argued that Tenniel also introduces the politician Benjamin Disraeli as the passenger clad in the paper hat in this scene, in keeping with his long-standing history of representing the prime minister for *Punch*

---

[21] M. Gardner (ed.), *The Annotated Alice: The Definitive Edition* (New York: Norton, 1999), 297.

[22] See Gardner (ed.), *Annotated Alice*, 293–308.

[23] See W. Weaver, 'Ink and Pen used by Lewis Carroll', *Jabberwocky*, 4/1 (1975), 3–4; and S. Goodacre, 'Consideration of Physical Factors', *Jabberwocky*, 7/2 (1978), 71–4, at 73.

[24] Gardner (ed.), *Annotated Alice*, 301.

[25] Gardner (ed.), *Annotated Alice*, 297.

magazine.[26] Tenniel requested that Carroll change 'The Walrus and the Carpenter | Were walking hand-in-hand' to 'close at hand', and chose the Carpenter for the Walrus's companion out of Carroll's proposed 'carpenter', 'baronet', or 'butterfly'.[27] Tenniel clearly held the power to add, remove, and alter characters, and we must assume that in other, now lost, correspondence and meetings there were further negotiations and changes. The text–image relationships found in *Through the Looking-Glass* therefore emerged slowly, but carefully. Even so, Carroll found cause to complain of the first print run 'that several of the pictures have [. . .] lost all *brilliance* of effect' because the ink was hastily dried to facilitate the quick binding required for Christmas sales.[28] Given the importance of the gift market, Macmillan did all they could to ensure the second *Alice* was published by December 1971.

The First Edition and Its Reception

The text and carefully placed illustrations were delivered late in 1871 and quickly printed, bound, and published in time for the Christmas 1871 market, with a first print run of 9,000 copies, far outstripping *Wonderland*'s 2,000-copy first edition. One 'trouble' with the publication of *Looking-Glass* was the near-simultaneous release of three separate issues in Britain and America: in Boston by Lee and Shepard, and New York by Lee, Shepard and Dillingham; separately by Macmillan's US office as 'London and New York'; and in London by Macmillan—which is usually regarded as the 'first' edition, but has no primacy over the US releases. These issues have different title pages, all dated 1872 (it was common practice to post-date December publications), but the body of the text is the same. The variant title pages and complete text were printed by Richard Clay in London by electrotype from formes of set type and woodblocks. The first 2,000

[26] For a discussion of the history of this identification, first proposed by William Empson in *Some Versions of Pastoral* (London: Chatto and Windus, 1935), see M. Hancher, *The Tenniel Illustrations to the 'Alice' Books* (2nd edn, Columbus, OH: Ohio State University Press, 2019), 115–16.

[27] See M. N. Cohen and E. Wakeling (eds), *Lewis Carroll and His Illustrators: Collaboration and Correspondence, 1865–1898* (New York: Cornell University Press, 2003), 170–1.

[28] Cohen and Gandolfo (eds), *House of Macmillan*, 97.

sets of sheets were shipped by steamer to Lee and Shepard on 2 December 1871. The US publishers had ordered a total of 3,000 initial copies.[29] Carroll received his own copies on 6 December 1871, which can be roughly accounted the UK publication date.[30]

The book was designed to match the physical format of *Wonderland*. Clay printed it in octavo, measuring 190 mm by 13.5 mm to match the format of *Wonderland*, but, at 224 pages, it is longer than the first 'Alice'. It is also more complex in its make-up, not only with eight additional images, but also with the paratextual components of Dramatis Personæ and chess schema, and tissue paper protecting the frontispiece. UK copies are bound in red cloth and black endpapers by Burn and Company, who also bound *Wonderland*. The stern Red Queen appears on the front cover (replicating Tenniel's 'Live Flowers' illustration) and the bedraggled White Queen (from 'Wool and Water') on the rear in gold inlay, surrounded by triple-lined cartouches. The spine reads 'THROUGH THE LOOKING GLASS' in a size slightly larger than the 'ALICE'S ADVENTURES IN WONDERLAND' of the first book, but otherwise they are a matched pair. The US copies were probably bound by Lee and Shepard to imitate the Macmillan bindings, but were offered in red, green, or blue cloth. The format, in keeping with Carroll's wishes, is what we might today consider adult-centric, a formal and restrained aesthetic, but it is very much in keeping with Macmillan's house style, similar to Edwin Abbott's *The Good Voices* (1872) or Charles Kingsley's *Glaucus* (1873), even if competing publishers like Thomas Nelson, Routledge, and Frederick Warne were by 1871 producing books with brighter covers, using more gold or, indeed, full-colour pictures. Most importantly, the cover is modelled on *Wonderland*, which itself imitated the format, but not the green colour, of Charles Kingsley's *The Water-Babies* of 1863.

While the US edition did not sell particularly well—Lee and Shepard did not request additional copies—UK sales exceeded expectations, outstripping even *Wonderland*, at least in terms of sales in the first month. Six thousand additional copies had to be printed in haste. Carroll's diary records his excitement about early sales: 'Heard

---

[29] H. Bohem, 'The First Edition of Through the Looking-Glass', *Jabberwocky*, 13 (1984), 87–95.

[30] Bohem, 'First Edition', 92.

from Macmillan that they already have orders for 7,500 Looking-Glasses (they printed 9,000), and are at once going to print 6,000 more!'[31] (In comparison, the first edition of *Harry Potter and the Philosopher's Stone* was printed in only 5,500 copies.) The first edition of *Looking-Glass* was carefully crafted, and because of its high print run widely read and reviewed, making it an especially important document in children's literature, with a secure textual history. It therefore differs substantially from the rejected first edition of *Wonderland*, which was dispatched to America as faulty goods.

Early reviewers were waiting expectantly, and, owing to Macmillan's expert marketing and distribution channels, a variety of periodicals promoted the book. The *British Quarterly Review* noted that 'no Christmas book this year has been anticipated with anything like the eagerness excited by the announcement of this new story by the author of "Alice's Adventures in Wonderland"', calling the sequel 'delicious allegorical nonsense'.[32] As Carroll and Macmillan hoped, *Looking-Glass* was singled out as an ideal Christmas gift: 'It is a beautiful little book, illustrated, printed, and bound with extremely good taste, and just the thing for a Christmas present.'[33] Carroll's attention to detail and efforts in securing Tenniel's illustration met wide acclaim.

The Athenaeum was struck by the Jabberwock illustration, and, assuaging Carroll's fears, saw it as especially appropriate for young people: 'Much young blood will run cold with fright—children dearly love to be frightened—at the awe-inspiring portrait of the Apollyon-like Jabberwocky.'[34] Many, like the reviewer of *The Athenaeum*, celebrated Tenniel's pencil as much as Carroll's pen:

Mr. Tenniel's designs are masterpieces of wise absurdity. We may refer, for instance, to that in which the Oysters, incarnations of old-womanishness, are listening to the dulcet speech of the Walrus and the Carpenter [. . .] not to speak of some drawings which deserve still higher and more serious praise, such as that in which Alice is rowing the boat along the stream which is half river and half grocer's shop.[35]

[31] *Diaries*, vi. 189–90.
[32] 'Contemporary Literature', *British Quarterly Review*, 44 (Jan. 1872), 148.
[33] 'Things to Buy', *Judy, or the London Serio-Comic Journal*, 20 Dec. 1871, 79.
[34] 'Through the Looking-Glass, and What Alice Found There', *The Athenaeum*, 16 Dec. 1871, 787–8, at 787.
[35] *The Athenaeum*, 16 Dec. 1871, 787.

On 21 December 1871, *The Standard* writes, 'here are Mr. Carroll and Mr. Tenniel again in company, in a sequel called *Through the Looking-Glass, and What Alice Found There* (Macmillan). We do not know which is the better, that or this.' Time and again, Tenniel emerges as a champion of Carroll's style: 'the delicious refined nonsense of his present illustrations generally comes up to if it does not surpass what he drew in "Alice" aforetime'.[36]

Early reviewers were also drawn to the 'Jabberwocky' poem, sometimes seeing it as the jewel in Alice's crown. The *Pall-Mall Gazette* thought it excellent poetry: 'The vigour of this ballad in some places is as remarkable as its tender gravity in others [. . .] what pleases us most is the stanza with which the ballad begins and ends. Anything more affecting than those lines we rarely meet in the poetry of our day.'[37] Since Carroll's *Phantasmagoria* of 1869—also aimed at children but in verse instead of prose—was poorly reviewed and did not sell well, critics seemed surprised that he had a talent for poetry.

Not all reviewers were convinced that Carroll had quite lived up to the reputation of *Wonderland* in his sequel. The same paper that praised its poetry found *Looking-Glass* 'not, perhaps, quite so good, as a whole, as "Alice's Adventures in Wonderland," but there is not much to choose between them'.[38] The *Manchester Guardian* judged that 'we cannot say that we think Alice's last adventures by any means equal to her previous ones', but concluded that 'the author has surpassed all modern writers of children's books except himself'.[39] The *Saturday Review* thought that Carroll here 'has fallen but very little short of that most delightful of children's stories', at least to an adult ear, but that was not necessarily the case from a child's perspective: 'We have tried it by the best of all criticism; for we have had it read aloud to a number of little folk and have heard a dismal outcry raised, as the nurse, like a returning wave on a rising tide, kept sweeping them ruthlessly off one by one'.[40] This simultaneous agelessness and age-appropriateness had also been found in responses to *Wonderland*, but here it seems mixed with a slight taint of second-rate status, which thus makes it more appropriate for children alone. *The Examiner*

---

[36] *The Standard*, 21 Dec. 1871, 2.
[37] *Pall Mall Gazette*, 14 Dec. 1871, 11.
[38] *Pall Mall Gazette*, 14 Dec. 1871, 11.
[39] 'Literature', *Manchester Guardian*, 27 Dec. 1871, 3.
[40] 'Christmas Books', *Saturday Review*, 30 Dec. 1871, 859–60, at 860.

thought that *Looking-Glass*, 'though hardly as good as that altogether delightful book [*Wonderland*], is quite good enough to delight every sensible reader of any age [. . .]. And the best of all is that the book has no moral, and is nothing but a capital jumble of fun.'[41] *Turning Over New Leaves* had a similar take: 'The marvels Alice meets with in her rambles are of the utterly illogical and hidden-moral-less kind that delights children, while the interspersed bits of verse are highly ludicrous'.[42] *The Times* almost protests too much: 'there is literally no sense in it, no lurking moral, no covert satire, no meaning, so far as we read it, of any sort whatever'.[43] Just as Carroll's *Wonderland* was seen as a much-needed response to the heavily moralized novels then popular for children, like Charles Kingsley's *The Water-Babies*, *Looking-Glass* satisfied reviewers for being of a similar style. Few, however, perhaps owing to the pressures of reviewing books quickly for Christmas buyers, were able to spot Carroll's novel innovations that emerged in his sequel text.

A New World of Language and Verse

Readers have long debated the relative merits of *Wonderland* versus *Looking-Glass*, but arguably the second book shows signs of a more seasoned author of fantasy. Importantly, this book is conceived as a book (without the oral origins of *Wonderland*), and Carroll was able to devote more attention to its development in that form. A more literary approach is especially signalled by the inclusion of more startlingly original verse. As in *Wonderland*, Carroll mixes parodies of nursery rhymes and famous poems with his own compositions, but *Looking-Glass* takes special care not only to include new and better poetry, but also to discuss its relevance and meaning, as a metacommentary on his own practice.

'Jabberwocky' remains a favourite, memorized by generations of schoolchildren, and it is also Carroll's most original poem. It deploys an 8–8–8–6 structure to give pace and drama to the mortal combat. Carroll generally favoured 8- or 6-syllable lines, and *Looking-Glass*'s other original poems, like 'The Walrus and the Carpenter', alternate

---

[41] 'Christmas Books', *The Examiner*, 16 Dec. 1871, 1249–50, at 1250.

[42] *Turning Over New Leaves*, 6 Jan. 1872, 14

[43] 'Christmas Books', *The Times*, 25 Dec. 1871, 4.

trimeter and tetrameter lines. Carroll notes of such rhythm: 'In writing "The Walrus and the Carpenter," I had no particular poem in my
mind. The metre is a common one'.[44] When the composer William
Boyd asked to set music for the *Looking-Glass* poems (he had already
done so for *Wonderland*), Carroll responded in a letter of 1 December
1871: 'You are very welcome to set to music any of the verses in Through
the Looking-Glass. I'm afraid, however, that you will find the same difficulty in your way as in the case of the former volume—namely, that all
the verses at all like songs have well-known tunes already.'[45] As the
author acknowledges, he shows little metrical originality, keeping
rhythms straightforward and memorable for child audiences. That
being said, the vocabulary and philosophies of some of his *Looking-Glass*
poems are far more challenging than their *Wonderland* precursors.

Carroll builds upon the tradition of nonsense poetry, made especially popular by Edward Lear's *A Book of Nonsense* (1846), through
the juxtaposition of made-up words and inconceivable encounters.
Alice serves as a test case for how far Carroll can push these boundar-
ies, and she frequently has dubious responses to the verse she hears.
When Tweedledee asks, 'You like poetry?', Alice 'doubtfully' responds:
'Ye-es, pretty well—*some* poetry' (p. 43). The word 'poetry' appears
ten times in *Looking-Glass* (as opposed to zero occurrences in
Wonderland), providing a running commentary on verse form and
contents. On the one hand, Alice's knowledge of nursery rhymes, and
more importantly how they end, offers her some contextual comfort,
giving 'her the self-assurance and predictive powers of a Sybil' when
characters cite well-known rhymes to her.[46] On the other, Carroll's
nonsense creations and adaptations work to discombobulate the heroine, and no doubt most readers. That feeling of familiarity and unex-
pected confusion is a deliberate rhythm of Carroll's overall chess
framework, and the poems satisfyingly add to it.

Carroll's 'Jabberwocky' is a work that predates even *Wonderland*,
and his keenness to foreground it in the frontispiece shows that he
saw it, as did his reviewers, as a particularly important part of *Looking-
Glass*. Carroll first 'published' the opening of 'Jabberwocky' as

---

[44] *The Letters of Lewis Carroll*, ed. M. N. Cohen, 2 vols, (London: Macmillan, 1979), i. 168.
[45] *Letters*, i. 168.
[46] U. C. Knoeplfmacher, *Ventures into Childhood: Victorians, Fairy Tales, and Femininity*
(Chicago: University of Chicago Press, 1998), 217.

a 'Stanza of Anglo-Saxon Poetry' in the 1855 edition of *Mischmasch*, a journal he produced with his siblings for private circulation. In this early outing Carroll also glossed his portmanteau and invented words, but slightly differently from the meanings given by Humpty Dumpty in *Looking-Glass*. For instance, 'wabe' is 'the side of a hill' and 'mome' is 'grave' (i.e. solemn). The origins of the poem, therefore, make light fun of not only the serious canon of English letters, but also philology-driven attempts to parse nonsense. Humpty Dumpty embodies that overdetermined confidence in interpretation: 'I can explain all the poems that ever were invented—and a good many that haven't been invented just yet' (p. 69). He also exposes himself when his reading breaks down: ' "*mome*" I'm not certain about. I think it's short for "from home"—meaning that they'd lost their way, you know' (p. 71). And Alice, too, wryly rejects both more poetry and literary criticism when Humpty Dumpty offers further recitation, and she exclaims: ' "Oh, it needn't come to that!" [. . .] hoping to keep him from beginning' (p. 71). Humpty Dumpty does of course continue, but he manages to strip "meaning" from real words as well as nonsense ones:

'But "glory" doesn't mean "a nice knock-down argument," ' Alice objected. 'When *I* use a word,' Humpty Dumpty said in rather a scornful tone, 'it means just what I choose it to mean—neither more nor less.' (p. 68)

Power ultimately shapes discourse here, and Alice's knowledge of nursery rhymes or difficult words is defeated in favour of absolute rule: ' "The question is," said Humpty Dumpty, "which is to be master—that's all" ' (p. 68).

Other poetic encounters maintain Alice's droll stance of tempered enthusiasm and politeness, but she typically ends up disappointed and defeated by them. In the end the rewards of queenship come only through an enforced mastery over discourse, as Humpty Dumpty suggests they should. But Alice must have one final lesson about the meaninglessness of words. When Queen Alice approaches her own royal hall, there are two doorbells, the 'Visitors' Bell' and the 'Servants' Bell'. Alice is perplexed by this binary: 'There *ought* to be one marked "Queen," you know' (p. 105), while the nearby Frog explains that she should leave the door alone. Alice's 'I don't know what you mean' is met with the Frog's 'I speaks English, doesn't I?' (p. 106). Carroll then completely takes away Alice's direct powers of speech and comprehension, when Alice hears a song inside in her own voice.

> 'To the Looking-Glass world it was Alice that said,
> "I've a sceptre in hand, I've a crown on my head; (p. 106)

Alice finally gains queenship not through her own discourse, but through silencing those around her and embracing the non-sensical. When she enters the banquet celebrating her coronation, 'there was a dead silence the moment she appeared' (p. 107). The Red and White Queens subsequently try to prompt Alice to speak: 'Make a remark' (p. 108) and 'You ought to return thanks in a neat speech' (p. 110). But before the speech begins, 'all sorts of things happened in a moment' (p. 110) to bring Alice back through the Looking-Glass, with an audience of only her pet kitten. Alice is never given her final say in the Looking-Glass world, returning to a land where she can take comfort in the fact that animals, as far as she perceives them at least, will listen to her but not answer back.

Significantly, the final mention of poetry in the book comes when Alice, back at home, recounts her adventures to Kitty: 'there was one thing you *would* have enjoyed—I had such a quantity of poetry said to me, all about fishes!' (p. 116). But this celebration of poetry arises only once Alice has absolute control over the conversation: 'On this occasion the kitten only purred: and it was impossible to guess whether it meant "yes" or "no"' (p. 115). Alice becomes the recounter of tales and verse, instead of its resistant recipient.

Playfulness, Games, and Chess

Alice's narrative and linguistic mastery is shaped by a dream frame-work of playful nonsense, with the titular theme of a looking-glass as magical gateway quickly subsumed by a world of life-sized chess (albeit one where reflections and inversions will play a crucial part). As a mathematician, Lewis Carroll took a long-standing interest in games and play, including inventing his own board games, like *The Game of Logic* in 1886, and producing mirror-imaged handwriting. As *Wonderland* depends upon anthropomorphized playing cards, *Looking-Glass* deploys chess-piece encounters, to offer, according to Robert Douglas-Fairhurst, 'a much more purposeful narrative structure than the picaresque wanderings of Wonderland'.[47] Yet even the seeming rigorous rules of chess are deployed flexibly to ensure that there is more wonder and 'romps' to her adventure than rigid set-pieces. The narrative opens with Alice trying to wind up her worsted wool and the black kitten unrolling and entangling it by playing this 'grand game of romps' (p. 9). This moment introduces a more grown-up Alice than the girl of *Wonderland*, here engaging in female domestic labour—set in opposition to 'the boys getting in sticks for the bonfire' outside (p. 11). She starts with a task, firmly detached from childhood play, similar to the history lesson that opens *Wonderland*, but with a considerably more grown-up attitude. Alice is also firmly positioned indoors—no longer rowing in a boat or playing croquet, or even outside in a garden with the playing cards. She is, instead, pointedly isolated. It is also significant that the season is now winter, far removed from the July day of *Wonderland*. The seasonal shift makes chess, easily an indoor pursuit, particularly appropriate for *Looking-Glass*'s framework of play.

In talking to the black kitten, Alice mentions that she had just been playing chess, and she 'might have won, if it hadn't been for that nasty Knight' (p. 12). Chess was a popular game for adults and children in Victorian England, and Carroll, too, played chess and liked to solve chess problems. The 'real' Alice Liddell recalls learning chess in the period she associated with Carroll, and in fact learned the game from him before the creation of the story of *Wonderland*:

Much of *Through the Looking-Glass* is made up of [stories Carroll told the children], particularly the ones to do with chessmen, which are dated by the period when we were excitedly learning chess.[48]

Like the boat ride that presages *Wonderland*, then, the chess of *Looking-Glass* is part of a real-life connection between Carroll and the young Alice.

However, children (or adults) do not need to have much comprehension of the technicalities of chess to understand the *Looking-Glass* narrative, which has only the loosest of connections to the formal

[47] R. Douglas-Fairhurst, *The Story of Alice: Lewis Carroll and the Secret History of Wonderland* (London: Vintage, 2015), 190.

[48] Alice's recollections of Carrollian days, as told to her son, *Cornhill Magazine* (July 1932), 1–12; repr. in M. N. Cohen (ed.), *Lewis Carroll: Interviews and Recollections* (London: Macmillan, 1989), 83–8.

rules of the game. *Looking-Glass* is structured to trace Alice's advancement, as a white pawn, to the final rank of the board, thereby allowing
her to be promoted to queen. Only six moves are required for a pawn
to reach an opponent's back row, and in Carroll's version, Alice as
pawn advances the permitted, but not mandated, two squares in her
first move through the queen's third to the queen's fourth in her journey on the train.

Carroll's list of eleven moves defies chess logic, and is incomplete,
so it has frequently puzzled chess players. By adding missing moves
or completing the game with additional ones it is possible to show
various checkmates, as Carroll later insisted, but the point here is
Alice's direct journey from pawn to being 'Queened', by advancing to
the eighth row. It is not strictly speaking about whether white or red
wins or loses the purported match. In a note dated December 1896
Carroll explains his thinking behind the play:

As the chess-problem, given on the previous page, has puzzled some of my
readers, it may be well to explain that it is correctly worked out, so far as the
moves are concerned. The alternation of Red and White is perhaps not so
strictly observed as it might be, and the 'castling' of the three Queens is
merely a way of saying that they entered the palace: but the 'check' of the
White King at move 6, the capture of the Red Knight at move 7, and the
final 'checkmate' of the Red King, will be found, by any one who will take
the trouble to set the pieces and play the moves as directed, to be strictly in
accordance with the laws of the game.[49]

Carroll's narrative structure, with the moves according roughly to
Alice's advancement as pawn, is more important here than the strict
rules of the chess game. As with the playing cards of *Wonderland*, chess
allows Carroll to explore rigid social hierarchies and ranks. Alice disrupts in this book, however, not by denying those structures ('You're
nothing but a pack of cards'), but by playing the rules of them to gain
supremacy. This regimented play also means that Alice is generally
a politer and more engaged character in *Looking-Glass*—with the
order of the chess board offsetting the greater rowdiness of the card
table. Unlike the vertigo-inducing randomness she experiences in
Wonderland, Alice is also quite resolute in her aims here: 'Despite the
problems with multiple queenships, and despite the examples of both

the Red and White Queens (neither seem the sort of queen one would aspire to be), Alice is single-minded in her pursuit of becoming a queen'.[50] So the chess framework provides an order and narrative drive not present in the first book, but that does not mean that the formality is meant to be rigidly unexciting. As the Red Queen says: 'in the Eighth Square, we shall be Queens together, and it's all feasting and fun!' (p. 30) The question becomes—how 'fun' is the final success that Alice so doggedly pursues?

The Girlhood of Alice

Alice's *Looking-Glass* movement from pawn to queen is framed by a series of brief encounters with fantastical beings, much as it was in *Wonderland*, or as James R. Kincaid puts it, she faces 'a series of good-byes'.[51] These meetings and departures chiefly serve to teach Alice manners, often by telling her off for poor comportment. Of course, the reader is not meant to take such moments of chastisement at face value: the book plays with appropriate models of Victorian girlhood while also at times setting up challenges to that behaviour, revelling in modest transgression and the adultist fantasy of the polished, but slightly cheeky child. Importantly, Alice is sufficiently everyday to be identifiable. As Kiera Vaclavik points out, Alice's very clothes are designed to provide 'a degree of camouflage and inconspicuousness, ensuring that she blends in rather than stands out'.[52] Alice therefore becomes a kind of shorthand for the typical Victorian girl.

Although *Looking-Glass* was not published or received as a book 'for girls'—there is in fact much evidence that it was bought for and read by boys—the encounters of Alice are frequently gendered ones. *The Times* specifically praises Tenniel's 'thousand girlish gestures and sweet ways'.[53] Confrontations with knights, kings, Tweedledum and Tweedledee, Humpty Dumpty, and the Lion and the Unicorn are

---

[50] L. Mooneyham White, 'Domestic Queen, Queenly Domestic: Queenly Contradictions in Carroll's *Through the Looking-Glass*', *Children's Literature Association Quarterly*, 32 (2007), 110–28, at 117.

[51] J. R. Kincaid, *Child-Loving: The Erotic Child and Victorian Culture* (London: Routledge, 1992), 297.

[52] K. Vaclavik, *Fashioning Alice: The Career of Lewis Carroll's Icon, 1860–1901* (London: Bloomsbury, 2019), 62.

[53] 'Christmas Books', *The Times*, 25 Dec. 1871, 4.

framed as meetings with authority-figure males—even if they also
are figures of fun, or 'insane' as *The Times* puts it. In meetings with
female figures, like the flowers and queens, she is continually told off
for her appearance and deportment, and 'Alice didn't like being
criticised' (p. 24). While the male characters are quite comfortable
with their own ineptitudes, they do not hesitate to judge Alice,
too. Although they are for the most part non-threatening figures,
Tweedledum and Tweedledee give Alice a dressing-down when they
first meet: 'if you think we're alive, you ought to speak'. '"I'm sure
I'm very sorry," was all Alice could say' (pp. 41–2), indicating her
initial disempowerment when faced with even the most fanciful
males. Humpty Dumpty tells her that at 7 years and 6 months she
is 'An uncomfortable sort of age' (p. 67) and calls her name 'stupid'
(p. 65). The Unicorn regards Alice 'with an air of the deepest disgust'
(p. 81). These awkward situations, mimicking those of *Wonderland*,
can make it seem like Alice is 'in various ways bullied'.[54] Nonetheless,
it is possible to focus instead on Alice's pleasure and growth in
responding against such harsh words, as Douglas-Fairhurst does in
noting: 'Most of the time she appears to relish her new authority,
as she bosses around Tweedledum and Tweedledee, or deals with
a bunch of noisy flowers'.[55]

When the characters are not directly engaged in questioning or
mocking Alice's conduct, they show an unusual propensity towards
violence, which Alice regards with a mixture of bemusement and
timidity, but generally tries to circumvent with peaceful com-
promise. The words 'battle' and 'fight' are peppered throughout the
story; whenever two male figures encounter one another, as in chess,
they attempt a conquest. Significantly, Alice seems to regard this
fighting in gendered terms. When Tweedledee and Tweedledum prepare to battle: 'They looked so exactly like a couple of great schoolboys, that Alice couldn't help pointing her finger at Tweedledum,
and saying "First Boy!"' (p. 42). This ridiculous battle ends when
Alice proclaims 'you'd better not fight to-day', because of Tweedledee
and Tweedledum's respective headache and toothache. Alice here
hopes 'to make them a *little* ashamed of fighting for such a trifle' as

---

[54] F. D. Shi, '*Alice's Adventures in Wonderland* as an Anti-Feminist Text: Historical,
Psychoanalytical and Postcolonial Perspectives', *Women: A Cultural Review*, 27 (2016),
177–201, at 186.

[55] Douglas-Fairhurst, *The Story of Alice*, 192.

the rattle (p. 52). Although the fight of the Lion and the Unicorn largely happens outside Alice's company–'Alice could not make out which was which' (p. 79)–she similarly makes peace, or attempts to, by serving the plum cake to the Lion and the Unicorn in their break from battle, while 'the poor King was nearly shaking off his head, he trembled so much' (p. 83). When the Red Knight engages the White Knight in the final male contention, Alice again avoids intervention: ' "I wonder, now, what the Rules of Battle are," she said to herself, as she watched the fight, timidly peeping out from her hiding-place' (p. 86). Again, she explicitly wants to avoid both the conflict and its apparent results:

'It was a glorious victory, wasn't it?' said the White Knight, as he came up panting.

'I don't know,' Alice said doubtfully. 'I don't want to be anybody's prisoner. I want to be a Queen.' (p. 87)

The recurring violence, and Alice's resistance to it, becomes part of a narrative cycle that accords with the turn-based rules of chess—itself a game modelled on warfare—but alternates between emphasizing Alice's helplessness and agency as peacemaker.

Alice's encounters with female characters are, of course, no more satisfying, but are more heavily concerned with propriety. The word 'manners' is used only in female contexts, for instance, first prompted as Alice in her real world tells the kitten off: 'Really, Dinah ought to have taught you better manners!' (p. 10). Once she ventures through the Looking-Glass, in Alice's initial fantastical encounter, the flowers are particularly cruel. The Violet 'never saw anybody that looked stupider' (p. 24), while the Rose notes 'you're beginning to fade' (p. 25). Such criticisms prompt Alice's own threat of violence: 'I'll pick you!' (p. 24). In a recollection of powerful females from *Wonderland*, the Red Queen also is both harsh and heavily concerned with Alice's conduct: ' "Speak when you're spoken to!" the Queen sharply interrupted her' (p. 99). Yet Alice is more assertive in speaking with the females of *Looking-Glass*: ' "But if everybody obeyed that rule," said Alice, who was always ready for a little argument, "and if you only spoke when you were spoken to, and the other person always waited for *you* to begin, you see nobody would ever say anything——" ' (p. 99). Ultimately the Red Queen accuses Alice of having 'A nasty, vicious temper' (p. 100).

Critics have understandably read these various encounters in gendered terms. Interpretations range from promoting Alice as a feminist hero to critiquing her as a mundane middle-class Victorian girl. As William Empson, who was not a fan of Alice, notes: 'It depends what you expect of a child of seven.'[56] On the side of seeing Alice as protofeminist, Megan S. Lloyd endorses her potential as a role model for contemporary young women, because 'Alice bravely enters into a new world and takes care of herself.'[57] She is certainly undaunted by most situations, however dangerous or preposterous, in these books. For readers focusing on Alice's final victory, there is a great deal of satisfaction in the way in which she disentangles herself from the trials of (and by) the other characters. Her triumph appears easy and liberating: 'Alice has no need to kiss the frog beside her so as to reach the banquet beyond.'[58]

Other critics have, however, doubted Alice's agency or empowered status. Her chief characteristics of curiosity and adventurousness are, for Victorians, strongly associated with childhood vivacity, but this characterization was explicitly disassociated from expectations for adult women—a key consideration, as Lewis Carroll certainly preferred the company of young girls to even teenagers. It therefore might be misleading to find in Alice's assertiveness anything particularly radical. As Flair Donglai Shi points out, if Alice is 'seen as a girl belonging to a separate social group of innocent middle-class female children, rather than a general category of Victorian women, her "unconventional" characteristics actually do not breach any essential social norms of the mid-Victorian era'.[59] If, however, Alice is seen as a girl on the path to adulthood, as Judith Little does, then 'the feminist implications of Alice's sceptical attitude as she advances toward, and ultimately resists, Victorian womanhood' become highlighted.[60] This kind of black-or-white interpretation in part depends upon the evidence selected, as Alice seesaws between cowered acceptance and active resistance in almost every encounter. As Nina Auerbach astutely

[56] Empson, *Some Versions of Pastoral*, 259.
[57] M. S. Lloyd, 'Unruly Alice: A Feminist View of Some Adventures in Wonderland', in R. B. Davis (ed.), *Alice in Wonderland and Philosophy: Curiouser and Curiouser* (Hoboken, NJ: John Wiley and Sons, 2010), 7–18, at 16.
[58] Vaclavik, *Fashioning Alice*, 66–7.
[59] Shi, '*Alice's Adventures in Wonderland* as an Anti-Feminist Text', 183.
[60] J. Little, 'Liberated Alice: Dodgson's Female Hero as Domestic Rebel', *Women's Studies*, 3 (1976), 195–205, at 195.

puts it, Alice is 'simultaneously Wonderland's slave and its queen, its creator and destroyer as well as its victim'.[61]

A key question here is whether we view Alice as agent or as pawn in Carroll's fantastical—and possibly puerile—imagination. Because of the author's notorious fascination with the real-life Alice Liddell, the model for Alice, critics have frequently blurred Alice's relationship with the adults represented in the story with her relationship with the author himself. This identification is of course encouraged by Carroll, both in the text—' "I *am* real!" said Alice and began to cry' (p. 49)—and more significantly in the final metatextual poem, an acrostic spelling out 'Alice Pleasance Liddell'. Karen Coats sees Carroll as indulging his fantasies of desire and ownership: 'Carroll has so designed Alice's adventures that she is never in control of who she is or what she does. Alice, as a pawn, may move only in certain directions and may see only what is in the squares directly adjacent to her.'[62] Maria Nikolajeva similarly sees Alice as being demeaned by the author, who seems focused on 'making her lose her mental capacity and control of her body, and subjecting her to unlimited power from creatures that would normally be inferior to her'.[63]

Such contemporary criticisms were not fully available to original readers, who were largely ignorant of Carroll's relationship to Alice Liddell. Early reviewers instead saw the *Looking-Glass* hero as a character responding to fantastical situations. The reviewer for the *Manchester Guardian* noted that 'Alice is charmingly depicted throughout, sometimes grave, sometimes amused, sometimes alarmed. But nothing graces her better than the air of dainty dignity with which she is represented wearing her royal honours on becoming a Queen "in the eighth square".'[64] Alice certainly expresses a great deal of care in certain moments. She twice worries about hurting the feelings of others, with Tweedledum and Tweedledee and the White Queen (p. 42, p. 103), for instance. But if one might place a teleological reading upon such

---

[61] N. Auerbach, 'Falling Alice, Fallen Women, and Victorian Dream Children', *English Language Notes*, 20/2 (1982), 46–64, at 49.

[62] K. Coats, *Looking Glasses and Neverlands: Lacan, Desire, and Subjectivity in Children's Literature* (Iowa City: University of Iowa Press, 2004), 87.

[63] M. Nikolajeva, 'The Development of Children's Fantasy', in E. James and F. Mendlesohn (eds), *The Cambridge Companion to Fantasy Literature* (Cambridge: Cambridge University Press, 2012), 50–61, at 51.

[64] 'Literature', *Manchester Guardian*, 27 Dec. 1871, 3.

a series of vignettes, as the *Manchester Guardian* reviewer does, then Alice being crowned is not quite the end of her story.

The Ending and Continuation of Alice

In *Wonderland* Alice completes her adventures by famously declaring 'You're nothing but a pack of cards!' and waking up from her dream.[65] She transitions out of the *Looking-Glass* world through a somewhat more violent action:

'I can't stand this any longer!' she cried as she jumped up and seized the table-cloth with both hands: one good pull, and plates, dishes, guests, and candles came crashing down together in a heap on the floor. (p. 111)

Her royal banquet ends abruptly, owing to her frustration at the guests 'lying down in the dishes' and generally misbehaving (p. 110). This situation of course differs from the ending of *Wonderland*, too, in that Alice is not being herself threatened with the violence of 'Off with her head!'[66] Alice's *Looking-Glass* passion intensifies as she grabs the shrunken Red Queen and exclaims 'I'll shake you into a kitten, that I will!' (p. 112), and then wakes up in her chair with Kitty. Given the violence of this shaking, Tenniel's penultimate illustration of Alice holding the kitten might be seen as a particularly frightening instance of animal abuse. But Carroll's text, and Tenniel's final illustration, are gentler, peaceful even. Back through the Looking-Glass, Alice's final acts involve playful admonishments of the cats for their behaviour, mimicking the Red Queen: 'Sit up a little more stiffly, dear! [. . .] And curtsey while you're thinking what to—what to purr' (p. 115). Alice here is still very much the queen of her make-believe environment. Instead of wistfully watching the boys playing outside, or engaging with domestic work, she is able to play again.

Alice Liddell, 19 by the time *Through the Looking-Glass* was published, was unlikely to indulge in much childish play. Carroll's relationship with the real-life Alice had long since fizzled away—he hardly saw her—and the final acrostic ode is one of sad memory, instead of active anticipation. 'Still she haunts me, phantomwise' (p. 118) is certainly revealing here, alluding as directly as the author ever creatively gets to obsession. His poem quickly moves from Alice to

---

[65] Carroll, *Complete Works of Lewis Carroll* (London: The Nonsuch Press, 1939), 17.
[66] Carroll, *Complete Works*, 117.

more generic 'children yet, the tale to hear' (p. 118), and hear of course they would, over the decades, to the present day.

Alice's final concern with propriety and play is perfectly in keeping with Victorian notions of childhood, and how adults might benefit in turn from a kind of childish instruction: 'spending time [with children] allowed adults to feel that their own souls could be washed clean of the blots and scuff marks of experience, because if children were good for anything it was showing adults how to be good'.[67] Those conceptions of childhood have not entirely disappeared, yet each generation takes its own meanings from Alice. In the 150 years following its publication, *Looking-Glass* has enjoyed extraordinary vitality, not least because it is often conflated with *Wonderland* in adaptations for the stage or screen. It is telling that the 1951 Disney animation, *Alice in Wonderland*, includes as its subtitle '*An Adaptation of Lewis Carrol's* [sic] The Adventures of Alice in Wonderland *and* Through the Looking Glass'. Both stories have largely merged into one in the public imagination. As Michael Hancher puts it: 'Like Mickey Mouse, Alice lives in popular culture; she does not need books.'[68] Tweedledum and Tweedledee and the Walrus and the Carpenter are major characters in the Disney adaptation, and Alice herself is considerably, if not misleadingly, more assertive than Carroll's hero, shouting to the Queen of Hearts that she is a "Fat, pompous, bad-tempered old tyrant". Such revisions continue in Disney's 2010 *Alice in Wonderland* and 2016 *Through the Looking-Glass*, both of which deploy elements of *Looking-Glass*, like the prominent roles given to the Jabberwock, Bandersnatch, Jubjub Bird, and Vorpal sword in the 2010 film, where Alice becomes the 'champion' in armour, enhancing a sense of her heroism and agency. Although Disney's 2016 *Through the Looking-Glass* surprisingly has little connection to the book, excepting Humpty Dumpty, these films spend a great deal of time outside the *Wonderland* or *Looking-Glass* world, and are heavily concerned with Alice's successful resistance to being married off, occupying the roles of champion or sea captain instead of following Victorian domestic expectations.

---

[67] Douglas-Fairhurst, *Story of Alice*, 110.

[68] M. Hancher, 'Alice's Adventures', in J. H. McGavran (ed.), *Romanticism and Children's Literature in Nineteenth-Century England* (Athens, GA: University of Georgia Press, 2009), 202.

These deliberately feminist revisions show that the tenacious qualities of Carroll's Alice continue to be an inspiration even for less straight-laced times. With its multiple layers of dreaming, reflection, and play, and its powerfully memorable vignettes, readers of *Through the Looking-Glass* have always been able to find their own version of the hero and her companions. This flexibility, although no longer seen as mere fun without a 'moral', gives the book a timeless quality that makes it a fully worthy successor to *Wonderland*.

NOTE ON THE TEXT

LEWIS CARROLL made a number of revisions to the text of both *Wonderland* and *Looking-Glass* during his lifetime. The most significant changes were made in 1887, for the People's Editions of the books published that year, and in 1896 for the 6s. Editions published in 1897 (a year before Carroll's death).

Editors of the *Alice* books tend to emphasize final authorial intentions, working from the 1897 editions as the most authoritative indication of Carroll's last word on textual corrections. For this 2021 Oxford World's Classics Edition, I take the 1871 edition as my copytext and have chosen not to preserve the bulk of Carroll's subsequent alterations for several reasons. Firstly, *Looking-Glass*, unlike its sister text, has a fairly stable early textual history. For the initial fifteen years of its publication *Looking-Glass* saw few alterations (generally corrections to misprints), ensuring that for the majority of Carroll's lifetime contemporary readers encountered the work largely in the form presented here. Secondly, Lewis Carroll's final corrections to the text introduce complex anomalies, owning to his unusual editing practices. When making what would be his final revisions in 1896, Carroll was reticent to make use of his printer's file copies for he felt 'it would be a pity to spoil them by marking and correcting', electing instead to borrow old copies 'the spoiling of which does not matter'.[1] The editions he worked from belonged to a child friend named May Barber, and included the text of the 1880 *Looking-Glass*, thus predating the extensive corrections and alterations Carroll had made for the 1887 People's Edition. This dual set of extensive authorial corrections, the latter of which overlooked or forgot those of the former, ensures that producing a definitive or authoritative edition based on the author's final intentions is largely a matter of speculation. As a final point, in celebration of the 150th anniversary of the publication of *Looking-Glass*, it seems fitting that the text should be presented here largely as originally published.

---

[1] M. N. Cohen and A. Gandolfo (eds), *Lewis Carroll and the House of Macmillan* (Cambridge: Cambridge University Press, 1987), 344.

My guiding principle therefore has been to maintain the 1871 text except where that original is disruptive to the reading experience or includes obvious misprints that were later corrected (such as, most famously, the printer's error of making 'wabe' into 'wade' in the first stanza of 'Jabberwocky'). I have not preserved incidentals (such as the full stop to follow the title and chapter headings or original page references to the chess moves that have no relevance to the typesetting of this edition). I have maintained Carroll's use of double inverted commas for quotation and dialogue. Although this does not conform with contemporary UK usage, it is typical of Victorian punctuation. I have kept Carroll's original contractions, as opposed to his famous subsequent alterations to 'wo'n't', 'ca'n't', and 'sha'n't'. The majority of Carroll's later changes are small rearrangements or revisions to punctuation (the addition, subtraction, or substitution of commas, for example). In cases where a significant revision to content was made at a later stage, I provide brief reference in the accompanying commentary.[2]

Illustrations have been typeset as close to the original placement as possible. Virginie Iché has pointed out that 'the page-turning mechanism is exploited in extremely diverse ways in the *Alice* books' so that the 'layout of the original editions [. . .] regularly empowers the reader, who has kinesthetic experiences while reading the books'.[3] Iché's case applies most particularly to the precise relational positioning of text and illustration in the first editions. Whilst it is not possible in the context of a modern standardized edition, with different pagination, to recreate the physical experience of reading the original text, such observations do reflect the carefulness of the first printed edition and emphasize the importance of retaining its content.

---

[2] For full details of the extensive changes made by Carroll to the text of *Looking-Glass*, see S. Goodacre's 'Lewis Carroll's 1887 Corrections to *Alice*' (*The Library*, 28 (June 1973), 121–46) and 'Lewis Carroll's Alterations for the 1897 6s Edition of *Through the Looking-Glass*' (*The Carrollian*, 22 (2008), 11–24).

[3] V. Iché, 'Submission and Agency, or the Role of the Reader in the First Editions of Lewis Carroll's *Alice's Adventures in Wonderland* (1865) and *Through the Looking-Glass* (1871)', *Cahiers victoriens et édouardiens*, 16 (2016), 1–13, at 9.

SELECT BIBLIOGRAPHY

THROUGH THE LOOKING-GLASS is rarely critically read as a stand-alone text, and far more ink has been spent interpreting its older sister. Below is a selective bibliography of texts and articles from Carroll studies, which include discussion of both 'Alice' books as well as the broader biographical history and literary interests of Lewis Carroll. For specific attention to *Looking-Glass*, articles in *The Carrollian* (formerly *Jabberwocky*), which is the journal of the Lewis Carroll Society, are recommended.

Biographical

Bakewell, M., *Lewis Carroll: A Biography* (London: Heinemann, 1996).

Carroll, Lewis, *The Letters of Lewis Carroll*, ed. M. N. Cohen, 2 vols, (London: Macmillan, 1979).

Carroll, Lewis, *Lewis Carroll's Diaries: The Private Journals of Charles Lutwidge Dodgson*, ed. E. Wakeling, 10 vols, (Luton: Lewis Carroll Society, 1992–2007).

Clark, A., *Lewis Carroll: A Biography* (Dent: London, 1979).

Cohen, M. N. (ed.), *Lewis Carroll: Interviews and Recollections* (London: Macmillan, 1989).

Cohen, M. N., *Lewis Carroll: A Biography* (1995; London: Macmillan, 2015).

Collingwood, S. D., *The Life and Letters of Lewis Carroll* (London: Thomas Nelson, 1898).

Douglas-Fairhurst, R., *The Story of Alice: Lewis Carroll and the Secret History of Wonderland* (London: Vintage, 2015).

Hudson, D., *Lewis Carroll: An Illustrated Biography* (1954; London: Constable, 1976).

Leach, K., *In the Shadow of the Dreamchild: The Myth and Reality of Lewis Carroll* (1999; London: Peter Owen, 2009).

Stern, J., *Lewis Carroll: Bibliophile* (Luton: White Stone, 1997).

Taylor, R., and Wakeling, E., *Lewis Carroll, Photographer* (Princeton: Princeton University Press, 2002).

Thomas, D., *Lewis Carroll: A Portrait with Background* (London: John Murray, 1996).

Wilson, R., *Lewis Carroll in Numberland: His Fantastical Mathematical Logical Life* (London: Allen Lane, 2008).

Woolf, J., *The Mystery of Lewis Carroll*. (New York: St Martin's Press, 2010).

Textual History

Cohen, M. N., and Gandolfo, A. (eds), *Lewis Carroll and the House of Macmillan* (Cambridge: Cambridge University Press, 1987).

Godman, S., 'Lewis Carroll's Final Corrections to "Alice" ', *Times Literary Supplement*, 2 May 1958, 258.

Goodacre, S., 'Lewis Carroll's Alterations for the 1897 6s Edition of *Through the Looking-Glass*', *The Carrollian*, 22 (2008), 11–24.

Goodacre, S., 'Lewis Carroll's 1887 Corrections to *Alice*', *The Library*, 28 (June 1973), 121–46.

Iché, V., 'Submission and Agency, or the Role of the Reader in the First Editions of Lewis Carroll's *Alice's Adventures in Wonderland* (1865) and *Through the Looking-Glass* (1871)', *Cahiers victoriens et édouardiens*, 16 (2016), 1–13.

Jaques, Z., and Giddens, E., *Lewis Carroll's* Alice's Adventures in Wonderland *and* Through the Looking-Glass*: A Publishing History* (Aldershot: Ashgate, 2013).

Lovett, C., *Alice on Stage: A History of Early Theatrical Productions of 'Alice in Wonderland'* (Westport, CT: Meckler, 1978).

Reichertz, R., *The Making of the Alice Books: Lewis Carroll's Uses of Earlier Children's Literature* (Montreal: McGill-Queen's University Press, 1997).

Williams, S. H., Madan, F., and Green, R. L., *The Lewis Carroll Handbook* (1931; London: Oxford University Press, 1962).

Interpreting Alice

Beer, G., *Alice in Space: The Sideways Victorian World of Lewis Carroll* (Chicago: Chicago University Press, 2016).

Blake, K., *Play, Games and Sports: The Literary Works of Lewis Carroll* (New York: Cornell University Press, 1974).

Coats, K., *Looking Glasses and Neverlands: Lacan, Desire, and Subjectivity in Children's Literature* (Iowa City: University of Iowa Press, 2004).

Davis, R. B. (ed.), *Alice in Wonderland and Philosophy* (Hoboken, NJ: John Wiley & Sons, 2010).

Dusinberre, J., *Alice to the Lighthouse: Children's Books and Radical Experiments in Art* (London: Macmillan, 1999).

Fordyce, R. (ed.), *Semiotics and Linguistics in Alice's Worlds* (Berlin: de Gruyter, 1994).

Gardner, M. (ed.), *The Annotated Alice: The Definitive Edition* (London: Penguin, 2000).

Guiliano, E. (ed.), *Lewis Carroll: A Celebration* (New York: Clarkson N. Potter, 1982).

Hollingsworth, C. (ed.), *Alice Beyond Wonderland: Essays for the Twenty-First Century* (Iowa City: Iowa University Press, 2009).

Jones, J. E., and Gladstone, J. F., *The Red King's Dream; Or Lewis Carroll in Wonderland* (London: Pimlico, 1995).

Jones, J. E., and Gladstone, J. F., *The Alice Companion: A Guide to Lewis Carroll's Alice Books* (London: Macmillan, 1998).

Mooneyham White, L., 'Domestic Queen, Queenly Domestic: Queenly Contradictions in Carroll's *Through the Looking-Glass*', *Children's Literature Association Quarterly*, 32 (Summer 2007), 110–28.

Phillips, R. (ed.), *Aspects of Alice: Lewis Carroll's Dreamchild as seen through the Critics' Looking-Glasses 1865–1971* (London: Victor Gollancz, 1972).

Rackin, D., *Alice's Adventures in Wonderland and Through the Looking-Glass: Nonsense, Sense and Meaning* (New York: Twaync, 1991).

Schanoes, V., 'Queen Alice and the Monstrous Child: Alice through the Looking-Glass', *Children's Literature*, 45 (2017), 1–20.

Susina, J., *The Place of Lewis Carroll in Children's Literature* (London: Routledge, 2010).

Tosi, L., and Hunt, P., *The Fabulous Journeys of Alice and Pinocchio: Exploring Their Parallel Worlds* (Jefferson, NC: McFarland, 2018).

Turner, B., '"Which Is to Be Master?": Language as Power in *Alice in Wonderland* and *Through the Looking-Glass*', *Children's Literature Association Quarterly*, 35 (2010), 243–54.

Zirker, A., '"All about fishes"? The Riddle of Humpty Dumpty's Song and Recursive Understanding in Lewis Carroll's *Through the Looking-Glass and What Alice Found There*', *Victorian Poetry*, 56 (Spring 2018), 81–102.

Afterlives

Brooker, W., *Alice's Adventures: Lewis Carroll in Popular Culture* (New York: Continuum, 2004).

Sigler, C., *Alternative Alices: Visions and Revisions of Lewis Carroll's Alice Books* (Lexington, KY: University Press of Kentucky, 1999).

Weaver, W., *Alice in Many Tongues: The Translations of Alice in Wonderland* (Madison, WI: University of Wisconsin Press, 1964).

Illustration and the Visual Arts

Cohen, M., and Wakeling, E. (eds), *Lewis Carroll and His Illustrators: Collaboration and Correspondence, 1865–1898* (New York: Cornell University Press, 2003).

Delahunty, G., and Schulz, C. B. (eds), *Alice in Wonderland Through the Visual Arts* (London: Tate, 2011).

Hancher, M., *The Tenniel Illustrations to the 'Alice' Books* (2nd edn, Columbus, OH: Ohio State University Press, 2019).

Morris, F., *Artist of Wonderland: The Life, Political Cartoons, and Illustrations of Tenniel* (Charlottesville, VA: University of Virginia Press, 2005).

Ovenden, G. (ed.), *The Illustrators of Alice in Wonderland and Through the Looking Glass* (London: Academy Editions, 1979).

Simpson, R., *Sir John Tenniel: Aspects of His Work* (Rutherford, NJ: Fairleigh Dickinson University Press, 1994).

Stoffell, S. L., *The Art of Alice in Wonderland* (New York: Smithmark, 1998).

Vaclavik, K., *Fashioning Alice: The Career of Lewis Carroll's Icon, 1860–1901* (London: Bloomsbury Academic, 2019).

A CHRONOLOGY OF
C. L. DODGSON/'LEWIS CARROLL'

1827 The Revd Charles Dodgson marries Frances Jane Lutwidge, and is presented to the living of Daresbury, Cheshire.

1832 (27 Jan.) Charles Lutwidge Dodgson, third child and first son, born at Daresbury Parsonage.

1839 Catherine Sinclair, *Holiday House*.

1843 Family moves to Croft, near Richmond, Yorkshire; father becomes Rector.

1844–5 Attends Richmond School.

1845 Composes first 'family magazine', *Useful and Instructive Poetry* (published 1954).

1846 Edward Lear, *A Book of Nonsense*.

   Attends Rugby School.

1848 Heinrich Hoffman, *The English Struwwelpeter*.

1849 Returns to Croft to prepare for Oxford; has mumps, which leave him permanently deaf in his right ear; writes *The Rectory Umbrella* (to 1850).

1851 (24 Jan.) Comes into Residence at Christ Church, Oxford; death of his mother. John Ruskin, *King of the Golden River*.

1852 1st Class in Mathematical and 2nd in Classical Moderations; nominated by Dr Pusey to a studentship.

1854 1st Class in Mathematics (Final Schools); spends summer being coached by Bartholomew Price at Whitby for his mathematics examination; first publications, in *The Whitby Gazette*; BA; epidemic of cholera at Oxford.

1855 (1 Jan.) Begins diary; (8 Sept.) 'She's All My Fancy Painted Him' (first version of poem in *Alice's Adventures in Wonderland*, chapter 12) published in *Comic Times*; made 'A Master of the House' and Senior Student; 'Stanza of Anglo-Saxon Poetry' (first stanza of 'Jabberwocky') written in family magazine, *Mischmasch*; Henry George Liddell appointed Dean of Christ Church. W. M. Thackeray, *The Rose and the Ring*.

1855–7   Sub-librarian at Christ Church (salary £35).

1855–81   Lecturer in Mathematics at Christ Church.

1856   (Mar.) First uses pseudonym 'Lewis Carroll' to poem 'Solitude' in *The Train* (i. 154–5); (18 Mar.) buys first camera, made by Thomas Ottewill for £15 (delivered 1 May); (25 Apr.) meets Lorina, Alice, and Edith Liddell.

1857   Takes MA; (May) meets Thackeray; (June) meets Holman Hunt; (Sept.) meets Tennyson; (Oct.) meets Ruskin; (Dec.) 'Hiawatha's Photographing' published in *The Train*.

1858   Publication of his first book: *The Fifth Book of Euclid treated Algebraically*, 'By a College Tutor'. George MacDonald's *Phantastes*.

1859   Begins therapy for his 'stammer' with Dr James Hunt at Hastings; meets George MacDonald.

1860   Publication of his first acknowledged book, *A Syllabus of Plane Algebraical Geometry*, 'by Charles Lutwidge Dodgson'; publishes 'A Photographer's Day Out' in the *South Shields Amateur Magazine*.

1861   (22 Dec.) Admitted to Deacon's Orders ('regard myself . . . as practically a layman') by Samuel Wilberforce, Bishop of Oxford.

1862   River trips with Liddell sisters: genesis of *Alice's Adventures in Wonderland*; (13 Nov.) begins writing. Christina Rossetti, *Goblin Market*.

1863   (10 Feb.) Completes *Alice's Adventures under Ground*; (May) sends MS of *Alice's Adventures in Wonderland* to the Mac-Donalds; (June) estrangement from Liddell family; (Sept.) first visits Dante Gabriel Rossetti at Cheyne Walk, Chelsea; (Oct.) meets Alexander Macmillan; John Tenniel agrees to illustrate the book. Charles Kingsley's *The Water Babies*.

1864   (26 Nov.) Sends hand-lettered copy of *Alice's Adventures under Ground* to Alice Liddell.

1865   (27 June) Receives first copies of *Alice's Adventures in Wonderland*; (14 July) photographs Ellen Terry; (2 Aug.) orders reprint of *Alice*; (14 Dec.) sends copy to Alice Liddell.

1866 (June) Meets Charlotte M. Yonge.

1867 (12 July–14 Sept.) Travels with Henry Parry Litton to Moscow (his only trip abroad); (Dec.) publishes 'Bruno's Revenge' in *Aunt Judy's Magazine*, iv; Electoral Reform Act. 'Hesba Stretton', *Jessica's First Prayer*.

1868 (21 June) Death of his father: 'the greatest blow that has ever fallen on my life'; moves into rooms on Tom quad, which he occupies for the rest of his life; leases 'The Chestnuts', Guildford; begins *Through the Looking-Glass*. Louisa May Alcott, *Little Women*.

1869 (Jan.) Publication of *Phantasmagoria, and Other Poems*; (12 Jan.) 'Finished and sent to Macmillan the first chapter of *Behind the Looking-Glass, and What Alice Saw There*'; first German and French translations of *Alice's Adventures in Wonderland*. Jean Ingelow, *Mopsa the Fairy*.

1870 (4 Jan.) 'Finished the MS of *Through the Looking-Glass*'.

1871 (Dec.) *Through the Looking-Glass* published (9,000 copies, dated 1872).

1872 First Italian translation of *Alice's Adventures in Wonderland*; *The New Belfry of Christ Church, Oxford*.

1874 First Dutch translation of *Alice's Adventures in Wonderland*; publication of *Notes by an Oxford Chiel*. Christina Rossetti, *Speaking Likenesses*.

1875 (June) 'Some Popular Fallacies about Vivisection', *Fortnightly Review*. Tom Hood, *From Nowhere to the North Pole*.

1876 (29 Mar.) Publication of *The Hunting of the Snark*.

1877 (31 July) Takes rooms at 27 Lushington Road, Eastbourne, for the summer; he returns to them each summer for the rest of his life.

1878 45th thousand of *Through the Looking-Glass*.

1879 (Mar.) Publication of *Euclid and his Modern Rivals*; *Doublets, a Word Puzzle*.

1880 (July) Gives up photography; marriage of Alice Liddell to Reginald Hargreaves; begins *A Tangled Tale* in *The Monthly Packet*.

1882–92 Curator of Christ Church Common Room.

1882 Richard Jefferies, *Bevis*.

1883   (6 Dec.) Publication of *Rhyme? and Reason?* Robert Louis
        Stevenson, *Treasure Island*.

1884   (Nov.) *The Principles of Parliamentary Representation*.

1885   Criminal Law Amendment Act raises age of consent to 16;
        (22 Dec.) publication of *A Tangled Tale*.

1886   (22 Dec.) Publication of *Alice's Adventures under Ground*;
        (23 Dec.) first night of Henry Savile Clarke's 'Dream Play',
        Alice in Wonderland (Prince of Wales Theatre; the play was
        published in early 1887—dated 1886). Frances Hodgson
        Burnett, *Little Lord Fauntleroy*.

1887   (21 Feb.) Publication of *The Game of Logic* (an edition printed
        in 1886 was cancelled and sold to America).

1888   *Curiosa Mathematica: A New Theory of Parallels*.

1889   (12 Dec.) Publication of *Sylvie and Bruno*. Andrew Lang, *The
        Blue Fairy Book*.

1890   Publication of *The Nursery Alice, Eight or Nine Wise Words
        about Letter-Writing*, and (July) the *Wonderland Stamp Case*.

1893   (29 Dec.) Publication of *Sylvie and Bruno Concluded*; *Pillow
        Problems (Curiosa Mathematica II)*.

1894   Rudyard Kipling, *The Jungle Book*.

1895   G. E. Farrow, *The Wallypug of Why*; Kenneth Grahame, *The
        Golden Age*.

1896   (21 Feb.) Publication of *Symbolic Logic, Part 1*.

1898   (14 Jan.) Dies at 'The Chestnuts', Guildford; (Feb.) pub-
        lication of *Three Sunsets and Other Poems*; (Dec.) *The Life and
        Letters of Lewis Carroll* (dated 1899).

THROUGH THE
LOOKING-GLASS,
AND WHAT ALICE
FOUND THERE

RED.

WHITE.

White Pawn (Alice) to play, and win in eleven moves.

DRAMATIS PERSONÆ

(As arranged before commencement of game.)

WHITE.			RED.
PIECES.	PAWNS.	PAWNS.	PIECES.
Tweedledee	Daisy.	Daisy	Humpty Dumpty.
Unicorn	Haigha.	Messenger	Carpenter.
Sheep	Oyster.	Oyster	Walrus.
W. Queen	"Lily."	Tiger-lily	R. Queen.
W. King	Fawn.	Rose	R. King.
Aged man	Oyster.	Oyster	Crow.
W. Knight	Hatta.	Frog	R. Knight.
Tweedledum	Daisy.	Daisy	Lion.

CHILD of the pure unclouded brow*
 And dreaming eyes of wonder!
Though time be fleet, and I and thou
 Are half a life asunder,*
Thy loving smile will surely hail
The love-gift of a fairy-tale.*

I have not seen thy sunny face,
 Nor heard thy silver laughter;*
No thought of me shall find a place
 In thy young life's hereafter—*
Enough that now thou wilt not fail
To listen to my fairy-tale.

A tale begun in other days,
 When summer suns were glowing—
A simple chime, that served to time
 The rhythm of our rowing—*
Whose echoes live in memory yet,
Though envious years would say 'forget.'

Come, hearken then, ere voice of dread,
 With bitter tidings laden,
Shall summon to unwelcome bed
 A melancholy maiden!
We are but older children,* dear,
Who fret to find our bedtime* near.

Without, the frost, the blinding snow,
 The storm-wind's moody madness—
Within, the firelight's ruddy glow,
 And childhood's nest of gladness.*
The magic words shall hold thee fast:
Thou shalt not heed the raving blast.

And, though the shadow of a sigh
 May tremble through the story,
For 'happy summer days'* gone by,
 And vanish'd summer glory—
It shall not touch with breath of bale*
The pleasance* of our fairy-tale.

CONTENTS

CHAPTER I

LOOKING-GLASS HOUSE

ONE thing was certain,* that the *white* kitten had had nothing to do with it:—it was the black kitten's* fault entirely. For the white kitten had been having its face washed by the old cat* for the last quarter of an hour (and bearing it pretty well, considering); so you see that it *couldn't* have had any hand in the mischief.

The way Dinah washed her children's faces was this: first she held the poor thing down by its ear with one paw, and then with the other paw she rubbed its face all over, the wrong way, beginning at the nose: and just now, as I said, she was hard at work on the white kitten, which was lying quite still and trying to purr—no doubt feeling that it was all meant for its good.

But the black kitten had been finished with earlier in the afternoon, and so, while Alice was sitting curled up in a corner of the great arm-chair, half talking to herself and half asleep, the kitten had been having a grand game of romps with the ball of worsted* Alice had been trying to wind up, and had been rolling it up and down till it had all come undone again; and there it was, spread over the hearth-rug, all knots and tangles, with the kitten running after its own tail in the middle.

"Oh, you wicked* wicked little thing!" cried Alice, catching up the kitten, and giving it a little kiss to make it understand that it was in disgrace. "Really, Dinah ought to have taught you better manners! You *ought*, Dinah, you know you ought!" she added, looking reproach-fully at the old cat, and speaking in as cross a voice as she could manage—and then she scrambled back into the arm-chair, taking the kitten and the worsted with her, and began winding up the ball again. But she didn't get on very fast, as she was talking all the time, some-times to the kitten, and sometimes to herself. Kitty sat very demurely on her knee, pretending to watch the progress of the winding, and now and then putting out one paw and gently touching the ball, as if it would be glad to help if it might.

"Do you know what to-morrow is, Kitty?" Alice began. "You'd have guessed if you'd been up in the window with me—only Dinah was making you tidy, so you couldn't. I was watching the boys getting in sticks for the bonfire—and it wants plenty of sticks, Kitty! Only it got so cold, and it snowed so, they had to leave off. Never mind, Kitty, we'll go and see the bonfire to-morrow."* Here Alice wound two or three turns of the worsted round the kitten's neck, just to see how it would look: this led to a scramble, in which the ball rolled down upon the floor, and yards and yards of it got unwound again.

"Do you know, I was so angry, Kitty," Alice went on, as soon as they were comfortably settled again, "when I saw all the mischief you had been doing, I was very nearly opening the window, and putting you out into the snow! And you'd have deserved it, you little mischievous darling! What have you got to say for yourself? Now don't interrupt me!" she went on, holding up one finger. "I'm going to tell you all your faults. Number one: you squeaked twice while Dinah was washing your face this morning. Now you can't deny it, Kitty: I heard you! What's that you say?" (pretending that the kitten was speaking.) "Her paw went into your eye? Well, that's *your* fault, for keeping your eyes open—if you'd shut them tight up, it wouldn't have happened. Now don't make any more excuses, but listen! Number two: you pulled Snowdrop* away by the tail just as I had put down the saucer of milk before her! What, you were thirsty, were you? How do you know she wasn't thirsty too? Now for number three: you unwound every bit of the worsted while I wasn't looking!

"That's three faults, Kitty, and you've not been punished* for any of them yet. You know I'm saving up all your punishments for Wednesday week*—Suppose they had saved up all *my* punishments!" she went on, talking more to herself than the kitten. "What *would* they do at the end of a year? I should be sent to prison, I suppose, when the day came. Or—let me see—suppose each punishment was to be going without a dinner: then, when the miserable day came, I should have to go without fifty dinners at once! Well, I shouldn't mind *that* much! I'd far rather go without them than eat them!

"Do you hear the snow against the window-panes, Kitty? How nice and soft it sounds! Just as if some one was kissing the window all over outside. I wonder if the snow *loves* the trees and fields, that it kisses them so gently? And then it covers them up snug, you know, with a white quilt; and perhaps it says, 'Go to sleep, darlings, till the summer comes again.'* And when they wake up in the summer, Kitty, they dress themselves all in green, and dance about—whenever the wind blows—oh, that's very pretty!" cried Alice, dropping the ball of worsted to clap her hands. "And I do so *wish* it was true! I'm sure the woods look sleepy in the autumn, when the leaves are getting brown.

"Kitty, can you play chess? Now, don't smile, my dear, I'm asking it seriously. Because, when we were playing just now, you watched just as if you understood it: and when I said 'Check!' you purred! Well, it *was* a nice check, Kitty, and really I might have won, if it hadn't been for that nasty Knight, that came wriggling down among my pieces. Kitty, dear, let's pretend——" And here I wish I could tell you half the things Alice used to say, beginning with her favourite phrase "Let's pretend." She had had quite a long argument with her sister only the day before—all because Alice had begun with "Let's pretend we're kings and queens;" and her sister, who liked being very exact, had argued that they couldn't, because there were only two of them, and Alice had been reduced at last to say, "Well, *you* can be one of them then, and *I'll* be all the rest."* And once she had really frightened her old nurse by shouting suddenly in her ear, "Nurse! Do let's pretend that I'm a hungry hyæna, and you're a bone!"*

But this is taking us away from Alice's speech to the kitten. "Let's pretend that you're the Red Queen, Kitty! Do you know, I think if you sat up and folded your arms, you'd look exactly like her. Now do try, there's a dear!" And Alice got the Red Queen off the table, and set it up before the kitten as a model for it to imitate: however, the thing didn't succeed, principally, Alice said, because the kitten wouldn't fold its arms properly. So, to punish it, she held it up to the Looking-glass, that it might see how sulky it was—"and if you're not good directly," she added, "I'll put you through into Looking-glass House. How would you like *that?*

"Now, if you'll only attend, Kitty, and not talk so much, I'll tell you all my ideas* about Looking-glass House. First, there's the room you can see through the glass—that's just the same as our drawing-room, only the things go the other way. I can see all of it when I get upon a chair—all but the bit just behind the fireplace. Oh! I do so wish I could see *that* bit! I want so much to know whether they've a fire in the winter: you never *can* tell, you know, unless our fire smokes, and then smoke comes up in that room too—but that may be only pretence, just to make it look as if they had a fire. Well then, the books are something like our books, only the words go the wrong way;* I know that, because I've held up one of our books to the glass, and then they hold up one in the other room.

"How would you like to live in Looking-glass House, Kitty? I wonder if they'd give you milk in there? Perhaps Looking-glass milk* isn't good to drink—But oh, Kitty! now we come to the passage. You can just see a little *peep* of the passage in Looking-glass House, if you leave the door of our drawing-room* wide open: and it's very like our passage as far as you can see, only you know it may be quite different on beyond. Oh, Kitty! how nice it would be if we could only get through into Looking-glass House! I'm sure it's got, oh! such beautiful things in it! Let's pretend there's a way of getting through into it*, somehow, Kitty. Let's pretend the glass has got all soft like gauze, so that we can get through. Why, it's turning into a sort of mist now, I declare! It'll be easy enough

to get through——" She was up on the chimney-piece* while she said this, though she hardly knew how she had got there. And certainly the glass *was* beginning to melt away, just like a bright silvery mist.

In another moment Alice was through the glass, and had jumped lightly down into the Looking-glass room. The very first thing she did was to look whether there was a fire in the fireplace, and she was quite pleased to find that there was a real one, blazing away as brightly as the one she had left behind. "So I shall be as warm here as I was in the old room," thought Alice: "warmer, in fact, because there'll be no one here to scold me away from the fire. Oh, what fun it'll be, when they see me through the glass in here, and can't get at me!"*

Then she began looking about, and noticed that what could be seen from the old room was quite common and uninteresting, but that all the rest was as different as possible. For instance, the pictures on the wall next the fire seemed to be all alive, and the very clock on the chimney-piece (you know you can only see the back of it in the Looking-glass) had got the face of a little old man,* and grinned at her.

"They don't keep this room so tidy as the other," Alice thought to herself, as she noticed several of the chessmen down in the hearth among the cinders: but in another moment, with a little "Oh!" of surprise, she was down on her hands and knees watching them. The chessmen were walking about, two and two!

"Here are the Red King and the Red Queen," Alice said (in a whisper, for fear of frightening them), "and there are the White King and the White Queen sitting on the edge of the shovel—and here are two Castles walking arm in arm—I don't think they can hear me," she went on, as she put her head closer down, "and I'm nearly sure they can't see me. I feel somehow as if I were invisible——"*

Here something began squeaking on the table behind Alice, and made her turn her head just in time to see one of the White Pawns roll over and begin kicking: she watched it with great curiosity* to see what would happen next.

"It is the voice of my child!"* the White Queen cried out, as she rushed past the King, so violently that she knocked him over among the cinders. "My precious Lily!* My imperial kitten!" and she began scrambling wildly up the side of the fender.*

"Imperial fiddlestick!"* said the King, rubbing his nose, which had been hurt by the fall. He had a right to be a *little* annoyed with the Queen, for he was covered with ashes from head to foot.

Alice was very anxious to be of use, and, as the poor little Lily was nearly screaming herself into a fit, she hastily picked up the Queen and set her on the table by the side of her noisy little daughter.

The Queen gasped, and sat down: the rapid journey through the air had quite taken away her breath, and for a minute or two she could do nothing but hug the little Lily in silence. As soon as she had recovered her breath a little, she called out to the White King, who was sitting sulkily among the ashes, "Mind the volcano!"*

"What volcano?" said the King, looking up anxiously into the fire, as if he thought that was the most likely place to find one.

"Blew—me—up," panted the Queen, who was still a little out of breath. "Mind you come up—the regular way—don't get blown up!"

Alice watched the White King as he slowly struggled up from bar to bar,* till at last she said, "Why, you'll be hours and hours getting to the table, at that rate. I'd far better help you, hadn't I?" But the King took no notice of the question: it was quite clear that he could neither hear her nor see her.

So Alice picked him up very gently, and lifted him across more slowly than she had lifted the Queen, that she mightn't take his breath away: but, before she put him on the table, she thought she might as well dust him a little, he was so covered with ashes.

She said afterwards that she had never seen in all her life such a face as the King made, when he found himself held in the air by an invisible hand, and being dusted: he was far too much astonished to cry out, but his eyes and his mouth went on getting larger and larger, and rounder and rounder, till her hand shook so with laughing that she nearly let him drop upon the floor.

"Oh! *please* don't make such faces, my dear!" she cried out, quite forgetting that the King couldn't hear her. "You make me laugh so that I can hardly hold you! And don't keep your mouth so wide open! All the ashes will get into it—there, now I think you're tidy enough!" she added, as she smoothed his hair, and set him upon the table near the Queen.

The King immediately fell flat on his back, and lay perfectly still: and Alice was a little alarmed at what she had done, and went round the room to see if she could find any water to throw over him. However, she could find nothing but a bottle of ink, and when she got back with it she found he had recovered, and he and the Queen were talking together in a frightened whisper—so low, that Alice could hardly hear what they said.

The King was saying, "I assure you, my dear, I turned cold to the very ends of my whiskers!"*

To which the Queen replied, "You haven't got any whiskers."

"The horror of that moment," the King went on, 'I shall never, *never* forget!"

"You will, though," the Queen said, "if you don't make a memorandum* of it."

Alice looked on with great interest as the King took an enormous memorandum-book out of his pocket, and began writing. A sudden thought struck her, and she took hold of the end of the pencil, which came some way over his shoulder, and began writing for him.

The poor King looked puzzled and unhappy, and struggled with the pencil for some time without saying anything; but Alice was too strong for him, and at last he panted out, "My dear! I really *must* get a thinner pencil. I can't manage this one a bit; it writes all manner of things that I don't intend——"

"What manner of things?" said the Queen, looking over the book (in which Alice had put '*The White Knight is sliding down the poker. He balances very badly*'). "That's not a memorandum of *your* feelings!"

There was a book lying near Alice on the table, and while she sat watching the White King (for she was still a little anxious about him, and had the ink all ready to throw over him, in case he fainted again), she turned over the leaves, to find some part that she could read, "——for it's all in some language I don't know," she said to herself.

It was like this.

*ЈАВВЕᴙWOCKY.

'Twas brillig, and the slithy toves
Did gyre and gimble in the wabe:
All mimsy were the borogoves,
And the mome raths outgrabe.

She puzzled over this for some time, but at last a bright thought struck her. "Why, it's a Looking-glass book, of course! And if I hold it up to a glass, the words will all go the right way again."

This was the poem that Alice read.

JABBERWOCKY.*

'Twas brillig, and the slithy toves
    Did gyre and gimble in the wabe;*
All mimsy were the borogoves,
    And the mome raths outgrabe.

"Beware the Jabberwock, my son!
    The jaws that bite, the claws that catch!
Beware the Jubjub bird, and shun
    The frumious Bandersnatch!"*

He took his vorpal sword in hand:
    Long time the manxome foe he sought—
So rested he by the Tumtum tree,
    And stood awhile in thought.

And as in uffish thought he stood,
    The Jabberwock, with eyes of flame,
Came whiffling through the tulgey wood,
    And burbled as it came!

One, two! One, two! And through and through
    The vorpal blade went snicker-snack!
He left it dead, and with its head
    He went galumphing back.

"And hast thou slain the Jabberwock?
    Come to my arms, my beamish boy!
O frabjous day! Callooh! Callay!"
    He chortled in his joy.

'Twas brillig, and the slithy toves
    Did gyre and gimble in the wabe;
All mimsy were the borogoves,
    And the mome raths outgrabe.

"It seems very pretty," she said when she had finished it, "but it's *rather* hard to understand!" (You see she didn't like to confess, even to herself, that she couldn't make it out at all.) "Somehow it seems to fill my head with ideas—only I don't exactly know what they are! However, *somebody* killed *something*:* that's clear, at any rate——"

"But oh!" thought Alice, suddenly jumping up, "if I don't make haste I shall have to go back through the Looking-glass, before I've seen what the rest of the house is like! Let's have a look at the garden first!"* She was out of the room in a moment, and ran down stairs—or, at least, it wasn't exactly running, but a new invention for getting down stairs quickly and easily, as Alice said to herself. She just kept the tips of her fingers on the hand-rail, and floated gently down without even touching the stairs with her feet; then she floated on through the hall, and would have gone straight out at the door in the same way, if she hadn't caught hold of the door-post. She was getting a little giddy* with so much floating in the air, and was rather glad to find herself walking again in the natural way.

CHAPTER II

THE GARDEN OF LIVE FLOWERS

"I SHOULD see the garden far better," said Alice to herself, "if I could get to the top of that hill: and here's a path that leads straight to it—at least, no, it doesn't do that——" (after going a few yards along the path, and turning several sharp corners), "but I suppose it will at last. But how curiously it twists! It's more like a corkscrew than a path! Well, *this* turn goes to the hill, I suppose—no, it doesn't! This goes straight back to the house! Well then, I'll try it the other way."

And so she did: wandering up and down, and trying turn after turn, but always coming back to the house, do what she would. Indeed, once, when she turned a corner rather more quickly than usual, she ran against it before she could stop herself.

"It's no use talking about it," Alice said, looking up at the house and pretending it was arguing with her. "I'm *not* going in again yet. I know I should have to get through the Looking-glass again—back into the old room—and there'd be an end of all my adventures!"

So, resolutely turning her back upon the house, she set out once more down the path, determined to keep straight on till she got to the hill. For a few minutes all went on well, and she was just saying, "I really *shall* do it this time——" when the path gave a sudden twist and shook itself (as she described it afterwards), and the next moment she found herself actually walking in at the door.

"Oh, it's too bad!" she cried. "I never saw such a house for getting in the way! Never!"

However, there was the hill full in sight, so there was nothing to be done but start again. This time she came upon a large flower-bed, with a border of daisies, and a willow-tree growing in the middle.

"O Tiger-lily,"* said Alice, addressing herself to one that was waving gracefully about in the wind, "I *wish* you could talk!"

"We *can* talk,"* said the Tiger-lily: "when there's anybody worth talking to."

Alice was so astonished* that she couldn't speak for a minute: it quite seemed to take her breath away. At length, as the Tiger-lily only went on waving about, she spoke again, in a timid voice—almost in a whisper. "And can *all* the flowers talk?"

"As well as *you* can," said the Tiger-lily. "And a great deal louder."

"It isn't manners* for us to begin, you know," said the Rose, "and I really was wondering when you'd speak! Said I to myself, 'Her face has got *some* sense in it, though it's not a clever one!' Still, you're the right colour,* and that goes a long way."

"I don't care about the colour," the Tiger-lily remarked. "If only her petals curled up a little more, she'd be all right."

Alice didn't like being criticised, so she began asking questions. "Aren't you sometimes frightened at being planted out here, with nobody to take care of you?"

"There's the tree in the middle," said the Rose: "what else is it good for?"

"But what could it do, if any danger came?" Alice asked.

"It could bark," said the Rose.

"It says 'Bough-wough!'" cried a Daisy: "that's why its branches are called boughs!"

"Didn't you know *that?*" cried another Daisy, and here they all began shouting together, till the air seemed quite full of little shrill voices. "Silence, every one of you!" cried the Tiger-lily, waving itself passionately from side to side, and trembling with excitement. "They know I can't get at them!" it panted, bending its quivering head towards Alice, "or they wouldn't dare to do it!"

"Never mind!" Alice said in a soothing tone, and stooping down to the daisies, who were just beginning again, she whispered, "If you don't hold your tongues, I'll pick you!"*

There was silence in a moment, and several of the pink daisies turned white.*

"That's right!" said the Tiger-lily. "The daisies are worst of all. When one speaks, they all begin together, and it's enough to make one wither to hear the way they go on!"

"How is it you can all talk so nicely?" Alice said, hoping to get it into a better temper by a compliment. "I've been in many gardens before, but none of the flowers could talk."

"Put your hand down, and feel the ground," said the Tiger-lily. "Then you'll know why."

Alice did so. "It's very hard," she said, "but I don't see what that has to do with it."

"In most gardens," the Tiger-lily said, "they make the beds too soft—so that the flowers are always asleep."

This sounded a very good reason, and Alice was quite pleased to know it. "I never thought of that before!" she said.

"It's *my* opinion that you never think *at all*," the Rose said in a rather severe tone.

"I never saw anybody that looked stupider," a Violet* said, so suddenly, that Alice quite jumped; for it hadn't spoken before.

"Hold *your* tongue!" cried the Tiger-lily. "As if *you* ever saw anybody! You keep your head under the leaves, and snore away there, till you know no more what's going on in the world, than if you were a bud!"

"Are there any more people in the garden besides me?" Alice said, not choosing to notice the Rose's last remark.

"There's one other flower in the garden that can move about like you," said the Rose. "I wonder how you do it——" ("You're always wondering," said the Tiger-lily), "but she's more bushy than you are."

"Is she like me?" Alice asked eagerly, for the thought crossed her mind, "There's another little girl in the garden, somewhere!"

"Well, she has the same awkward shape as you," the Rose said: 'but she's redder—and her petals are shorter,* I think."

"Her petals are done up close, almost like a dahlia," the Tiger-lily interrupted: "not tumbled about anyhow, like yours."

"But that's not *your* fault," the Rose added kindly: "you're beginning to fade, you know—and then one can't help one's petals getting a little untidy."*

Alice didn't like this idea at all: so, to change the subject, she asked "Does she ever come out here?"

"I daresay you'll see her soon," said the Rose. "She's one of the thorny kind."*

"Where does she wear the thorns?" Alice asked with some curiosity.

"Why, all round her head, of course," the Rose replied. "I was wondering *you* hadn't got some too. I thought it was the regular rule."

"She's coming!" cried the Larkspur. "I hear her footstep,* thump, thump, along the gravel walk!"

Alice looked round eagerly, and found that it was the Red Queen. "She's grown a good deal!"* was her first remark. She had indeed: when Alice first found her in the ashes, she had been only three inches high—and here she was, half a head taller than Alice herself!

"It's the fresh air that does it," said the Rose: "wonderfully fine air it is, out here."

"I think I'll go and meet her," said Alice, for, though the flowers were interesting enough, she felt that it would be far grander to have a talk with a real Queen.

"You can't possibly do that," said the Rose: "*I* should advise you to walk the other way."

This sounded nonsense to Alice, so she said nothing, but set off at once towards the Red Queen. To her surprise, she lost sight of her in a moment, and found herself walking in at the front-door again.

A little provoked, she drew back, and after looking everywhere for the Queen (whom she spied out at last, a long way off), she thought she would try the plan, this time, of walking in the opposite direction.

It succeeded beautifully.* She had not been walking a minute before she found herself face to face with the Red Queen,* and full in sight of the hill she had been so long aiming at.

"Where do you come from?" said the Red Queen. "And where are you going? Look up, speak nicely, and don't twiddle your fingers all the time."

Alice attended to all these directions, and explained, as well as she could, that she had lost her way.

"I don't know what you mean by *your* way," said the Queen: "all the ways about here belong to *me*—but why did you come out here at all?" she added in a kinder tone. "Curtsey while you're thinking what to say. It saves time."

Alice wondered a little at this, but she was too much in awe of the Queen to disbelieve it. "I'll try it when I go home," she thought to herself, "the next time I'm a little late for dinner."

"It's time for you to answer now," the Queen said, looking at her watch: "open your mouth a *little* wider when you speak, and always say 'your Majesty.' "

"I only wanted to see what the garden was like, your Majesty——"

"That's right," said the Queen, patting her on the head, which Alice didn't like at all: "though, when you say 'garden,'—*I've* seen gardens, compared with which this would be a wilderness."

Alice didn't dare to argue the point, but went on: "—and I thought I'd try and find my way to the top of that hill——"

"When you say 'hill,' " the Queen interrupted, "*I* could show you hills, in comparison with which you'd call that a valley."

"No, I shouldn't," said Alice, surprised into contradicting her at last: "a hill *can't* be a valley, you know. That would be nonsense——"

The Red Queen shook her head. "You may call it 'nonsense' if you like," she said, "but *I've* heard nonsense, compared with which that would be as sensible as a dictionary!"*

Alice curtseyed again, as she was afraid from the Queen's tone that she was a *little* offended: and they walked on in silence till they got to the top of the little hill.*

For some minutes Alice stood without speaking, looking out in all directions over the country—and a most curious country it was. There were a number of tiny little brooks running straight across it

from side to side, and the ground between was divided up into squares by a number of little green hedges, that reached from brook to brook.

"I declare it's marked out just like a large chess-board!" Alice said at last. "There ought to be some men moving about somewhere—and so there are!" she added in a tone of delight, and her heart began to beat quick with excitement as she went on. "It's a great huge game of chess* that's being played—all over the world—if this *is* the world at all, you know. Oh, what fun it is! How I *wish* I was one of them! I wouldn't mind being a Pawn, if only I might join—though of course I should *like* to be a Queen, best."*

She glanced rather shyly at the real Queen as she said this, but her companion only smiled pleasantly, and said, "That's easily managed. You can be the White Queen's Pawn, if you like, as Lily's too young to play;* and you're in the Second Square to begin with: when you get to the Eighth Square you'll be a Queen——"* Just at this moment, somehow or other, they began to run.

Alice never could quite make out, in thinking it over afterwards, how it was that they began: all she remembers is, that they were running hand in hand, and the Queen went so fast* that it was all she could do to keep up with her: and still the Queen kept crying "Faster! Faster!" but Alice felt she *could not* go faster, though she had no breath left to say so.

The most curious part of the thing was, that the trees and the other things round them never changed their places at all: however

fast they went, they never seemed to pass anything. "I wonder if all the things move along with us?" thought poor puzzled Alice. And the Queen seemed to guess her thoughts, for she cried, "Faster! Don't try to talk!"

Not that Alice had any idea of doing *that*. She felt as if she would never be able to talk again, she was getting so much out of breath: and still the Queen cried "Faster! Faster!" and dragged her along. "Are we nearly there?" Alice managed to pant out at last.

"Nearly there!" the Queen repeated. "Why, we passed it ten minutes ago! Faster!" And they ran on for a time in silence, with the wind whistling in Alice's ears, and almost blowing her hair off her head, she fancied.

"Now! Now!" cried the Queen. "Faster! Faster!" And they went so fast that at last they seemed to skim through the air, hardly touching the ground with their feet, till suddenly, just as Alice was getting quite exhausted, they stopped, and she found herself sitting on the ground, breathless and giddy.

The Queen propped her up against a tree, and said kindly, "You may rest a little now."

Alice looked round her in great surprise. "Why, I do believe we've been under this tree the whole time! Everything's just as it was!"

"Of course it is," said the Queen: "what would you have it?"

"Well, in *our* country," said Alice, still panting a little, "you'd generally get to somewhere else—if you ran very fast for a long time, as we've been doing."

"A slow sort of country!" said the Queen. "Now, *here*, you see, it takes all the running *you* can do, to keep in the same place.* If you want to get somewhere else, you must run at least twice as fast as that!"

"I'd rather not try, please!" said Alice. "I'm quite content to stay here—only I *am* so hot and thirsty!"

"I know what *you'd* like!" the Queen said good-naturedly, taking a little box out of her pocket. "Have a biscuit?"*

Alice thought it would not be civil to say "No," though it wasn't at all what she wanted. So she took it, and ate it as well as she could: and it was *very* dry; and she thought she had never been so nearly choked in all her life.

"While you're refreshing yourself," said the Queen, "I'll just take the measurements." And she took a ribbon out of her pocket, marked in inches, and began measuring the ground, and sticking little pegs in here and there.

"At the end of two yards," she said, putting in a peg to mark the distance, "I shall give you your directions—have another biscuit?"

"No, thank you," said Alice: "one's *quite* enough!"

"Thirst quenched, I hope?" said the Queen.

Alice did not know what to say to this, but luckily the Queen did not wait for an answer, but went on. "At the end of *three* yards I shall repeat them—for fear of your forgetting them. At the end of *four*, I shall say good-bye. And at the end of *five*, I shall go!"

She had got all the pegs put in by this time, and Alice looked on with great interest as she returned to the tree, and then began slowly walking down the row.

At the two-yard peg she faced round, and said, "A pawn goes two squares in its first move, you know. So you'll go *very* quickly through the Third Square—by railway, I should think—and you'll find yourself in the Fourth Square in no time. Well, *that* square belongs to Tweedledum and Tweedledee—the Fifth is mostly water—the Sixth belongs to Humpty Dumpty—But you make no remark?"

"I—I didn't know I had to make one—just then," Alice faltered out.

"You *should* have said," the Queen went on in a tone of grave reproof, " 'It's extremely kind of you to tell me all this'—however, we'll suppose it said—the Seventh Square is all forest—however, one of the Knights will show you the way—and in the Eighth Square we shall be Queens together, and it's all feasting and fun!" Alice got up and curtseyed, and sat down again.

At the next peg the Queen turned again, and this time she said, "Speak in French when you can't think of the English for a thing—turn out your toes as you walk—and remember who you are!"* She did not wait for Alice to curtsey this time, but walked on quickly to the next peg, where she turned for a moment to say "good-bye," and then hurried on to the last.

How it happened, Alice never knew, but exactly as she came to the last peg, she was gone.* Whether she vanished into the air, or whether she ran quickly into the wood ("and she *can* run very fast!" thought Alice), there was no way of guessing, but she was gone, and Alice began to remember that she was a Pawn, and that it would soon be time for her to move.

CHAPTER III

LOOKING-GLASS INSECTS

Of course the first thing to do was to make a grand survey of the country she was going to travel through. "It's something very like learning geography," thought Alice, as she stood on tiptoe in hopes of being able to see a little further. "Principal rivers—there *are* none. Principal mountains—I'm on the only one, but I don't think it's got any name. Principal towns—why, what *are* those creatures, making honey down there? They can't be bees—nobody ever saw bees a mile off, you know——" and for some time she stood silent, watching one of them that was bustling about among the flowers, poking its proboscis* into them, "just as if it was a regular bee," thought Alice.

However, this was anything but a regular bee: in fact, it was an elephant—as Alice soon found out, though the idea quite took her breath away at first. "And what enormous flowers they must be!" was her next idea. "Something like cottages with the roofs taken off, and stalks put to them—and what quantities of honey they must make! I think I'll go down and—no, I won't go *just* yet," she went on, checking herself just as she was beginning to run down the hill, and trying to find some excuse for turning shy so suddenly. "It'll never do to go down among them without a good long branch to brush them away—and what fun it'll be when they ask me how I liked my walk. I shall say—'Oh, I liked it well enough——' (here came the favourite little toss of the head), 'only it was so dusty and hot, and the elephants did tease so!'"

"I think I'll go down the other way," she said after a pause: "and perhaps I may visit the elephants later on. Besides, I do so want to get into the Third Square!"

So with this excuse she ran down the hill and jumped over the first of the six little brooks.*

       *   *   *   *   *

         *   *   *   *

       *   *   *   *   *

"Tickets, please!" said the Guard, putting his head in at the window. In a moment everybody was holding out a ticket: they were about the same size as the people, and quite seemed to fill the carriage.

"Now then! Show your ticket, child!" the Guard went on, looking angrily at Alice. And a great many voices all said together ("like the chorus of a song," thought Alice), "Don't keep him waiting, child! Why, his time is worth a thousand pounds a minute!"

"I'm afraid I haven't got one," Alice said in a frightened tone: "there wasn't a ticket-office where I came from." And again the chorus of voices went on. "There wasn't room for one where she came from. The land there is worth a thousand pounds an inch!"

"Don't make excuses," said the Guard: "you should have bought one from the engine-driver." And once more the chorus of voices went on with "The man that drives the engine. Why, the smoke alone is worth a thousand pounds a puff!"

Alice thought to herself, "Then there's no use in speaking." The voices didn't join in this time, as she hadn't spoken, but, to her great surprise, they all *thought* in chorus (I hope you understand what *thinking in chorus* means—for I must confess that *I* don't),* "Better say nothing at all. Language is worth a thousand pounds a word!"

"I shall dream about a thousand pounds to-night, I know I shall!" thought Alice.

All this time the Guard was looking at her, first through a telescope, then through a microscope, and then through an opera-glass.* At last he said, "You're travelling the wrong way," and shut up the window and went away.

"So young a child," said the gentleman sitting opposite to her, (he was dressed in white paper,) "ought to know which way she's going, even if she doesn't know her own name!"

A Goat, that was sitting next to the gentleman in white, shut his eyes and said in a loud voice, "She ought to know her way to the ticket-office, even if she doesn't know her alphabet!"

There was a Beetle sitting next the Goat (it was a very queer carriage-full of passengers* altogether), and, as the rule seemed to be that they should all speak in turn, *he* went on with "She'll have to go back from here as luggage!"

Alice couldn't see who was sitting beyond the Beetle, but a hoarse voice spoke next. "Change engines——" it said, and there it choked and was obliged to leave off.

"It sounds like a horse," Alice thought to herself. And an extremely small voice,* close to her ear, said, "you might make a joke on that—something about 'horse' and 'hoarse,' you know."

Then a very gentle voice in the distance said, "She must be labelled 'Lass, with care,'* you know——"

And after that other voices went on ("What a number of people there are in the carriage!" thought Alice), saying, "She must go by post, as she's got a head on her——"* "She must be sent as a message by the telegraph——" "She must draw the train herself the rest of the way——," and so on.

But the gentleman dressed in white paper leaned forwards and whispered in her ear, "Never mind what they all say, my dear, but take a return-ticket every time the train stops."

"Indeed I shan't!" Alice said rather impatiently. "I don't belong to this railway journey at all—I was in a wood just now—and I wish I could get back there!"*

"You might make a joke on *that*," said the little voice close to her ear: "something about 'you would if you could,' you know."

"Don't tease so," said Alice, looking about in vain to see where the voice came from; "if you're so anxious to have a joke made, why don't you make one yourself?"

The little voice sighed deeply: it was *very* unhappy, evidently, and Alice would have said something pitying to comfort it, "if it would only sigh like other people!" she thought. But this was such a wonderfully small sigh, that she wouldn't have heard it at all, if it hadn't come *quite* close to her ear. The consequence of this was that it tickled her ear very much, and quite took off her thoughts from the unhappiness of the poor little creature.

"I know you are a friend," the little voice went on; "a dear friend, and an old friend. And you won't hurt me, though I am an insect."

"What kind of insect?" Alice inquired a little anxiously. What she really wanted to know was, whether it could sting or not, but she thought this wouldn't be quite a civil question to ask.

"What, then you don't——" the little voice began, when it was drowned by a shrill scream from the engine, and everybody jumped up in alarm, Alice among the rest.

The Horse, who had put his head out of the window, quietly drew it in and said, "It's only a brook we have to jump over." Everybody seemed satisfied with this, though Alice felt a little nervous at the idea of trains jumping at all. "However, it'll take us into the Fourth Square,* that's some comfort!" she said to herself. In another moment she felt the carriage rise straight up into the air, and in her fright she caught at the thing nearest to her hand, which happened to be the Goat's beard.*

```
    *       *       *       *       *       *

        *       *       *       *       *

    *       *       *       *       *       *
```

But the beard seemed to melt away as she touched it, and she found herself sitting quietly under a tree—while the Gnat (for that was the insect she had been talking to) was balancing itself on a twig just over her head, and fanning her with its wings.

It certainly was a *very* large Gnat: "about the size of a chicken," Alice thought. Still, she couldn't feel nervous with it, after they had been talking together so long.

"—then you don't like all insects?" the Gnat went on, as quietly as if nothing had happened.

"I like them when they can talk," Alice said. "None of them ever talk, where *I* come from."

"What sort of insects do you rejoice in, where *you* come from?" the Gnat inquired.

"I don't *rejoice* in insects at all," Alice explained, "because I'm rather afraid of them—at least the large kinds. But I can tell you the names of some of them."*

"Of course they answer to their names?" the Gnat remarked carelessly.

"I never knew them do it."

"What's the use of their having names," the Gnat said, "if they won't answer to them?"

"No use to *them*," said Alice; "but it's useful to the people that name them, I suppose. If not, why do things have names at all?"*

"I can't say," the Gnat replied. "Further on, in the wood down there, they've got no names—however, go on with your list of insects: you're wasting time."

"Well, there's the Horse-fly," Alice began, counting off the names on her fingers.

"All right," said the Gnat: "half way up that bush, you'll see a Rocking-horse-fly,* if you look. It's made entirely of wood, and gets about by swinging itself from branch to branch."

"What does it live on?" Alice asked, with great curiosity.

"Sap and sawdust," said the Gnat. "Go on with the list."

Alice looked at the Rocking-horse-fly with great interest, and made up her mind that it must have been just repainted, it looked so bright and sticky; and then she went on.

"And there's the Dragon-fly."

"Look on the branch above your head," said the Gnat, "and there you'll find a Snap-dragon-fly.* Its body is made of plum-pudding,* its wings of holly-leaves, and its head is a raisin burning in brandy."

"And what does it live on?" Alice asked, as before.

"Frumenty* and mince-pie," the Gnat replied; "and it makes its nest in a Christmas-box."*

"And then there's the Butterfly," Alice went on, after she had taken a good look at the insect with its head on fire, and had thought to herself, "I wonder if that's the reason insects are so fond of flying into candles—because they want to turn into Snap-dragon-flies!"

"Crawling at your feet," said the Gnat (Alice drew her feet back in some alarm), "you may observe a Bread-and-butter-fly. Its wings are thin slices of bread-and-butter, its body is a crust, and its head is a lump of sugar."

"And what does *it* live on?"

"Weak tea with cream in it."

A new difficulty came into Alice's head. "Supposing it couldn't find any?" she suggested.

"Then it would die, of course."

"But that must happen very often," Alice remarked thoughtfully.

"It always happens,"* said the Gnat.

After this, Alice was silent for a minute or two, pondering.* The Gnat amused itself meanwhile by humming round and round her head: at last it settled again and remarked, "I suppose you don't want to lose your name?"

"No, indeed," Alice said, a little anxiously.

"And yet I don't know," the Gnat went on in a careless tone: "only think how convenient it would be if you could manage to go home without it! For instance, if the governess wanted to call you to your lessons, she would call out 'Come here——,' and there she would have to leave off, because there wouldn't be any name for her to call, and of course you wouldn't have to go, you know."

"That would never do, I'm sure," said Alice: "the governess would never think of excusing me lessons for that. If she couldn't remember my name, she'd call me 'Miss!' as the servants do."*

"Well, if she said 'Miss,' and didn't say anything more," the Gnat remarked, "of course you'd miss your lessons. That's a joke. I wish *you* had made it."

"Why do you wish *I* had made it?" Alice asked. "It's a very bad one."

But the Gnat only sighed deeply, while two large tears came rolling down its cheeks.

"You shouldn't make jokes," Alice said, "if it makes you so unhappy."

Then came another of those melancholy little sighs, and this time the poor Gnat really seemed to have sighed itself away, for, when Alice looked up, there was nothing whatever to be seen on the twig, and, as she was getting quite chilly with sitting still so long, she got up and walked on.

She very soon came to an open field, with a wood on the other side of it: it looked much darker than the last wood, and Alice felt a *little* timid about going into it. However, on second thoughts, she made up her mind to go on: "for I certainly won't go *back*," she thought to herself, and this was the only way to the Eighth Square.

"This must be the wood," she said thoughtfully to herself, "where things have no names. I wonder what'll become of *my* name when I go in? I shouldn't like to lose it at all——because they'd have to give me another, and it would be almost certain to be an ugly one.* But then the fun would be, trying to find the creature that had got my old name! That's just like the advertisements, you know, when people lose dogs——'*answers to the name of "Dash:"** had on a brass collar*'——just fancy calling everything you met 'Alice,' till one of them answered! Only they wouldn't answer at all, if they were wise."

She was rambling on in this way when she reached the wood: it looked very cool and shady. "Well, at any rate it's a great comfort," she said as she stepped under the trees, "after being so hot, to get into the—into the—into *what*?" she went on, rather surprised at not being able to think of the word. "I mean to get under the—under the—under *this*, you know!" putting her hand on the trunk of the tree. "What *does* it call itself, I wonder?* I do believe it's got no name—why, to be sure it hasn't!"

She stood silent for a minute, thinking: then she suddenly began again. "Then it really *has* happened, after all! And now, who am I?* I *will* remember, if I can! I'm determined to do it!" But being determined didn't help her much, and all she could say, after a great deal of puzzling, was, "L, I *know* it begins with L!"*

Just then a Fawn came wandering by:* it looked at Alice with its large gentle eyes, but didn't seem at all frightened. "Here then! Here then!" Alice said, as she held out her hand and tried to stroke it; but it only started back a little, and then stood looking at her again.

"What do you call yourself?" the Fawn said at last. Such a soft sweet voice it had!

"I wish I knew!" thought poor Alice. She answered, rather sadly, "Nothing, just now."

"Think again," it said: "that won't do."

Alice thought, but nothing came of it. "Please, would you tell me what *you* call yourself?" she said timidly. "I think that might help a little."

"I'll tell you, if you'll come a little further on," the Fawn said. "I can't remember here."

So they walked on together through the wood, Alice with her arms clasped lovingly round the soft neck of the Fawn, till they came out into another open field, and here the Fawn gave a sudden bound into the air, and shook itself free from Alice's arms. "I'm a Fawn!" it cried out in a voice of delight, "and, dear me! you're a human child!" A sudden look of alarm came into its beautiful brown eyes, and in another moment it had darted away at full speed.

Alice stood looking after it, almost ready to cry with vexation at having lost her dear little fellow-traveller so suddenly. "However, I know my name now," she said, "that's *some* comfort.*Alice—Alice— I won't forget it again. And now, which of these finger-posts ought I to follow, I wonder?"

It was not a very difficult question to answer, as there was only one road through the wood, and the two finger-posts both pointed along it. "I'll settle it," Alice said to herself, "when the road divides and they point different ways."

But this did not seem likely to happen.* She went on and on, a long way, but wherever the road divided there were sure to be two finger-posts pointing the same way, one marked 'TO TWEEDLEDUM'S HOUSE,' and the other 'TO THE HOUSE OF TWEEDLEDEE.'

"I do believe," said Alice at last, "that they live in the same house! I wonder I never thought of that before—But I can't stay there long. I'll just call and say 'How d'ye do?' and ask them the way out of the wood. If I could only get to the Eighth Square before it gets dark!" So she wandered on, talking to herself as she went, till, on turning a sharp corner, she came upon two fat little men*, so suddenly that she could not help starting back, but in another moment she recovered herself, feeling sure that they must be*

CHAPTER IV

TWEEDLEDUM AND TWEEDLEDEE

THEY were standing under a tree,* each with an arm round the other's neck, and Alice knew which was which in a moment, because one of them had 'DUM' embroidered on his collar, and the other 'DEE.' "I suppose they've each got 'TWEEDLE' round at the back of the collar," she said to herself.

They stood so still that she quite forgot they were alive, and she was just looking round to see if the word 'TWEEDLE' was written at the back of each collar, when she was startled by a voice coming from the one marked 'DUM.'

"If you think we're wax-works," he said, "you ought to pay, you know. Wax-works weren't made to be looked at for nothing.* Nohow!"*

"Contrariwise," added the one marked 'DEE,' "if you think we're alive, you ought to speak."

"I'm sure I'm very sorry," was all Alice could say; for the words of the old song* kept ringing through her head like the ticking of a clock, and she could hardly help saying them out loud:—

> *"Tweedledum and Tweedledee*
> *Agreed to have a battle;*
> *For Tweedledum said Tweedledee*
> *Had spoiled his nice new rattle.*
>
> *Just then flew down a monstrous crow,*
> *As black as a tar-barrel;*
> *Which frightened both the heroes so,*
> *They quite forgot their quarrel."*

"I know what you're thinking about," said Tweedledum: "but it isn't so, nohow."

"Contrariwise," continued Tweedledee, "if it was so, it might be; and if it were so, it would be; but as it isn't, it ain't. That's logic."*

"I was thinking," Alice said very politely, "which is the best way out of this wood: it's getting so dark. Would you tell me, please?"

But the fat little men only looked at each other and grinned.

They looked so exactly like a couple of great schoolboys, that Alice couldn't help pointing her finger at Tweedledum, and saying "First Boy!"*

"Nohow!" Tweedledum cried out briskly, and shut his mouth up again with a snap.

"Next Boy!" said Alice, passing on to Tweedledee, though she felt quite certain he would only shout out "Contrariwise!" and so he did.

"You've begun wrong!"* cried Tweedledum. "The first thing in a visit is to say 'How d'ye do?' and shake hands!" And here the two brothers gave each other a hug, and then they held out the two hands that were free, to shake hands with her.

Alice did not like shaking hands with either of them first, for fear of hurting the other one's feelings; so, as the best way out of the difficulty, she took hold of both hands at once: the next moment they were dancing round in a ring. This seemed quite natural (she remembered afterwards), and she was not even surprised to hear music playing: it seemed to come from the tree under which they were dancing, and it was done (as well as she could make it out) by the branches rubbing one across the other, like fiddles and fiddle-sticks.

"But it certainly *was* funny," (Alice said afterwards, when she was telling her sister the history of all this,) "to find myself singing '*Here we go round the mulberry bush.*'* I don't know when I began it, but somehow I felt as if I'd been singing it a long long time!"

The other two dancers were fat, and very soon out of breath. "Four times round is enough for one dance," Tweedledum panted out, and they left off dancing as suddenly as they had begun: the music stopped at the same moment.

Then they let go of Alice's hands, and stood looking at her for a minute: there was a rather awkward pause, as Alice didn't know how to begin a conversation with people she had just been dancing with. "It would never do to say 'How d'ye do?' *now*," she said to herself: "we seem to have got beyond that, somehow!"

"I hope you're not much tired?" she said at last.

"Nohow. And thank you *very* much for asking," said Tweedledum.

"So *much* obliged!" added Tweedledee. "You like poetry?"

"Ye-es, pretty well—*some* poetry," Alice said doubtfully.* "Would you tell me which road leads out of the wood?"

"What shall I repeat to her?" said Tweedledee, looking round at Tweedledum with great solemn eyes, and not noticing Alice's question.

"'*The Walrus and the Carpenter*'* is the longest," Tweedledum replied, giving his brother an affectionate hug.

Tweedledee began instantly:

> "*The sun was shining——*"

Here Alice ventured to interrupt him. "If it's *very* long," she said, as politely as she could, "would you please tell me first which road——"

Tweedledee smiled gently, and began again:

> "*The sun was shining on the sea,*
> *Shining with all his might:*
> *He did his very best to make*
> *The billows* smooth and bright—*
> *And this was odd, because it was*
> *The middle of the night.*
>
> *The moon was shining sulkily,*
> *Because she thought* the sun*

Had got no business to be there
 After the day was done—
'It's very rude of him,' she said,
 'To come and spoil the fun!'

The sea was wet as wet could be,
 The sands were dry as dry.
You could not see a cloud, because
 No cloud was in the sky:
No birds were flying overhead—
 There were no birds to fly.

The Walrus and the Carpenter
 Were walking close at hand;*
They wept like anything to see
 Such quantities of sand:
'If this were only cleared away,'
 They said, 'it *would* be grand!'

'If seven maids with seven mops
 Swept it for half a year,

Do you suppose,' the Walrus said,
    'That they could get it clear?'
'I doubt it,' said the Carpenter,
    And shed a bitter tear.

'O Oysters, come and walk with us!'
    The Walrus did beseech.
'A pleasant walk, a pleasant talk,
    Along the briny* beach:
We cannot do with more than four,
    To give a hand to each.'

The eldest Oyster looked at him,
    But never a word he said:
The eldest Oyster winked his eye,
    And shook his heavy head—
Meaning to say he did not choose
    To leave the oyster-bed.

But four young Oysters* hurried up,
    All eager for the treat:
Their coats were brushed, their faces washed,
    Their shoes were clean and neat—
And this was odd, because, you know,
    They hadn't any feet.*

Four other Oysters followed them,
    And yet another four;
And thick and fast they came at last,
    And more, and more, and more—
All hopping through the frothy waves,
    And scrambling to the shore.

The Walrus and the Carpenter
    Walked on a mile or so,
And then they rested on a rock
    Conveniently low:
And all the little Oysters stood
    And waited in a row.

'*The time has come,*' the Walrus said,
  '*To talk of many things:*
Of shoes—and ships—and sealing-wax—
  Of cabbages—and kings—
And why the sea is boiling hot—
  And whether pigs have wings.'*

'*But wait a bit,*' the Oysters cried,
  '*Before we have our chat;*
For some of us are out of breath,
  And all of us are fat!'
'*No hurry!*' said the Carpenter.
  They thanked him much for that.

'*A loaf of bread,*' the Walrus said,
  '*Is what we chiefly need:*
Pepper and vinegar besides
  Are very good indeed—
Now if you're ready, Oysters dear,
  We can begin to feed.'

'*But not on us!*' the Oysters cried,
  Turning a little blue.

*'After such kindness, that would be
   A dismal thing to do!'*
*'The night is fine,' the Walrus said.
   'Do you admire the view?*

*'It was so kind of you to come!
   And you are very nice!'*
*The Carpenter said nothing but
   'Cut us another slice:*
*I wish you were not quite so deaf—
   I've had to ask you twice!'*

*'It seems a shame,' the Walrus said,
   'To play them such a trick,*
*After we've brought them out so far,
   And made them trot so quick!'*
*The Carpenter said nothing but
   'The butter's spread too thick!'*

*'I weep for you,' the Walrus said:
   'I deeply sympathize.'*
*With sobs and tears he sorted out
   Those of the largest size,*

> Holding his pocket-handkerchief
> Before his streaming eyes.
>
> 'O Oysters,' said the Carpenter,
>   'You've had a pleasant run!
> Shall we be trotting home again?'
>   But answer came there none—
> And this was scarcely odd, because
>   They'd eaten every one."*

"I like the Walrus best," said Alice: "because you see he was a *little* sorry for the poor oysters."

"He ate more than the Carpenter, though," said Tweedledee. "You see he held his handkerchief in front, so that the Carpenter couldn't count how many he took: contrariwise."

"That was mean!" Alice said indignantly. "Then I like the Carpenter best—if he didn't eat so many as the Walrus."

"But he ate as many as he could get," said Tweedledum.

This was a puzzler. After a pause, Alice began, "Well! They were *both* very unpleasant characters——"* Here she checked herself in some alarm, at hearing something that sounded to her like the puffing of a large steam-engine in the wood near them, though she feared it was more likely to be a wild beast. "Are there any lions or tigers about here?" she asked timidly.

"It's only the Red King snoring," said Tweedledee.

"Come and look at him!" the brothers cried, and they each took one of Alice's hands, and led her up to where the King was sleeping.

"Isn't he a *lovely* sight?" said Tweedledum.

Alice couldn't say honestly that he was. He had a tall red night-cap on, with a tassel, and he was lying crumpled up into a sort of untidy heap, and snoring loud——"fit to snore his head off!" as Tweedledum remarked.

"I'm afraid he'll catch cold with lying on the damp grass," said Alice, who was a very thoughtful little girl.

"He's dreaming now," said Tweedledee: "and what do you think he's dreaming about?"

Alice said "Nobody can guess that."

"Why, about *you!*" Tweedledee exclaimed, clapping his hands triumphantly. "And if he left off dreaming about you, where do you suppose you'd be?"

"Where I am now, of course," said Alice.

"Not you!" Tweedledee retorted contemptuously. "You'd be nowhere. Why, you're only a sort of thing in his dream!"*

"If that there King was to wake," added Tweedledum, "you'd go out—bang!—just like a candle!"*

"I shouldn't!" Alice exclaimed indignantly. "Besides, if *I'm* only a sort of thing in his dream, what are *you*, I should like to know?"*

"Ditto," said Tweedledum.

"Ditto, ditto!" cried Tweedledee.

He shouted this so loud that Alice couldn't help saying, "Hush! You'll be waking him, I'm afraid, if you make so much noise."

"Well, it's no use *your* talking about waking him," said Tweedledum, "when you're only one of the things in his dream. You know very well you're not real."

"I *am* real!"* said Alice, and began to cry.

"You won't make yourself a bit realler by crying," Tweedledee remarked: "there's nothing to cry about."

"If I wasn't real," Alice said—half-laughing through her tears, it all seemed so ridiculous—"I shouldn't be able to cry."

"I hope you don't suppose those are real tears?" Tweedledum interrupted in a tone of great contempt.

"I know they're talking nonsense," Alice thought to herself: "and it's foolish to cry about it." So she brushed away her tears, and went on as cheerfully as she could, "At any rate I'd better be getting out of the wood, for really it's coming on very dark. Do you think it's going to rain?"

Tweedledum spread a large umbrella* over himself and his brother, and looked up into it. "No, I don't think it is," he said: "at least—not under *here*. Nohow."

"But it may rain *outside?*"

"It may—if it chooses," said Tweedledee: "we've no objection. Contrariwise."

"Selfish things!" thought Alice, and she was just going to say "Good-night" and leave them, when Tweedledum sprang out from under the umbrella, and seized her by the wrist.

"Do you see *that?*" he said, in a voice choking with passion, and his eyes grew large and yellow all in a moment, as he pointed with a trembling finger at a small white thing lying under the tree.

"It's only a rattle," Alice said, after a careful examination of the little white thing. "Not a rattle-*snake*, you know," she added hastily, thinking that he was frightened: "only an old rattle—quite old and broken."

"I knew it was!" cried Tweedledum, beginning to stamp about wildly and tear his hair. "It's spoilt, of course!" Here he looked at

Tweedledee, who immediately sat down on the ground, and tried to hide himself under the umbrella.

Alice laid her hand upon his arm, and said in a soothing tone, "You needn't be so angry about an old rattle."

"But it isn't old!" Tweedledum cried, in a greater fury than ever. "It's new, I tell you—I bought it yesterday—my nice NEW RATTLE!" and his voice rose to a perfect scream.

All this time Tweedledee was trying his best to fold up the umbrella, with himself in it: which was such an extraordinary thing to do, that it quite took off Alice's attention from the angry brother. But he couldn't quite succeed, and it ended in his rolling over, bundled up in the umbrella, with only his head out: and there he lay, opening and shutting his mouth and his large eyes——"looking more like a fish than anything else," Alice thought.

"Of course you agree to have a battle?" Tweedledum said in a calmer tone.

"I suppose so," the other sulkily replied, as he crawled out of the umbrella: "only *she* must help us to dress up, you know."

So the two brothers went off hand-in-hand into the wood, and returned in a minute with their arms full of things—such as bolsters,* blankets, hearth-rugs, table-cloths, dish-covers, and coal-scuttles. "I hope you're a good hand at pinning and tying strings?" Tweedledum remarked. "Every one of these things has got to go on, somehow or other."

Alice said afterwards she had never seen such a fuss made about anything in all her life—the way those two bustled about—and the quantity of things they put on—and the trouble they gave her in tying strings and fastening buttons——"Really they'll be more like bundles of old clothes than anything else, by the time they're ready!" she said to herself, as she arranged a bolster round the neck of Tweedledee, "to keep his head from being cut off,"* as he said.

"You know," he added very gravely, "it's one of the most serious things that can possibly happen to one in a battle—to get one's head cut off."

Alice laughed loud: but she managed to turn it into a cough, for fear of hurting his feelings.

"Do I look very pale?" said Tweedledum, coming up to have his helmet tied on. (He *called* it a helmet, though it certainly looked much more like a saucepan.)

"Well—yes—a *little*," Alice replied gently.

"I'm very brave generally," he went on in a low voice: "only to-day I happen to have a headache."

"And *I've* got a toothache!" said Tweedledee, who had overheard the remark. "I'm far worse than you!"

"Then you'd better not fight to-day," said Alice, thinking it a good opportunity to make peace.

"We *must* have a bit of a fight, but I don't care about going on long," said Tweedledum. "What's the time now?"

Tweedledee looked at his watch, and said "Half-past four."

"Let's fight till six, and then have dinner," said Tweedledum.

"Very well," the other said, rather sadly: "and *she* can watch us—only you'd better not come *very* close," he added: "I generally hit every thing I can see—when I get really excited."

"And *I* hit every thing within reach," cried Tweedledum, "whether I can see it or not!"

Alice laughed. "You must hit the *trees* pretty often, I should think," she said.

Tweedledum looked round him with a satisfied smile. "I don't suppose," he said, "there'll be a tree left standing, for ever so far round, by the time we've finished!"

"And all about a rattle!" said Alice, still hoping to make them a *little* ashamed of fighting for such a trifle.

"I shouldn't have minded it so much," said Tweedledum, "if it hadn't been a new one."

"I wish the monstrous crow* would come!" thought Alice.

"There's only one sword, you know," Tweedledum said to his brother: "but you can have the umbrella—it's quite as sharp. Only we must begin quick. It's getting as dark as it can."

"And darker," said Tweedledee.

It was getting dark so suddenly that Alice thought there must be a thunderstorm coming on. "What a thick black cloud that is!" she said. "And how fast it comes! Why, I do believe it's got wings!"

"It's the crow!" Tweedledum cried out in a shrill voice of alarm: and the two brothers took to their heels and were out of sight in a moment.

Alice ran a little way into the wood, and stopped under a large tree. "It can never get at me *here*," she thought: "it's far too large to squeeze itself in among the trees. But I wish it wouldn't flap its wings so—it makes quite a hurricane in the wood—here's somebody's shawl being blown away!"

CHAPTER V

WOOL AND WATER

SHE caught the shawl as she spoke, and looked about for the owner: in another moment the White Queen came running wildly through the wood, with both arms stretched out wide, as if she were flying, and Alice very civilly went to meet her with the shawl.*

"I'm very glad I happened to be in the way," Alice said, as she helped her to put on her shawl again.

The White Queen only looked at her in a helpless frightened sort of way, and kept repeating something in a whisper to herself that sounded like "Bread-and-butter, bread-and-butter,"* and Alice felt that if there was to be any conversation at all, she must manage it herself. So she began rather timidly: "Am I addressing the White Queen?"

"Well, yes, if you call that a-dressing," the Queen said. "It isn't *my* notion of the thing, at all."

Alice thought it would never do to have an argument at the very beginning of their conversation, so she smiled and said, "If your Majesty will only tell me the right way to begin, I'll do it as well as I can."

"But I don't want it done at all!" groaned the poor Queen. "I've been a-dressing myself for the last two hours."

It would have been all the better, as it seemed to Alice, if she had got some one else to dress her, she was so dreadfully untidy. "Every single thing's crooked," Alice thought to herself, "and she's all over pins!——May I put your shawl straight for you?" she added aloud.

"I don't know what's the matter with it!" the Queen said, in a melancholy voice. "It's out of temper, I think. I've pinned it here, and I've pinned it there, but there's no pleasing it!"

"It *can't* go straight, you know, if you pin it all on one side," Alice said, as she gently put it right for her; "and, dear me, what a state your hair is in!"

"The brush has got entangled in it!" the Queen said with a sigh. "And I lost the comb yesterday."

Alice carefully released the brush, and did her best to get the hair into order. "Come, you look rather better now!" she said, after altering most of the pins. "But really you should have a lady's-maid!"*

"I'm sure I'll take you with pleasure!" the Queen said. "Twopence a week, and jam every other day."

Alice couldn't help laughing, as she said, "I don't want you to hire *me*—and I don't care for jam."

"It's very good jam," said the Queen.

"Well, I don't want any *to-day*, at any rate."

"You couldn't have it if you *did* want it," the Queen said. "The rule is, jam to-morrow and jam yesterday—but never jam to-day."*

"It *must* come sometimes to 'jam to-day,'" Alice objected.

"No, it can't,' said the Queen. "It's jam every *other* day: to-day isn't any *other* day, you know."

"I don't understand you," said Alice. "It's dreadfully confusing!"

"That's the effect of living backwards," the Queen said kindly: "it always makes one a little giddy at first——"

"Living backwards!" Alice repeated in great astonishment. "I never heard of such a thing!"

"—but there's one great advantage in it, that one's memory works both ways."

"I'm sure *mine* only works one way," Alice remarked. "I can't remember things before they happen."

"It's a poor sort of memory that only works backwards," the Queen remarked.

"What sort of things do *you* remember best?" Alice ventured to ask.

"Oh, things that happened the week after next," the Queen replied in a careless tone. "For instance, now," she went on, sticking a large piece of plaster* on her finger as she spoke, "there's the King's Messenger. He's in prison now, being punished: and the trial doesn't even begin till next Wednesday:* and of course the crime comes last of all."

"Suppose he never commits the crime?" said Alice.

"That would be all the better, wouldn't it?" the Queen said, as she bound the plaster round her finger with a bit of ribbon.

Alice felt there was no denying *that*. "Of course it would be all the better," she said: "but it wouldn't be all the better his being punished."

"You're wrong *there*, at any rate," said the Queen: "were *you* ever punished?"

"Only for faults," said Alice.

"And you were all the better for it, I know!" the Queen said triumphantly.

"Yes, but then I *had* done the things I was punished for," said Alice: "that makes all the difference."

"But if you *hadn't* done them," the Queen said, "that would have been better still; better, and better, and better!" Her voice went higher with each "better," till it got quite to a squeak at last.

Alice was just beginning to say "There's a mistake

somewhere——," when the Queen began screaming, so loud that she had to leave the sentence unfinished. "Oh, oh, oh!" shouted the Queen, shaking her hand about as if she wanted to shake it off. "My finger's bleeding! Oh, oh, oh, oh!"

Her screams were so exactly like the whistle of a steam-engine, that Alice had to hold both her hands over her ears.

"What *is* the matter?" she said, as soon as there was a chance of making herself heard. "Have you pricked your finger?"

"I haven't pricked it *yet*," the Queen said, "but I soon shall*—oh, oh, oh!"

"When do you expect to do it?" Alice asked, feeling very much inclined to laugh.

"When I fasten my shawl again," the poor Queen groaned out: "the brooch will come undone directly. Oh, oh!" As she said the words the brooch flew open, and the Queen clutched wildly at it, and tried to clasp it again.

"Take care!" cried Alice. "You're holding it all crooked!" And she caught at the brooch; but it was too late: the pin had slipped, and the Queen had pricked her finger.

"That accounts for the bleeding, you see," she said to Alice with a smile. "Now you understand the way things happen here."

"But why don't you scream now?" Alice asked, holding her hands ready to put over her ears again.

"Why, I've done all the screaming already," said the Queen. "What would be the good of having it all over again?"

By this time it was getting light. "The crow must have flown away, I think," said Alice: "I'm so glad it's gone. I thought it was the night coming on."

"I wish *I* could manage to be glad!" the Queen said. "Only I never can remember the rule. You must be very happy, living in this wood, and being glad whenever you like!"

"Only it is so *very* lonely here!" Alice said in a melancholy voice; and at the thought of her loneliness two large tears came rolling down her cheeks.

"Oh, don't go on like that!" cried the poor Queen, wringing her hands in despair. "Consider what a great girl you are. Consider what a long way you've come to-day. Consider what o'clock it is. Consider anything, only don't cry!"

Alice could not help laughing at this, even in the midst of her tears. "Can *you* keep from crying by considering things?" she asked.

"That's the way it's done," the Queen said with great decision: "nobody can do two things at once, you know. Let's consider your age to begin with——how old are you?"

"I'm seven and a half exactly."*

"You needn't say 'exactually,'"* the Queen remarked: "I can believe it without that. Now I'll give *you* something to believe. I'm just one hundred and one, five months and a day."

"I can't believe *that!*" said Alice.

"Can't you?" the Queen said in a pitying tone. "Try again: draw a long breath, and shut your eyes."

Alice laughed. "There's no use trying," she said: "one *can't* believe impossible things."

"I daresay you haven't had much practice," said the Queen. "When I was your age, I always did it for half-an-hour a day. Why, sometimes I've believed as many as six impossible things before breakfast.* There goes the shawl again!"

The brooch had come undone as she spoke, and a sudden gust of wind blew the Queen's shawl across a little brook. The Queen spread out her arms again, and went flying after it,* and this time she succeeded in catching it for herself. "I've got it!" she cried in a triumphant tone. "Now you shall see me pin it on again, all by myself!"

"Then I hope your finger is better now?" Alice said very politely, as she crossed the little brook* after the Queen.

     *   *   *   *   *   *

       *   *   *   *   *

     *   *   *   *   *   *

"Oh, much better!" cried the Queen, her voice rising into a squeak as she went on. "Much be-etter! Be-etter! Be-e-e-etter! Be-e-ehh!" The last word ended in a long bleat, so like a sheep* that Alice quite started.

She looked at the Queen, who seemed to have suddenly wrapped herself up in wool.* Alice rubbed her eyes, and looked again. She couldn't make out what had happened at all. Was she in a shop? And was that really—was it really a *sheep* that was sitting on the other side of the counter? Rub as she would, she could make nothing more of it: she was in a little dark shop, leaning with her elbows on the counter, and opposite to her was an old Sheep, sitting in an arm-chair knitting,

and every now and then leaving off to look at her through a great pair
of spectacles.

"What is it you want to buy?" the Sheep said at last, looking up for
a moment from her knitting.

"I don't *quite* know yet," Alice said very gently. "I should like to
look all round me first, if I might."

"You may look in front of you, and on both sides, if you like," said
the Sheep; "but you can't look *all* round you—unless you've got eyes
at the back of your head."

But these, as it happened, Alice had *not* got: so she contented
herself with turning round, looking at the shelves as she came to
them.

The shop seemed to be full of all manner of curious things—but
the oddest part of it all was that, whenever she looked hard at any
shelf, to make out exactly what it had on it, that particular shelf was
always quite empty: though the others round it were crowded as full
as they could hold.

"Things flow about so here!" she said at last in a plaintive tone, after she had spent a minute or so in vainly pursuing a large bright thing,* that looked sometimes like a doll and sometimes like a work-box, and was always in the shelf next above the one she was looking at. "And this one is the most provoking of all—but I'll tell you what——" she added, as a sudden thought struck her, "I'll follow it up to the very top shelf of all. It'll puzzle it to go through the ceiling, I expect!"

But even this plan failed: the 'thing' went through the ceiling as quietly as possible, as if it were quite used to it.

"Are you a child or a teetotum?"* the Sheep said, as she took up another pair of needles. "You'll make me giddy soon, if you go on turning round like that." She was now working with fourteen pairs at once, and Alice couldn't help looking at her in great astonishment.

"How *can* she knit with so many?" the puzzled child thought to herself. "She gets more and more like a porcupine every minute!"

"Can you row?" the Sheep asked, handing her a pair of knitting-needles as she spoke.

"Yes, a little—but not on land—and not with needles——" Alice was beginning to say, when suddenly the needles turned into oars in her hands, and she found they were in a little boat, gliding along between banks: so there was nothing for it but to do her best.

"Feather!" cried the Sheep, as she took up another pair of needles.

This didn't sound like a remark that needed any answer, so Alice said nothing, but pulled away. There was something very queer about the water, she thought, as every now and then the oars got fast in it, and would hardly come out again.

"Feather!* Feather!" the Sheep cried again, taking more needles. "You'll be catching a crab* directly."

"A dear little crab!" thought Alice. "I should like that."

"Didn't you hear me say 'Feather'?" the Sheep cried angrily, taking up quite a bunch of needles.

"Indeed I did," said Alice: "you've said it very often—and very loud. Please, where *are* the crabs?"

"In the water, of course!" said the Sheep, sticking some of the needles into her hair, as her hands were full. "Feather, I say!"

"*Why* do you say 'Feather' so often?" Alice asked at last, rather vexed. "I'm not a bird!"

"You are," said the Sheep: "you're a little goose."*

This offended Alice a little, so there was no more conversation for a minute or two, while the boat glided gently on, sometimes among beds of weeds (which made the oars stick fast in the water, worse than ever), and sometimes under trees, but always with the same tall river-banks frowning over their heads.

"Oh, please! There are some scented rushes!" Alice cried in a sudden transport of delight. "There really are—and *such* beauties!"

"You needn't say 'please' to *me* about 'em," the Sheep said, without looking up from her knitting: "I didn't put 'em there, and I'm not going to take 'em away."

"No, but I meant—please, may we wait and pick some?" Alice pleaded. "If you don't mind stopping the boat for a minute."

"How am *I* to stop it?" said the Sheep. "If you leave off rowing, it'll stop of itself."

So the boat was left to drift down the stream as it would, till it glided gently in among the waving rushes. And then the little sleeves were carefully rolled up, and the little arms were plunged in elbow-deep, to get hold of the rushes a good long way down before breaking them off—and for a while Alice forgot all about the Sheep and the knitting, as she bent over the side of the boat, with just the ends of her tangled hair dipping into the water—while with bright eager eyes she caught at one bunch after another of the darling scented rushes.*

"I only hope the boat won't tipple over!" she said to herself. "Oh, *what* a lovely one! Only I couldn't quite reach it." And it certainly *did* seem a little provoking ("almost as if it happened on purpose," she thought) that, though she managed to pick plenty of beautiful rushes as the boat glided by, there was always a more lovely one that she couldn't reach.

"The prettiest are always further!"* she said at last, with a sigh at the obstinacy of the rushes in growing so far off, as, with flushed cheeks and dripping hair and hands, she scrambled back into her place, and began to arrange her new-found treasures.

What mattered it to her just then that the rushes had begun to fade, and to lose all their scent and beauty, from the very moment that she picked them? Even real scented rushes, you know, last only a very little while—and these, being dream-rushes, melted away almost like snow, as they lay in heaps at her feet—but Alice hardly noticed this, there were so many other curious things to think about.*

They hadn't gone much farther before the blade of one of the oars got fast in the water and *wouldn't* come out again (so Alice explained it afterwards), and the consequence was that the handle of it caught her under the chin, and, in spite of a series of little shrieks of 'Oh, oh, oh!' from poor Alice, it swept her straight off the seat, and down among the heap of rushes.

However, she wasn't a bit hurt,* and was soon up again: the Sheep went on with her knitting all the while, just as if nothing had happened. "That was a nice crab you caught!" she remarked, as

Alice got back into her place, very much relieved to find herself still in the boat.

"Was it? I didn't see it," said Alice, peeping cautiously over the side of the boat into the dark water. "I wish it hadn't let go—I should so like a little crab to take home with me!" But the Sheep only laughed scornfully, and went on with her knitting.

"Are there many crabs here?" said Alice.

"Crabs, and all sorts of things," said the Sheep: "plenty of choice, only make up your mind. Now, what *do* you want to buy?"

"To buy!" Alice echoed in a tone that was half astonished and half frightened—for the oars, and the boat, and the river, had vanished all in a moment, and she was back again in the little dark shop.

"I should like to buy an egg, please," she said timidly. "How do you sell them?"

"Fivepence farthing* for one—twopence for two," the Sheep replied.

"Then two are cheaper than one?" Alice said in a surprised tone, taking out her purse.

"Only you *must* eat them both, if you buy two," said the Sheep.

"Then I'll have *one*, please," said Alice, as she put the money down on the counter. For she thought to herself, "They mightn't be at all nice, you know."*

The Sheep took the money, and put it away in a box: then she said "I never put things into people's hands—that would never do—you must get it for yourself." And so saying, she went off* to the other end of the shop, and set the egg upright on a shelf.

"I wonder *why* it wouldn't do?" thought Alice, as she groped her way among the tables and chairs, for the shop was very dark towards the end. "The egg seems to get further away the more I walk towards it. Let me see, is this a chair? Why, it's got branches, I declare! How very odd to find trees growing here! And actually here's a little brook!* Well, this is the very queerest shop I ever saw!"

<pre>
    *   *   *   *   *

        *   *   *   *   *

    *   *   *   *   *
</pre>

So she went on, wondering more and more at every step, as everything turned into a tree the moment she came up to it, and she quite expected the egg to do the same.

CHAPTER VI

HUMPTY DUMPTY

HOWEVER, the egg only got larger and larger, and more and more human: when she had come within a few yards of it, she saw that it had eyes and a nose and mouth; and when she had come close to it, she saw clearly that it was HUMPTY DUMPTY himself.* "It can't be anybody else!" she said to herself. "I'm as certain of it, as if his name were written all over his face."

It might have been written a hundred times, easily, on that enormous face. Humpty Dumpty was sitting with his legs crossed, like a Turk, on the top of a high wall*—such a narrow one that Alice quite wondered how he could keep his balance—and, as his eyes were steadily fixed in the opposite direction, and he didn't take the least notice of her, she thought he must be a stuffed figure after all.

"And how exactly like an egg he is!" she said aloud, standing with her hands ready to catch him, for she was every moment expecting him to fall.

"It's *very* provoking," Humpty Dumpty said after a long silence, looking away from Alice as he spoke, "to be called an egg—*very*!"

"I said you *looked* like an egg, Sir," Alice gently explained. "And some eggs are very pretty, you know," she added, hoping to turn her remark into a sort of compliment.

"Some people," said Humpty Dumpty, looking away from her as usual, "have no more sense than a baby!"

Alice didn't know what to say to this: it wasn't at all like conversation, she thought, as he never said anything to *her*; in fact, his last remark was evidently addressed to a tree—so she stood and softly repeated* to herself:—

> "*Humpty Dumpty sat on a wall:*
> *Humpty Dumpty had a great fall.*
> *All the King's horses and all the King's men*
> *Couldn't put Humpty Dumpty in his place again.*"

"That last line* is much too long for the poetry," she added, almost out loud, forgetting that Humpty Dumpty would hear her.

"Don't stand chattering to yourself like that," Humpty Dumpty said, looking at her for the first time, "but tell me your name and your business."

"My *name* is Alice, but——"

"It's a stupid name enough!" Humpty Dumpty interrupted impatiently. "What does it mean?"

"*Must* a name mean something?"* Alice asked doubtfully.

"Of course it must," Humpty Dumpty said with a short laugh: "*my* name means the shape I am—and a good handsome shape it is, too.* With a name like yours, you might be any shape, almost."

"Why do you sit out here all alone?" said Alice, not wishing to begin an argument.

"Why, because there's nobody with me!" cried Humpty Dumpty. "Did you think I didn't know the answer to *that?* Ask another."

"Don't you think you'd be safer down on the ground?" Alice went on, not with any idea of making another riddle, but simply in her good-natured anxiety for the queer creature. "That wall is so *very* narrow!"

"What tremendously easy riddles you ask!" Humpty Dumpty growled out. "Of course I don't think so! Why, if ever I *did* fall off—which there's no chance of—but *if* I did——" Here he pursed up his lips, and looked so solemn and grand that Alice could hardly help laughing. "*If* I did fall," he went on, "*the King has promised me*—ah, you may turn pale, if you like! You didn't think I was going to say that, did you? *The King has promised me—with his very own mouth*—to—to——"

"To send all his horses and all his men," Alice interrupted, rather unwisely.

"Now I declare that's too bad!" Humpty Dumpty cried, breaking into a sudden passion. "You've been listening at doors—and behind trees—and down chimneys—or you couldn't have known it!"

"I haven't, indeed!" Alice said very gently. "It's in a book."

"Ah, well! They may write such things in a *book*," Humpty Dumpty said in a calmer tone. "That's what you call a History of England,* that is. Now, take a good look at me! I'm one that has spoken to a King, *I* am: mayhap you'll never see such another: and to show you I'm not proud,* you may shake hands with me!" And he grinned almost from ear to ear, as he leant forwards (and as nearly as possible fell off the

wall in doing so) and offered
Alice his hand. She watched him
a little anxiously as she took it.
"If he smiled much more, the
ends of his mouth might meet
behind," she thought: "and then
I don't know what would happen
to his head! I'm afraid it would
come off!"

"Yes, all his horses and all his
men," Humpty Dumpty went on.
"They'd pick me up again in
a minute, *they* would! However, this conversation is going on a little
too fast: let's go back to the last remark but one."

"I'm afraid I can't quite remember it," Alice said very politely.

"In that case we start fresh," said Humpty Dumpty, "and it's my
turn to choose a subject——" ("He talks about it just as if it was
a game!" thought Alice.) "So here's a question for you. How old did
you say you were?"

Alice made a short calculation, and said "Seven years and six
months."

"Wrong!" Humpty Dumpty exclaimed triumphantly. "You never
said a word like it!"

"I thought you meant 'How old *are* you?'" Alice explained.

"If I'd meant that, I'd have said it," said Humpty Dumpty.

Alice didn't want to begin another argument, so she said nothing.

"Seven years and six months!" Humpty Dumpty repeated thoughtfully. "An uncomfortable sort of age. Now if you'd asked *my* advice, I'd have said 'Leave off at seven'——but it's too late now."

"I never ask advice about growing," Alice said indignantly.

"Too proud?" the other enquired.

Alice felt even more indignant at this suggestion. "I mean," she said, "that one can't help growing older."

"*One* can't, perhaps," said Humpty Dumpty, "but *two* can. With proper assistance, you might have left off at seven."*

"What a beautiful belt you've got on!" Alice suddenly remarked. (They had had quite enough of the subject of age, she thought: and if they really were to take turns in choosing subjects, it was her turn now.) "At least," she corrected herself on second thoughts, "a beautiful cravat, I should have said—no, a belt, I mean—I beg your pardon!" she added in dismay, for Humpty Dumpty looked thoroughly offended, and she began to wish she hadn't chosen that subject. "If only I knew," she thought to herself, "which was neck and which was waist!"

Evidently Humpty Dumpty was very angry, though he said nothing for a minute or two. When he *did* speak again, it was in a deep growl.

"It is a—*most*—*provoking*—thing," he said at last, "when a person doesn't know a cravat from a belt!"

"I know it's very ignorant of me," Alice said, in so humble a tone that Humpty Dumpty relented.

"It's a cravat, child, and a beautiful one, as you say. It's a present from the White King and Queen. There now!"

"Is it really?" said Alice, quite pleased to find that she *had* chosen a good subject, after all.

"They gave it me," Humpty Dumpty continued thoughtfully, as he crossed one knee over the other and clasped his hands round it, "they gave it me—for an un-birthday present."*

"I beg your pardon?" Alice said with a puzzled air.

"I'm not offended," said Humpty Dumpty.

"I mean, what *is* an un-birthday present?"

"A present given when it isn't your birthday, of course."

Alice considered a little. "I like birthday presents best," she said at last.

"You don't know what you're talking about!" cried Humpty Dumpty. "How many days are there in a year?"

"Three hundred and sixty-five," said Alice.

"And how many birthdays have you?"

"One."

"And if you take one from three hundred and sixty-five, what remains?"

"Three hundred and sixty-four, of course."

Humpty Dumpty looked doubtful. "I'd rather see that done on paper," he said.

Alice couldn't help smiling as she took out her memorandum-book, and worked the sum for him:*

$$
\begin{array}{r}
365 \\
1 \\
\hline
364 \\
\hline
\end{array}
$$

Humpty Dumpty took the book, and looked at it carefully. "That seems to be done right——" he began.

"You're holding it upside down!" Alice interrupted.

"To be sure I was!" Humpty Dumpty said gaily, as she turned it round for him. "I thought it looked a little queer. As I was saying, that *seems* to be done right—though I haven't time to look it over thoroughly just now—and that shows that there are three hundred and sixty-four days when you might get un-birthday presents——"

"Certainly," said Alice.

"And only *one* for birthday presents, you know. There's glory for you!"

"I don't know what you mean by 'glory,' " Alice said.

Humpty Dumpty smiled contemptuously. "Of course you don't—till I tell you. I meant 'there's a nice knock-down argument for you!' "

"But 'glory' doesn't mean 'a nice knock-down argument,' "* Alice objected.

"When *I* use a word," Humpty Dumpty said in rather a scornful tone, "it means just what I choose it to mean—neither more nor less."

"The question is," said Alice, "whether you *can* make words mean so many different things."

"The question is," said Humpty Dumpty, "which is to be master——that's all."*

Alice was too much puzzled to say anything, so after a minute Humpty Dumpty began again. "They've a temper, some of them—particularly verbs, they're the proudest—adjectives you can do anything with, but not verbs—however, *I* can manage the whole lot of them!* Impenetrability! That's what *I* say!"

"Would you tell me, please," said Alice, "what that means?"

"Now you talk like a reasonable child," said Humpty Dumpty, looking very much pleased. "I meant by 'impenetrability' that we've had enough of that subject, and it would be just as well if you'd mention what you mean to do next, as I suppose you don't mean to stop here all the rest of your life."

"That's a great deal to make one word mean," Alice said in a thoughtful tone.

"When I make a word do a lot of work like that," said Humpty Dumpty, "I always pay it extra."

"Oh!" said Alice. She was too much puzzled to make any other remark.

"Ah, you should see 'em come round me of a Saturday night," Humpty Dumpty went on, wagging his head gravely from side to side: "for to get their wages, you know."

(Alice didn't venture to ask what he paid them with; and so you see I can't tell *you*.)

"You seem very clever at explaining words, Sir," said Alice. "Would you kindly tell me the meaning of the poem called 'Jabberwocky'?"*

"Let's hear it," said Humpty Dumpty. "I can explain all the poems that ever were invented—and a good many that haven't been invented just yet."

This sounded very hopeful, so Alice repeated the first verse:

> " *'Twas brillig, and the slithy toves*
> *Did gyre and gimble in the wabe:*
> *All mimsy were the borogoves,*
> *And the mome raths outgrabe.*"

"That's enough to begin with," Humpty Dumpty interrupted: "there are plenty of hard words there. '*Brillig*' means four o'clock in the afternoon—the time when you begin *broiling* things for dinner."

"That'll do very well," said Alice: "and '*slithy*'?"

"Well, '*slithy*' means 'lithe and slimy.' 'Lithe' is the same as 'active.' You see it's like a portmanteau—there are two meanings packed up into one word."*

"I see it now," Alice remarked thoughtfully: "and what are '*toves*'?"

"Well, '*toves*' are something like badgers—they're something like lizards—and they're something like corkscrews."

"They must be very curious-looking creatures."

"They are that," said Humpty Dumpty: "also they make their nests under sun-dials—also they live on cheese."

"And what's to '*gyre*' and to '*gimble*'?"

"To '*gyre*' is to go round and round like a gyroscope.* To '*gimble*' is to make holes like a gimblet."*

"And '*the wabe*' is the grass-plot round a sun-dial, I suppose?" said Alice, surprised at her own ingenuity.

"Of course it is. It's called '*wabe*,' you know, because it goes a long way before it, and a long way behind it——"

"And a long way beyond it on each side," Alice added.

"Exactly so. Well then, '*mimsy*' is 'flimsy and miserable' (there's another portmanteau for you). And a '*borogove*' is a thin shabby-looking bird with its feathers sticking out all round—something like a live mop."

"And then '*mome raths*'?" said Alice. "I'm afraid I'm giving you a great deal of trouble."

"Well, a '*rath*' is a sort of green pig: but '*mome*' I'm not certain about. I think it's short for 'from home'—meaning that they'd lost their way, you know."

"And what does '*outgrabe*' mean?"

"Well, '*outgribing*' is something between bellowing and whistling, with a kind of sneeze in the middle: however, you'll hear it done, maybe—down in the wood yonder—and when you've once heard it you'll be *quite* content. Who's been repeating all that hard stuff to you?"

"I read it in a book," said Alice. "But I had some poetry repeated to me, much easier than that, by—Tweedledee, I think it was."

"As to poetry, you know," said Humpty Dumpty, stretching out one of his great hands, "*I* can repeat poetry as well as other folk, if it comes to that——"

"Oh, it needn't come to that!" Alice hastily said, hoping to keep him from beginning.*

"The piece I'm going to repeat," he went on without noticing her remark, "was written entirely for your amusement."

Alice felt that in that case she really *ought* to listen to it, so she sat down, and said "Thank you" rather sadly.

> "*In winter, when the fields are white,**
> *I sing this song for your delight*——

only I don't sing it," he added, as an explanation.

"I see you don't," said Alice.

"If you can *see* whether I'm singing or not, you've sharper eyes than most," Humpty Dumpty remarked severely. Alice was silent.

> "*In spring, when woods are getting green,*
> *I'll try and tell you what I mean.*"

"Thank you very much," said Alice.

> "*In summer, when the days are long,*
> *Perhaps you'll understand the song:*
>
> *In autumn, when the leaves are brown,*
> *Take pen and ink, and write it down.*"

"I will, if I can remember it so long," said Alice.

"You needn't go on making remarks like that," Humpty Dumpty said: "they're not sensible, and they put me out."

> "*I sent a message to the fish:*
> *I told them 'This is what I wish.'*
>
> *The little fishes of the sea,*
> *They sent an answer back to me.*
>
> *The little fishes' answer was*
> '*We cannot do it, Sir, because———*' "

"I'm afraid I don't quite understand," said Alice.

"It gets easier further on," Humpty Dumpty replied.

> "*I sent to them again to say*
> '*It will be better to obey.*'
>
> *The fishes answered with a grin,*
> '*Why, what a temper you are in!*'
>
> *I told them once, I told them twice:*
> *They would not listen to advice.*
>
> *I took a kettle large and new,*
> *Fit for the deed I had to do.*

My heart went hop, my heart went thump;
I filled the kettle at the pump.

Then some one came to me and said,
'The little fishes are in bed.'

I said to him, I said it plain,
'Then you must wake them up again.'

I said it very loud and clear;
I went and shouted in his ear."

Humpty Dumpty raised his voice almost to a scream as he repeated
this verse, and Alice thought with a shudder, "I wouldn't have been
the messenger* for *anything!*"

"But he was very stiff and proud;
He said 'You needn't shout so loud!'

And he was very proud and stiff;
He said 'I'd go and wake them, if——'

I took a corkscrew from the shelf:
I went to wake them up myself.

And when I found the door was locked,
I pulled and pushed and kicked and knocked.

And when I found the door was shut,
I tried to turn the handle, but——"

There was a long pause.

"Is that all?"* Alice timidly asked.

"That's all," said Humpty Dumpty. "Good-bye."

This was rather sudden, Alice thought: but, after such a *very* strong hint that she ought to be going, she felt that it would hardly be civil to stay. So she got up, and held out her hand. "Good-bye, till we meet again!" she said as cheerfully as she could.

"I shouldn't know you again if we *did* meet," Humpty Dumpty replied in a discontented tone, giving her one of his fingers to shake;* "you're so exactly like other people."

"The face is what one goes by, generally," Alice remarked in a thoughtful tone.

"That's just what I complain of," said Humpty Dumpty. "Your face is the same as everybody has—the two eyes, so——" (marking their places in the air with his thumb) "nose in the middle, mouth under. It's always the same. Now if you had the two eyes on the same side of the nose, for instance—or the mouth at the top—that would be *some* help."

"It wouldn't look nice," Alice objected. But Humpty Dumpty only shut his eyes and said "Wait till you've tried."

Alice waited a minute to see if he would speak again, but as he never opened his eyes or took any further notice of her, she said "Good-bye!" once more, and, getting no answer to this, she quietly walked away: but she couldn't help saying to herself as she went, "Of all the unsatisfactory——" (she repeated this aloud, as it was a great comfort to have such a long word to say) "of all the unsatisfactory people I *ever* met——" She never finished the sentence,* for at this moment a heavy crash shook the forest from end to end.

CHAPTER VII

THE LION AND THE UNICORN

THE next moment soldiers came running through the wood, at first in twos and threes, then ten or twenty together, and at last in such crowds that they seemed to fill the whole forest. Alice got behind a tree, for fear of being run over, and watched them go by.

She thought that in all her life she had never seen soldiers so uncertain on their feet: they were always tripping over something or other, and whenever one went down, several more always fell over him, so that the ground was soon covered with little heaps of men.

Then came the horses. Having four feet, these managed rather better than the foot-soldiers: but even *they* stumbled now and then; and it seemed to be a regular rule that, whenever a horse stumbled, the rider fell off instantly. The confusion got worse every moment, and Alice was very glad to get out of the wood into an open place, where she found the White King seated on the ground, busily writing in his memorandum-book.*

"I've sent them all!" the King cried in a tone of delight, on seeing Alice. "Did you happen to meet any soldiers, my dear, as you came through the wood?"

"Yes, I did," said Alice: "several thousand, I should think."

"Four thousand two hundred and seven,* that's the exact number," the King said, referring to his book. "I couldn't send all the horses, you know, because two of them are wanted in the game.* And I haven't sent the two Messengers,* either. They're both gone to the town. Just look along the road, and tell me if you can see either of them."

"I see nobody on the road," said Alice.

"I only wish *I* had such eyes," the King remarked in a fretful tone. "To be able to see Nobody! And at that distance too! Why, it's as much as *I* can do to see real people, by this light!"

All this was lost on Alice, who was still looking intently along the road, shading her eyes with one hand. "I see somebody now!" she

exclaimed at last. "But he's coming very slowly—and what curious attitudes he goes into!" (For the Messenger kept skipping up and down, and wriggling like an eel, as he came along, with his great hands spread out like fans on each side.)

"Not at all," said the King. "He's an Anglo-Saxon Messenger—and those are Anglo-Saxon attitudes.* He only does them when he's happy. His name is Haigha."* (He pronounced it so as to rhyme with 'mayor.')

"I love my love with an H,"* Alice couldn't help beginning, "because he is Happy. I hate him with an H, because he is Hideous.

I fed him with—with—with Ham-sandwiches and Hay. His name is Haigha, and he lives——"

"He lives on the Hill," the King remarked simply, without the least idea that he was joining in the game, while Alice was still hesitating for the name of a town beginning with H. "The other Messenger's called Hatta.* I must have *two*,* you know—to come and go. One to come, and one to go."

"I beg your pardon?" said Alice.

"It isn't respectable to beg," said the King.

"I only meant that I didn't understand," said Alice. "Why one to come and one to go?"

"Don't I tell you?" the King repeated impatiently. "I must have *two*—to fetch and carry. One to fetch, and one to carry."

At this moment the Messenger arrived: he was far too much out of breath to say a word, and could only wave his hands about, and make the most fearful faces at the poor King.

"This young lady loves you with an H," the King said, introducing Alice in the hope of turning off the Messenger's attention from himself—but it was of no use—the Anglo-Saxon attitudes only got more extraordinary every moment, while the great eyes rolled wildly from side to side.*

"You alarm me!" said the King. "I feel faint——Give me a ham sandwich!"

On which the Messenger, to Alice's great amusement, opened a bag that hung round his neck, and handed a sandwich to the King, who devoured it greedily.

"Another sandwich!" said the King.

"There's nothing but hay left now," the Messenger said, peeping into the bag.

"Hay, then,"* the King murmured in a faint whisper.

Alice was glad to see that it revived him a good deal. "There's nothing like eating hay when you're faint," he remarked to her, as he munched away.

"I should think throwing cold water over you* would be better," Alice suggested: "—or some sal-volatile."*

"I didn't say there was nothing *better*," the King replied. "I said there was nothing *like* it." Which Alice did not venture to deny.

"Who did you pass on the road?" the King went on, holding out his hand to the Messenger for some more hay.

"Nobody," said the Messenger.

"Quite right," said the King: "this young lady saw him too. So of course Nobody walks slower than you."

"I do my best," the Messenger said in a sullen tone. "I'm sure nobody walks much faster than I do!"

"He can't do that," said the King, "or else he'd have been here first. However, now you've got your breath, you may tell us what's happened in the town."

"I'll whisper it," said the Messenger, putting his hands to his mouth in the shape of a trumpet, and stooping so as to get close to the King's ear. Alice was sorry for this, as she wanted to hear the news too. However, instead of whispering, he simply shouted at the top of his voice, "They're at it again!"

"Do you call *that* a whisper?" cried the poor King, jumping up and shaking himself. "If you do such a thing again, I'll have you buttered!* It went through and through my head like an earthquake!"

"It would have to be a very tiny earthquake!" thought Alice. "Who are at it again?" she ventured to ask.

"Why, the Lion and the Unicorn,* of course," said the King.

"Fighting for the crown?"

"Yes, to be sure," said the King: "and the best of the joke is, that it's *my* crown all the while! Let's run and see them." And they trotted off, Alice repeating to herself, as she ran, the words of the old song:—*

> *"The Lion and the Unicorn were fighting for the crown:*
> *The Lion beat the Unicorn all round the town.*
> *Some gave them white bread, some gave them brown;*
> *Some gave them plum-cake and drummed them out of town."*

"Does——the one——that wins——get the crown?" she asked, as well as she could, for the run was putting her quite out of breath.

"Dear me, no!" said the King. "What an idea!"

"Would you—be good enough——" Alice panted out, after running a little further, "to stop a minute—just to get—one's breath again?"

"I'm *good* enough," the King said, "only I'm not strong enough. You see, a minute goes by so fearfully quick. You might as well try to stop a Bandersnatch!"*

Alice had no more breath for talking, so they trotted on in silence, till they came in sight of a great crowd, in the middle of which the Lion and Unicorn were fighting. They were in such a cloud of dust, that at first Alice could not make out which was which: but she soon managed to distinguish the Unicorn by his horn.

They placed themselves close to where Hatta, the other Messenger, was standing watching the fight, with a cup of tea in one hand and a piece of bread-and-butter in the other.

"He's only just out of prison, and he hadn't finished his tea when he was sent in," Haigha whispered to Alice: "and they only give them oyster-shells* in there—so you see he's very hungry and thirsty. How are you, dear child?" he went on, putting his arm affectionately round Hatta's neck.

Hatta looked round and nodded, and went on with his bread-and-butter.

"Were you happy in prison, dear child?" said Haigha.

Hatta looked round once more, and this time a tear or two trickled down his cheek: but not a word would he say.

"Speak, can't you!" Haigha cried impatiently. But Hatta only munched away, and drank some more tea.

"Speak, won't you!" cried the King. "How are they getting on with the fight?"

Hatta made a desperate effort, and swallowed a large piece of bread-and-butter. "They're getting on very well," he said in a choking voice: "each of them has been down about eighty-seven times."

"Then I suppose they'll soon bring the white bread and the brown?" Alice ventured to remark.

"It's waiting for 'em now," said Hatta: "this is a bit of it as I'm eating."

There was a pause in the fight just then, and the Lion and the Unicorn sat down, panting, while the King called out "Ten minutes allowed for refreshments!" Haigha and Hatta set to work at once, carrying round trays of white and brown bread. Alice took a piece to taste, but it was *very* dry.*

"I don't think they'll fight any more to-day," the King said to Hatta: "go and order the drums to begin." And Hatta went bounding away like a grasshopper.

For a minute or two Alice stood silent, watching him. Suddenly she brightened up. "Look, look!" she cried, pointing eagerly. "There's

the White Queen running across the country! She came flying out of the wood over yonder——How fast those Queens *can* run!"

"There's some enemy after her,* no doubt," the King said, without even looking round. "That wood's full of them."

"But aren't you going to run and help her?" Alice asked, very much surprised at his taking it so quietly.

"No use, no use!" said the King. "She runs so fearfully quick. You might as well try to catch a Bandersnatch! But I'll make a memorandum about her, if you like——She's a dear good creature," he repeated softly to himself, as he opened his memorandum-book. "Do you spell 'creature' with a double 'e'?"

At this moment the Unicorn sauntered by them, with his hands in his pockets. "I had the best of it this time?" he said to the King, just glancing at him as he passed.

"A little—a little," the King replied, rather nervously. "You shouldn't have run him through with your horn, you know."

"It didn't hurt him," the Unicorn said carelessly, and he was going on, when his eye happened to fall upon Alice: he turned round instantly, and stood for some time looking at her with an air of the deepest disgust.

"What—is—this?" he said at last.

"This is a child!" Haigha replied eagerly, coming in front of Alice to introduce her, and spreading out both his hands towards her in an Anglo-Saxon attitude. "We only found it to-day. It's as large as life, and twice as natural!"*

"I always thought they were fabulous monsters!"* said the Unicorn. "Is it alive?"*

"It can talk," said Haigha, solemnly.

The Unicorn looked dreamily at Alice, and said "Talk, child."

Alice could not help her lips curling up into a smile as she began: "Do you know, I always thought Unicorns were fabulous monsters, too! I never saw one alive before!"

"Well, now that we *have* seen each other," said the Unicorn, "if you'll believe in me, I'll believe in you. Is that a bargain?"*

"Yes, if you like," said Alice.

"Come, fetch out the plum-cake, old man!" the Unicorn went on, turning from her to the King. "None of your brown bread for me!"

"Certainly—certainly!" the King muttered, and beckoned to Haigha. "Open the bag!" he whispered. "Quick! Not that one—that's full of hay!"

Haigha took a large cake out of the bag, and gave it to Alice to hold, while he got out a dish and carving-knife. How they all came out of it Alice couldn't guess. It was just like a conjuring-trick, she thought.

The Lion had joined them while this was going on: he looked very tired and sleepy, and his eyes were half shut. "What's this!" he said, blinking lazily at Alice, and speaking in a deep hollow tone that sounded like the tolling of a great bell.*

"Ah, what *is* it, now?" the Unicorn cried eagerly. "You'll never guess! *I* couldn't."

The Lion looked at Alice wearily. "Are you animal—or vegetable—or mineral?"* he said, yawning at every other word.

"It's a fabulous monster!"* the Unicorn cried out, before Alice could reply.

"Then hand round the plum-cake, Monster," the Lion said, lying down and putting his chin on his paws. "And sit down, both of you," (to the King and the Unicorn): "fair play with the cake, you know!"

The King was evidently very uncomfortable at having to sit down between the two great creatures; but there was no other place for him.

"What a fight we might have for the crown, *now!*' the Unicorn said, looking slyly up at the crown, which the poor King was nearly shaking off his head, he trembled so much.

"I should win easy," said the Lion.

"I'm not so sure of that," said the Unicorn.

"Why, I beat you all round the town, you chicken!"* the Lion replied angrily, half getting up as he spoke.

Here the King interrupted, to prevent the quarrel going on: he was very nervous, and his voice quite quivered. "All round the town?" he said. "That's a good long way. Did you go by the old bridge, or the market-place? You get the best view by the old bridge."

"I'm sure I don't know," the Lion growled out as he lay down again. "There was too much dust to see anything. What a time the Monster is, cutting up that cake!"

Alice had seated herself on the bank of a little brook, with the great dish on her knees, and was sawing away diligently with the knife. "It's very provoking!" she said, in reply to the Lion (she was getting quite used to being called 'the Monster'). "I've cut several slices already, but they always join on again!"

"You don't know how to manage Looking-glass cakes," the Unicorn remarked. "Hand it round first, and cut it afterwards."

This sounded nonsense, but Alice very obediently got up, and carried the dish round, and the cake divided itself into three pieces as she did so. "*Now* cut it up," said the Lion, as she returned to her place with the empty dish.

"I say, this isn't fair!" cried the Unicorn, as Alice sat with the knife in her hand, very much puzzled how to begin. "The Monster has given the Lion twice as much as me!"*

"She's kept none for herself, anyhow," said the Lion. "Do you like plum-cake, Monster?"

But before Alice could answer him, the drums began.

Where the noise came from, she couldn't make out: the air seemed full of it, and it rang through and through her head till she felt quite deafened. She started to her feet and sprang across the little brook in her terror,*

* * * * * *

* * * * *

* * * * * *

and had just time to see the Lion and the Unicorn rise to their feet, with angry looks at being interrupted in their feast, before she dropped to her knees, and put her hands over her ears, vainly trying to shut out the dreadful uproar.

"If *that* doesn't 'drum them out of town,'" she thought to herself, "nothing ever will!"

CHAPTER VIII

"IT'S MY OWN INVENTION"

AFTER a while the noise seemed gradually to die away, till all was dead silence, and Alice lifted up her head in some alarm. There was no one to be seen, and her first thought was that she must have been dreaming about the Lion and the Unicorn and those queer Anglo-Saxon Messengers. However, there was the great dish still lying at her feet, on which she had tried to cut the plum-cake, "So I wasn't dreaming, after all," she said to herself, "unless—unless we're all part of the same dream. Only I do hope it's *my* dream, and not the Red King's! I don't like belonging to another person's dream," she went on in a rather complaining tone: "I've a great mind to go and wake him, and see what happens!"*

At this moment her thoughts were interrupted by a loud shouting of "Ahoy! Ahoy! Check!" and a Knight, dressed in crimson armour,* came galloping down upon her, brandishing a great club. Just as he reached her, the horse stopped suddenly: "You're my prisoner!"* the Knight cried, as he tumbled off his horse.

Startled as she was, Alice was more frightened for him than for herself at the moment, and watched him with some anxiety as he mounted again. As soon as he was comfortably in the saddle, he began once more "You're my——" but here another voice broke in "Ahoy! Ahoy! Check!" and Alice looked round in some surprise for the new enemy.

This time it was a White Knight.* He drew up at Alice's side, and tumbled off his horse just as the Red Knight had done: then he got on again, and the two Knights sat and looked at each other for some time without speaking. Alice looked from one to the other in some bewilderment.*

"She's *my* prisoner, you know!" the Red Knight said at last.

"Yes, but then *I* came and rescued her!" the White Knight replied.

"Well, we must fight for her, then," said the Red Knight, as he took up his helmet (which hung from the saddle, and was something the shape of a horse's head), and put it on.

"You will observe the Rules of Battle,* of course?" the White Knight remarked, putting on his helmet too.

"I always do," said the Red Knight, and they began banging away at each other with such fury that Alice got behind a tree to be out of the way of the blows.

"I wonder, now, what the Rules of Battle are," she said to herself, as she watched the fight, timidly peeping out from her hiding-place: "one Rule seems to be, that if one Knight hits the other, he knocks him off his horse, and if he misses, he tumbles off himself—and another Rule seems to be that they hold their clubs with their arms, as if they were Punch and Judy*——What a noise they make when they tumble! Just like a whole set of fire-irons falling into the fender! And how quiet the horses are!* They let them get on and off them just as if they were tables!"

Another Rule of Battle, that Alice had not noticed, seemed to be that they always fell on their heads, and the battle ended with their both falling off in this way, side by side: when they got up again, they shook hands, and then the Red Knight mounted and galloped off.

"It was a glorious victory,* wasn't it?" said the White Knight, as he came up panting.

"I don't know," Alice said doubtfully. "I don't want to be anybody's prisoner. I want to be a Queen."

"So you will, when you've crossed the next brook," said the White Knight. "I'll see you safe to the end of the wood—and then I must go back, you know. That's the end of my move."*

"Thank you very much," said Alice. "May I help you off with your helmet?"* It was evidently more than he could manage by himself; however, she managed to shake him out of it at last.

"Now one can breathe more easily," said the Knight, putting back his shaggy hair with both hands, and turning his gentle face and large mild eyes to Alice. She thought she had never seen such a strange-looking soldier in all her life.

He was dressed in tin armour, which seemed to fit him very badly, and he had a queer-shaped little deal box* fastened across his shoulders, upside-down, and with the lid hanging open. Alice looked at it with great curiosity.

"I see you're admiring my little box," the Knight said in a friendly tone. "It's my own invention*—to keep clothes and sandwiches in. You see I carry it upside-down, so that the rain can't get in."

"But the things can get *out*," Alice gently remarked. "Do you know the lid's open?"

"I didn't know it," the Knight said, a shade of vexation passing over his face. "Then all the things must have fallen out! And the box is no use without them." He unfastened it as he spoke, and was just going to throw it into the bushes, when a sudden thought seemed to strike him, and he hung it carefully on a tree. "Can you guess why I did that?" he said to Alice.

Alice shook her head.

"In hopes some bees may make a nest in it—then I should get the honey."

"But you've got a bee-hive—or something like one—fastened to the saddle," said Alice.

"Yes, it's a very good bee-hive," the Knight said in a discontented tone, "one of the best kind. But not a single bee has come near it yet. And the other thing is a mouse-trap. I suppose the mice keep the bees out—or the bees keep the mice out, I don't know which."

"I was wondering what the mouse-trap was for," said Alice. "It isn't very likely there would be any mice on the horse's back."

"Not very likely, perhaps," said the Knight; "but if they *do* come, I don't choose to have them running all about."

"You see," he went on after a pause, "it's as well to be provided for *everything*. That's the reason the horse has all those anklets round his feet."

"But what are they for?" Alice asked in a tone of great curiosity.

"To guard against the bites of sharks," the Knight replied. "It's an invention of my own. And now help me on. I'll go with you to the end of the wood——What's that dish for?"

"It's meant for plum-cake," said Alice.

"We'd better take it with us," the Knight said. "It'll come in handy if we find any plum-cake.* Help me to get it into this bag."

This took a long time to manage, though Alice held the bag open very carefully, because the Knight was so *very* awkward in putting in the dish: the first two or three times that he tried he fell in himself instead. "It's rather a tight fit, you see," he said, as they got it in at last; "there are so many candlesticks in the bag." And he hung it to the saddle, which was already loaded with bunches of carrots, and fire-irons, and many other things.

"I hope you've got your hair well fastened on?" he continued, as they set off.

"Only in the usual way," Alice said, smiling.

"That's hardly enough," he said, anxiously. "You see the wind is so *very* strong here. It's as strong as soup."

"Have you invented a plan for keeping the hair from being blown off?" Alice enquired.

"Not yet," said the Knight. "But I've got a plan for keeping it from *falling* off."

"I should like to hear it, very much."

"First you take an upright stick," said the Knight. "Then you make your hair creep up it, like a fruit-tree. Now the reason hair falls off is because it hangs *down*—things never fall *upwards*, you know. It's a plan of my own invention. You may try it if you like."

It didn't sound a comfortable plan, Alice thought, and for a few minutes she walked on in silence, puzzling over the idea, and every now and then stopping to help the poor Knight, who certainly was *not* a good rider.*

Whenever the horse stopped (which it did very often), he fell off in front; and whenever it went on again (which it generally did rather suddenly), he fell off behind. Otherwise he kept on pretty well,* except that he had a habit of now and then falling off sideways; and as he generally did this on the side on which Alice was walking, she soon found that it was the best plan not to walk *quite* close to the horse.

"I'm afraid you've not had much practice in riding," she ventured to say, as she was helping him up from his fifth tumble.

The Knight looked very much surprised, and a little offended at the remark. "What makes you say that?" he asked, as he scrambled back into the saddle, keeping hold of Alice's hair with one hand, to save himself from falling over on the other side.

"Because people don't fall off quite so often, when they've had much practice."

"I've had plenty of practice," the Knight said very gravely: "plenty of practice!"

Alice could think of nothing better to say than "Indeed?" but she said it as heartily as she could. They went on a little way in silence after this, the Knight with his eyes shut, muttering to himself, and Alice watching anxiously for the next tumble.

"The great art of riding," the Knight suddenly began in a loud voice, waving his right arm as he spoke, "is to keep——" Here the sentence ended as suddenly as it had begun, as the Knight fell heavily on the top of his head exactly in the path where Alice was walking. She was quite frightened this time, and said in an anxious tone, as she picked him up, "I hope no bones are broken?"

"None to speak of," the Knight said, as if he didn't mind breaking two or three of them. "The great art of riding, as I was saying, is—to keep your balance properly. Like this, you know——"

He let go the bridle, and stretched out both his arms to show Alice what he meant, and this time he fell flat on his back, right under the horse's feet.

"Plenty of practice!" he went on repeating, all the time that Alice was getting him on his feet again. "Plenty of practice!"

"It's too ridiculous!" cried Alice, losing all her patience this time. "You ought to have a wooden horse on wheels, that you ought!"

"Does that kind go smoothly?"* the Knight asked in a tone of great interest, clasping his arms round the horse's neck as he spoke, just in time to save himself from tumbling off again.

"Much more smoothly than a live horse," Alice said, with a little scream of laughter, in spite of all she could do to prevent it.

"I'll get one," the Knight said thoughtfully to himself. "One or two—several."

There was a short silence after this, and then the Knight went on again. "I'm a great hand at inventing things. Now, I daresay you noticed, the last time you picked me up, that I was looking rather thoughtful?"

"You *were* a little grave," said Alice.

"Well, just then I was inventing a new way of getting over a gate—would you like to hear it?"

"Very much indeed," Alice said politely.

"I'll tell you how I came to think of it," said the Knight. "You see, I said to myself, 'The only difficulty is with the feet: the *head* is high enough already.' Now, first I put my head on the top of the gate—then the head's high enough—then I stand on my head—then the feet are high enough, you see—then I'm over, you see."

"Yes, I suppose you'd be over when that was done," Alice said thoughtfully: "but don't you think it would be rather hard?"

"I haven't tried it yet," the Knight said, gravely: "so I can't tell for certain—but I'm afraid it *would* be a little hard."

He looked so vexed at the idea, that Alice changed the subject hastily. "What a curious helmet you've got!" she said cheerfully. "Is that your invention too?"

The Knight looked down proudly at his helmet, which hung from the saddle. "Yes," he said, "but I've invented a better one than that—like a sugar-loaf.* When I used to wear it, if I fell off the horse, it always touched the ground directly. So I had a *very* little way to fall, you see—But there *was* the danger of falling *into* it, to be sure. That happened to me once—and the worst of it was, before I could get out again, the other White Knight came and put it on. He thought it was his own helmet."

The Knight looked so solemn about it that Alice did not dare to laugh. "I'm afraid you must have hurt him," she said in a trembling voice, "being on the top of his head."

"I had to kick him, of course," the Knight said, very seriously. "And then he took the helmet off again—but it took hours and hours to get me out. I was as fast as—as lightning, you know."

"But that's a different kind of fastness," Alice objected.

The Knight shook his head. "It was all kinds of fastness with me, I can assure you!" he said. He raised his hands in some excitement as he said this, and instantly rolled out of the saddle, and fell headlong into a deep ditch.

Alice ran to the side of the ditch to look for him. She was rather startled by the fall, as for some time he had kept on very well, and she was afraid that he really *was* hurt this time. However, though she could see nothing but the soles of his feet, she was much relieved to hear that he was talking on in his usual tone. "All kinds of fastness," he repeated: "but it was careless of him to put another man's helmet on—with the man in it, too."

"How *can* you go on talking so quietly, head downwards?" Alice asked, as she dragged him out by the feet, and laid him in a heap on the bank.

The Knight looked surprised at the question. "What does it matter where my body happens to be?" he said. "My mind goes on working all the same. In fact, the more head downwards I am, the more I keep inventing new things."

"Now the cleverest thing of the sort that I ever did," he went on after a pause, "was inventing a new pudding during the meat-course."

"In time to have it cooked for the next course?" said Alice. "Well, that *was* quick work, certainly!"

"Well, not the *next* course," the Knight said in a slow thoughtful tone: "no, certainly not the next *course*."

"Then it would have to be the next day. I suppose you wouldn't have two pudding-courses in one dinner?"

"Well, not the *next* day," the Knight repeated as before: "not the next *day*. In fact," he went on, holding his head down, and his voice getting lower and lower, "I don't believe that pudding ever *was* cooked! In fact, I don't believe that pudding ever *will* be cooked! And yet it was a very clever pudding to invent."

"What did you mean it to be made of?" Alice asked, hoping to cheer him up, for the poor Knight seemed quite low-spirited about it.

"It began with blotting-paper," the Knight answered with a groan.

"That wouldn't be very nice, I'm afraid——"

"Not very nice *alone*," he interrupted, quite eagerly: "but you've no idea what a difference it makes, mixing it with other things—such as gunpowder and sealing-wax. And here I must leave you." They had just come to the end of the wood.

Alice could only look puzzled: she was thinking of the pudding.

"You are sad," the Knight said in an anxious tone: "let me sing you a song to comfort you."

"Is it very long?"* Alice asked, for she had heard a good deal of poetry that day.

"It's long," said the Knight, "but it's very, *very* beautiful. Everybody that hears me sing it—either it brings the *tears* into their eyes, or else——"

"Or else what?" said Alice, for the Knight had made a sudden pause.

"Or else it doesn't, you know. The name of the song is called '*Haddocks' Eyes.*' "

"Oh, that's the name of the song, is it?" Alice said, trying to feel interested.

"No, you don't understand," the Knight said, looking a little vexed. "That's what the name is *called*. The name really *is* '*The Aged Aged Man.*' "

"Then I ought to have said 'That's what the *song* is called'?" Alice corrected herself.

"No, you oughtn't: that's quite another thing! The *song* is called '*Ways And Means*': but that's only what it's *called*, you know!"*

"Well, what *is* the song, then?" said Alice, who was by this time completely bewildered.

"I was coming to that," the Knight said. "The song really *is* '*A-sitting On A Gate*': and the tune's my own invention."

So saying, he stopped his horse and let the reins fall on its neck: then, slowly beating time with one hand, and with a faint smile lighting up his gentle foolish face, as if he enjoyed the music of his song, he began.

Of all the strange things that Alice saw in her journey Through The Looking-Glass, this was the one that she always remembered most clearly. Years afterwards she could bring the whole scene back again, as if it had been only yesterday—the mild blue eyes and kindly smile of the Knight—the setting sun gleaming through his hair, and shining on his armour in a blaze of light that quite dazzled her—the horse quietly moving about, with the reins hanging loose on his neck, cropping the grass at her feet—and the black shadows of the forest behind—all this she took in like a picture, as, with one hand shading her eyes, she leant against a tree, watching the strange pair, and listening, in a half dream, to the melancholy music of the song.*

"But the tune *isn't* his own invention," she said to herself: "it's '*I give thee all, I can no more.*' "* She stood and listened very attentively, but no tears came into her eyes.*

> "*I'll tell thee everything I can;**
>   *There's little to relate.*
> *I saw an aged aged man,**
>   *A-sitting on a gate.*
> '*Who are you, aged man?' I said.*
>   '*And how is it you live?'*
> *And his answer trickled through my head*
>   *Like water through a sieve.*
>
> *He said 'I look for butterflies*
>   *That sleep among the wheat:*
> *I make them into mutton-pies,*
>   *And sell them in the street.*
> *I sell them unto men,' he said,*
>   '*Who sail on stormy seas;*
> *And that's the way I get my bread—*
>   *A trifle, if you please.'*
>
> *But I was thinking of a plan*
>   *To dye one's whiskers green,*
> *And always use so large a fan*
>   *That they could not be seen.*
>
> *So, having no reply to give*
>   *To what the old man said,*
> *I cried 'Come, tell me how you live!'*
>   *And thumped him on the head.*
>
> *His accents mild took up the tale:*
>   *He said 'I go my ways,*
> *And when I find a mountain-rill,**
>   *I set it in a blaze;*
> *And thence they make a stuff they call*
>   *Rowland's Macassar Oil—**

Yet twopence-halfpenny is all
    They give me for my toil.'

But I was thinking of a way
    To feed oneself on batter,
And so go on from day to day
    Getting a little fatter.
I shook him well* from side to side,
    Until his face was blue:
'Come, tell me how you live,' I cried,
    'And what it is you do!'

He said 'I hunt for haddocks' eyes
    Among the heather bright,
And work them into waistcoat-buttons
    In the silent night.
And these I do not sell for gold
    Or coin of silvery shine,
But for a copper halfpenny,
    And that will purchase nine.

'I sometimes dig for buttered rolls,
    Or set limed twigs for crabs;*

I sometimes search the grassy knolls
     *For wheels of Hansom-cabs.**
And that's the way' (he gave a wink)
     'By which I get my wealth—
And very gladly will I drink
     Your Honour's noble health.'
I heard him then, for I had just
     Completed my design
To keep the Menai bridge from rust*
     By boiling it in wine.
I thanked him much for telling me
     The way he got his wealth,
But chiefly for his wish that he
     Might drink my noble health.

And now, if e'er by chance I put
     My fingers into glue,
Or madly squeeze a right-hand foot
     Into a left-hand shoe,
Or if I drop upon my toe
     A very heavy weight,
I weep, for it reminds me so
Of that old man I used to know—
Whose look was mild, whose speech was slow,
Whose hair was whiter than the snow,
Whose face was very like a crow,
With eyes, like cinders, all aglow,
Who seemed distracted with his woe,
Who rocked his body to and fro,
And muttered mumblingly and low,
As if his mouth were full of dough,
Who snorted like a buffalo——
That summer evening, long ago,
     A-sitting on a gate."

As the Knight sang the last words of the ballad, he gathered up the
reins, and turned his horse's head along the road by which they had
come. "You've only a few yards to go," he said, "down the hill and

over that little brook, and then you'll be a Queen——But you'll stay and see me off first?" he added as Alice turned with an eager look in the direction to which he pointed. "I shan't be long. You'll wait and wave your handkerchief when I get to that turn in the road? I think it'll encourage me, you see."*

"Of course I'll wait," said Alice: "and thank you very much for coming so far—and for the song—I liked it very much."

"I hope so," the Knight said doubtfully: "but you didn't cry so much* as I thought you would."

So they shook hands, and then the Knight rode slowly away into the forest. "It won't take long to see him *off*, I expect," Alice said to herself, as she stood watching him. "There he goes! Right on his head as usual! However, he gets on again pretty easily—that comes of having so many things hung round the horse——" So she went on talking to herself, as she watched the horse walking leisurely along the road, and the Knight tumbling off, first on one side and then on the other. After the fourth or fifth tumble he reached the turn, and then she waved her handkerchief to him, and waited till he was out of sight.*

"I hope it encouraged him," she said, as she turned to run down the hill: "and now for the last brook, and to be a Queen! How grand it sounds!" A very few steps brought her to the edge of the brook.* "The Eighth Square at last!" she cried as she bounded across,*

```
  *       *       *       *       *       *

      *       *       *       *       *

  *       *       *       *       *       *
```

and threw herself down to rest on a lawn as soft as moss, with little flower-beds dotted about it here and there. "Oh, how glad I am to get here! And what *is* this on my head?" she exclaimed in a tone of dismay,* as she put her hands up to something very heavy, that fitted tight all round her head.

"But how *can* it have got there without my knowing it?" she said to herself, as she lifted it off, and set it on her lap to make out what it could possibly be.

It was a golden crown.

CHAPTER IX

QUEEN ALICE

"WELL, this *is* grand!" said Alice. "I never expected I should be a Queen so soon—and I'll tell you what it is, your Majesty," she went on in a severe tone (she was always rather fond of scolding herself), "it'll never do for you to be lolling about on the grass like that! Queens have to be dignified,* you know!"

So she got up and walked about—rather stiffly just at first, as she was afraid that the crown might come off: but she comforted herself with the thought that there was nobody to see her, "and if I really am a Queen," she said as she sat down again, "I shall be able to manage it quite well in time."

Everything was happening so oddly that she didn't feel a bit surprised at finding the Red Queen and the White Queen sitting close to her, one on each side:* she would have liked very much to ask them how they came there, but she feared it would not be quite civil. However, there would be no harm, she thought, in asking if the game was over. "Please, would you tell me——" she began, looking timidly at the Red Queen.

"Speak when you're spoken to!" the Queen sharply interrupted her.

"But if everybody obeyed that rule," said Alice, who was always ready for a little argument, "and if you only spoke when you were spoken to, and the other person always waited for *you* to begin, you see nobody would ever say anything, so that——"

"Ridiculous!" cried the Queen. "Why, don't you see, child——" here she broke off with a frown, and, after thinking for a minute, suddenly changed the subject of the conversation. "What do you mean by 'If you really are a Queen'? What right have you to call yourself so? You can't be a Queen, you know, till you've passed the proper examination.* And the sooner we begin it, the better."

"I only said 'if'!" poor Alice pleaded in a piteous tone.

The two Queens looked at each other, and the Red Queen remarked, with a little shudder, "She *says* she only said 'if'——"

"But she said a great deal more than that!" the White Queen moaned, wringing her hands. "Oh, ever so much more than that!"

"So you did, you know," the Red Queen said to Alice. "Always speak the truth—think before you speak—and write it down afterwards."

"I'm sure I didn't mean——" Alice was beginning, but the Red Queen interrupted her impatiently.

"That's just what I complain of! You *should* have meant! What do you suppose is the use of a child without any meaning? Even a joke should have some meaning—and a child's more important than a joke, I hope. You couldn't deny that, even if you tried with both hands."

"I don't deny things with my *hands*," Alice objected.

"Nobody said you did," said the Red Queen. "I said you couldn't if you tried."

"She's in that state of mind," said the White Queen, "that she wants to deny *something*—only she doesn't know what to deny!"

"A nasty, vicious temper," the Red Queen remarked; and then there was an uncomfortable silence for a minute or two.

The Red Queen broke the silence by saying to the White Queen, "I invite you to Alice's dinner-party this afternoon."

The White Queen smiled feebly, and said "And I invite *you*."

"I didn't know I was to have a party at all," said Alice; "but if there is to be one, I think *I* ought to invite the guests."

"We gave you the opportunity of doing it," the Red Queen remarked: "but I daresay you've not had many lessons in manners* yet?"

"Manners are not taught in lessons," said Alice. "Lessons teach you to do sums, and things of that sort."

"Can you do Addition?" the White Queen asked. "What's one and one and one and one and one and one and one and one and one and one?"

"I don't know," said Alice. "I lost count."

"She can't do Addition," the Red Queen interrupted. "Can you do Subtraction? Take nine from eight."

"Nine from eight I can't, you know," Alice replied very readily: "but——"

"She can't do Substraction,"* said the White Queen. "Can you do Division? Divide a loaf by a knife—what's the answer to that?"

"I suppose——" Alice was beginning, but the Red Queen answered for her. "Bread-and-butter, of course. Try another Subtraction sum. Take a bone from a dog: what remains?"

Alice considered. "The bone wouldn't remain, of course, if I took it—and the dog wouldn't remain; it would come to bite me—and I'm sure *I* shouldn't remain!"

"Then you think nothing would remain?" said the Red Queen.

"I think that's the answer."

"Wrong, as usual," said the Red Queen: "the dog's temper would remain."

"But I don't see how——"

"Why, look here!" the Red Queen cried. "The dog would lose its temper, wouldn't it?"

"Perhaps it would," Alice replied cautiously.

"Then if the dog went away, its temper would remain!"* the Queen exclaimed triumphantly.

Alice said, as gravely as she could, "They might go different ways." But she couldn't help thinking to herself, "What dreadful nonsense we *are* talking!"

"She can't do sums a *bit!*" the Queens said together, with great emphasis.

"Can *you* do sums?" Alice said, turning suddenly on the White Queen, for she didn't like being found fault with so much.

The Queen gasped and shut her eyes. "I can do Addition," she said, "if you give me time—but I can't do Substraction, under *any* circumstances!"

"Of course you know your ABC?" said the Red Queen.

"To be sure I do," said Alice.

"So do I," the White Queen whispered: "we'll often say it over together, dear. And I'll tell you a secret—I can read words of one letter! Isn't *that* grand? However, don't be discouraged. You'll come to it in time."

Here the Red Queen began again. "Can you answer useful questions?"* she said. "How is bread made?"

"I know *that!*" Alice cried eagerly. "You take some flour——"

"Where do you pick the flower?" the White Queen asked. "In a garden, or in the hedges?"

"Well, it isn't *picked* at all," Alice explained: "it's *ground*——"

"How many acres of ground?" said the White Queen. "You mustn't leave out so many things."

"Fan her head!" the Red Queen anxiously interrupted. "She'll be feverish after so much thinking." So they set to work and fanned her with bunches of leaves, till she had to beg them to leave off, it blew her hair about so.

"She's all right again now," said the Red Queen. "Do you know Languages? What's the French for fiddle-de-dee?"*

"Fiddle-de-dee's not English," Alice replied gravely.

"Who ever said it was?" said the Red Queen.

Alice thought she saw a way out of the difficulty this time. "If you'll tell me what language 'fiddle-de-dee' is, I'll tell you the French for it!" she exclaimed triumphantly.

But the Red Queen drew herself up rather stiffly, and said "Queens never make bargains."

"I wish Queens never asked questions," Alice thought to herself.

"Don't let us quarrel," the White Queen said in an anxious tone. "What is the cause of lightning?"

"The cause of lightning," Alice said very decidedly, for she felt quite certain about this, "is the thunder—no, no!" she hastily corrected herself. "I meant the other way."

"It's too late to correct it,"* said the Red Queen: "when you've once said a thing, that fixes it, and you must take the consequences."

"Which reminds me——" the White Queen said, looking down and nervously clasping and unclasping her hands, "we had *such* a thunderstorm last Tuesday—I mean one of the last set of Tuesdays, you know."

Alice was puzzled. "In *our* country," she remarked, "there's only one day at a time."

The Red Queen said "That's a poor thin way of doing things. Now *here*, we mostly have days and nights two or three at a time, and sometimes in the winter we take as many as five nights together—for warmth, you know."

"Are five nights warmer than one night, then?" Alice ventured to ask.

"Five times as warm, of course."

"But they should be five times as *cold*, by the same rule——"

"Just so!" cried the Red Queen. "Five times as warm, *and* five times as cold—just as I'm five times as rich as you are, *and* five times as clever!"*

Alice sighed and gave it up. "It's exactly like a riddle with no answer!"* she thought.

"Humpty Dumpty saw it too," the White Queen went on in a low voice, more as if she were talking to herself. "He came to the door with a corkscrew in his hand——"

"What did he want?" said the Red Queen.

"He said he *would* come in," the White Queen went on, "because he was looking for a hippopotamus. Now, as it happened, there wasn't such a thing in the house, that morning."

"Is there generally?" Alice asked in an astonished tone.

"Well, only on Thursdays," said the Queen.

"I know what he came for," said Alice: "he wanted to punish the fish, because——"*

Here the White Queen began again. "It was *such* a thunderstorm, you can't think!" ("She *never* could, you know," said the Red Queen.) "And part of the roof came off, and ever so much thunder got in—and it went rolling round the room in great lumps—and knocking over the tables and things—till I was so frightened, I couldn't remember my own name!"

Alice thought to herself, "I never should *try* to remember my name in the middle of an accident! Where would be the use of it?" but she did not say this aloud, for fear of hurting the poor Queen's feelings.*

"Your Majesty* must excuse her," the Red Queen said to Alice, taking one of the White Queen's hands in her own, and gently stroking it: "she means well, but she can't help saying foolish things, as a general rule."

The White Queen looked timidly at Alice, who felt she *ought* to say something kind, but really couldn't think of anything at the moment.

"She never was really well brought up," the Red Queen went on: "but it's amazing how good-tempered she is! Pat her on the head, and see how pleased she'll be!" But this was more than Alice had courage to do.

"A little kindness—and putting her hair in papers*—would do wonders with her——"

The White Queen gave a deep sigh, and laid her head on Alice's shoulder. "I *am* so sleepy!" she moaned.

"She's tired, poor thing!" said the Red Queen. "Smooth her hair—lend her your nightcap—and sing her a soothing lullaby."

"I haven't got a nightcap with me," said Alice, as she tried to obey the first direction: "and I don't know any soothing lullabies."

"I must do it myself, then," said the Red Queen, and she began:

> *"Hush-a-by lady, in Alice's lap!**
> *Till the feast's ready, we've time for a nap:*
> *When the feast's over, we'll go to the ball—*
> *Red Queen, and White Queen, and Alice, and all!"*

"And now you know the words," she added, as she put her head down on Alice's other shoulder, "just sing it through to *me.* I'm getting sleepy too." In another moment both Queens were fast asleep, and snoring loud.

"What *am* I to do?" exclaimed Alice, looking about in great perplexity, as first one round head, and then the other, rolled down from her shoulder, and lay like a heavy lump in her lap. "I don't think it *ever* happened before, that any one had to take care of two Queens asleep at once! No, not in all the History of England*—it couldn't, you know, because there never was more than one Queen at a time. Do wake up, you heavy things!" she went on in an impatient tone; but there was no answer but a gentle snoring.

The snoring got more distinct every minute, and sounded more like a tune: at last she could even make out words, and she listened so eagerly that, when the two great heads suddenly vanished* from her lap, she hardly missed them.

She was standing before an arched doorway over which were the words QUEEN ALICE in large letters, and on each side of the arch there was a bell-handle; one was marked "Visitors' Bell," and the other "Servants' Bell."

"I'll wait till the song's over," thought Alice, "and then I'll ring the—the—*which* bell must I ring?"* she went on, very much puzzled by the names. "I'm not a visitor, and I'm not a servant. There *ought* to be one marked 'Queen,' you know——"

Just then the door opened a little way, and a creature with a long beak put its head out for a moment and said "No admittance till the week after next!"* and shut the door again with a bang.

Alice knocked and rang in vain for a long time, but at last a very old Frog,* who was sitting under a tree, got up and hobbled slowly towards her: he was dressed in bright yellow, and had enormous boots on.

"What is it, now?" the Frog said in a deep hoarse whisper.

Alice turned round, ready to find fault with anybody. "Where's the servant whose business it is to answer the door?" she began angrily.

"Which door?" said the Frog.

Alice almost stamped with irritation at the slow drawl in which he spoke. "*This* door, of course!"

The Frog looked at the door with his large dull eyes for a minute: then he went nearer and rubbed it with his thumb, as if he were trying whether the paint would come off; then he looked at Alice.

"To answer the door?" he said. "What's it been asking of?" He was so hoarse that Alice could scarcely hear him.

"I don't know what you mean," she said.

"I speaks English, doesn't I?" the Frog went on. "Or are you deaf? What did it ask you?"

"Nothing!" Alice said impatiently. "I've been knocking at it!"

"Shouldn't do that—shouldn't do that——" the Frog muttered. "Wexes it,* you know." Then he went up and gave the door a kick with one of his great feet. "You let *it* alone," he panted out, as he hobbled back to his tree, "and it'll let *you* alone, you know."

At this moment the door was flung open, and a shrill voice was heard singing:

> "*To the Looking-Glass world it was Alice that said,**
> '*I've a sceptre in hand, I've a crown on my head;*
> *Let the Looking-Glass creatures, whatever they be,*
> *Come and dine with the Red Queen, the White Queen, and me!*'"

And hundreds of voices joined in the chorus:

> *"Then fill up the glasses as quick as you can,*
> *And sprinkle the table with buttons and bran:*
> *Put cats in the coffee, and mice in the tea—**
> *And welcome Queen Alice with thirty-times-three!"*

Then followed a confused noise of cheering, and Alice thought to herself, "Thirty times three makes ninety. I wonder if any one's counting?" In a minute there was silence again, and the same shrill voice sang another verse:

> *"'O Looking-Glass creatures,' quoth Alice, 'draw near!*
> *'Tis an honour to see me, a favour to hear:*
> *'Tis a privilege high to have dinner and tea*
> *Along with the Red Queen, the White Queen, and me!'"*

Then came the chorus again:—

> *"Then fill up the glasses with treacle and ink,*
> *Or anything else that is pleasant to drink;*
> *Mix sand with the cider, and wool with the wine—*
> *And welcome Queen Alice with ninety-times-nine!"*

"Ninety times nine!" Alice repeated in despair. "Oh, that'll never be done! I'd better go in at once——" and in she went,* and there was a dead silence the moment she appeared.

Alice glanced nervously along the table, as she walked up the large hall, and noticed that there were about fifty guests, of all kinds: some were animals, some birds, and there were even a few flowers among them. "I'm glad they've come without waiting to be asked," she thought: "I should never have known who were the right people to invite!"*

There were three chairs at the head of the table; the Red and White Queens had already taken two of them, but the middle one was empty. Alice sat down in it, rather uncomfortable at the silence, and longing for some one to speak.

At last the Red Queen began. "You've missed the soup and fish," she said. "Put on the joint!" And the waiters set a leg of mutton before Alice, who looked at it rather anxiously, as she had never had to carve a joint before.

"You look a little shy; let me introduce you to that leg of mutton," said the Red Queen. "Alice——Mutton; Mutton——Alice." The leg of mutton got up in the dish and made a little bow to Alice; and Alice returned the bow, not knowing whether to be frightened or amused.

"May I give you a slice?" she said, taking up the knife and fork, and looking from one Queen to the other.

"Certainly not," the Red Queen said, very decidedly: "it isn't etiquette to cut any one you've been introduced to.* Remove the joint!" And the waiters carried it off, and brought a large plum-pudding in its place.

"I won't be introduced to the pudding, please," Alice said rather hastily, "or we shall get no dinner at all. May I give you some?"

But the Red Queen looked sulky, and growled "Pudding——Alice; Alice——Pudding. Remove the pudding!" and the waiters took it away so quickly that Alice couldn't return its bow.

However, she didn't see why the Red Queen should be the only one to give orders, so, as an experiment, she called out "Waiter! Bring back the pudding!" and there it was again in a moment, like a conjuring-trick. It was so large that she couldn't help feeling a *little* shy with it, as she had been with the mutton; however, she conquered her shyness by a great effort, and cut a slice and handed it to the Red Queen.

"What impertinence!" said the Pudding. "I wonder how you'd like it, if I were to cut a slice out of *you*, you creature!"*

It spoke in a thick, suety sort of voice, and Alice hadn't a word to say in reply: she could only sit and look at it and gasp.

"Make a remark," said the Red Queen: "it's ridiculous to leave all the conversation to the pudding!"

"Do you know, I've had such a quantity of poetry repeated to me to-day," Alice began, a little frightened at finding that, the moment she opened her lips, there was dead silence, and all eyes were fixed upon her; "and it's a very curious thing, I think—every poem was about fishes in some way.* Do you know why they're so fond of fishes, all about here?"

She spoke to the Red Queen, whose answer was a little wide of the mark. "As to fishes," she said, very slowly and solemnly, putting her mouth close to Alice's ear, "her White Majesty knows a lovely riddle—all in poetry—all about fishes. Shall she repeat it?"

"Her Red Majesty's very kind to mention it," the White Queen murmured into Alice's other ear, in a voice like the cooing of a pigeon. "It would be *such* a treat! May I?"

"Please do," Alice said very politely.

The White Queen laughed with delight, and stroked Alice's cheek. Then she began:

> "'*First, the fish must be caught.*'
> *That is easy: a baby, I think, could have caught it.*
> '*Next, the fish must be bought.*'
> *That is easy: a penny, I think, would have bought it.*
>
> '*Now cook me the fish!*'
> *That is easy, and will not take more than a minute.*
> '*Let it lie in a dish!*'
> *That is easy, because it already is in it.*
>
> '*Bring it here! Let me sup!*'
> *It is easy to set such a dish on the table.*
> '*Take the dish-cover up!*'
> *Ah, that is so hard that I fear I'm unable!*
>
> *For it holds it like glue—*
> *Holds the lid to the dish, while it lies in the middle:*
> *Which is easiest to do,*
> *Un-dish-cover the fish, or dishcover the riddle?*"*

"Take a minute to think about it, and then guess," said the Red Queen. "Meanwhile, we'll drink your health—Queen Alice's health!" she screamed at the top of her voice, and all the guests began drinking it directly, and very queerly they managed it: some of them put their glasses upon their heads like extinguishers,* and drank all that trickled down their faces—others upset the decanters, and drank the wine as it ran off the edges of the table—and three of them (who looked like kangaroos) scrambled into the dish of roast mutton, and began eagerly lapping up the gravy, "just like pigs in a trough!" thought Alice.

"You ought to return thanks in a neat speech," the Red Queen said, frowning at Alice as she spoke.

"We must support you, you know," the White Queen whispered, as Alice got up to do it, very obediently, but a little frightened.

"Thank you very much," she whispered in reply, "but I can do quite well without."

"That wouldn't be at all the thing," the Red Queen said very decidedly: so Alice tried to submit to it with a good grace.

("And they *did* push so!" she said afterwards, when she was telling her sister the history of the feast. "You would have thought they wanted to squeeze me flat!")

In fact it was rather difficult for her to keep in her place while she made her speech: the two Queens pushed her so, one on each side, that they nearly lifted her up into the air: "I rise to return thanks——" Alice began: and she really *did* rise as she spoke, several inches; but she got hold of the edge of the table, and managed to pull herself down again.

"Take care of yourself!" screamed the White Queen, seizing Alice's hair with both her hands. "Something's going to happen!"

And then (as Alice afterwards described it) all sorts of things happened in a moment. The candles all grew up to the ceiling, looking something like a bed of rushes with fireworks at the top. As to the bottles, they each took a pair of plates, which they hastily fitted on as wings, and so, with forks for legs, went fluttering about in all directions: "and very like birds they look," Alice thought to herself, as well as she could in the dreadful confusion that was beginning.

At this moment she heard a hoarse laugh at her side, and turned to see what was the matter with the White Queen; but, instead of the Queen, there was the leg of mutton sitting in the chair. "Here I am!" cried a voice from the soup-tureen, and Alice turned again, just in time to see the Queen's broad good-natured face grinning at her for a moment over the edge of the tureen, before she disappeared into the soup.*

There was not a moment to be lost. Already several of the guests were lying down in the dishes, and the soup-ladle was walking up the table towards Alice's chair, and beckoning to her impatiently to get out of its way.

"I can't stand this any longer!"* she cried as she jumped up and seized the tablecloth with both hands: one good pull, and plates, dishes, guests, and candles came crashing down together in a heap on the floor.

"And as for *you*," she went on, turning fiercely upon the Red Queen, whom she considered as the cause of all the mischief*—but the Queen was no longer at her side—she had suddenly dwindled down to the size of a little doll, and was now on the table, merrily running round and round after her own shawl,* which was trailing behind her.

At any other time, Alice would have felt surprised at this, but she was far too much excited to be surprised at anything *now.* "As for *you,*" she repeated, catching hold of the little creature in the very act of jumping over a bottle which had just lighted upon the table, "I'll shake you into a kitten, that I will!"

CHAPTER X

SHAKING

SHE took her off the table* as she spoke, and shook her backwards and forwards with all her might.

The Red Queen made no resistance whatever; only her face grew very small, and her eyes got large and green: and still, as Alice went on shaking her, she kept on growing shorter—and fatter—and softer—and rounder—and——

CHAPTER XI

WAKING

—— AND it really *was* a kitten, after all.*

CHAPTER XII

WHICH DREAMED IT?

"Your Red Majesty shouldn't purr so loud," Alice said, rubbing her eyes, and addressing the kitten,* respectfully, yet with some severity. "You woke me out of oh! such a nice dream! And you've been along with me, Kitty—all through the Looking-Glass world. Did you know it, dear?"

It is a very inconvenient habit of kittens (Alice had once made the remark) that, whatever you say to them, they *always* purr. "If they would only purr for 'yes,' and mew for 'no,' or any rule of that sort," she had said, "so that one could keep up a conversation! But how *can* you talk with a person if they always say the same thing?"

On this occasion the kitten only purred:* and it was impossible to guess whether it meant 'yes' or 'no.'

So Alice hunted among the chessmen on the table till she had found the Red Queen: then she went down on her knees on the hearth-rug, and put the kitten and the Queen to look at each other. "Now, Kitty!" she cried, clapping her hands triumphantly. "Confess that was what you turned into!"

("But it wouldn't look at it," she said, when she was explaining the thing afterwards to her sister: "it turned away its head, and pretended not to see it: but it looked a *little* ashamed of itself, so I think it *must* have been the Red Queen.")

"Sit up a little more stiffly, dear!" Alice cried with a merry laugh. "And curtsey while you're thinking what to—what to purr. It saves time, remember!" And she caught it up and gave it one little kiss, "just in honour of its having been a Red Queen."

"Snowdrop, my pet!" she went on, looking over her shoulder at the White Kitten, which was still patiently undergoing its toilet, "when *will* Dinah have finished with your White Majesty, I wonder? That must be the reason you were so untidy in my dream.——Dinah! Do you know that you're scrubbing a White Queen? Really, it's most disrespectful of you!

"And what did *Dinah* turn to, I wonder?" she prattled on, as she settled comfortably down, with one elbow on the rug, and her chin in her hand, to watch the kittens. "Tell me, Dinah, did you turn to Humpty Dumpty? I *think* you did—however, you'd better not mention it to your friends just yet, for I'm not sure.

"By the way, Kitty, if only you'd been really with me in my dream, there was one thing you *would* have enjoyed——I had such a quantity of poetry said to me, all about fishes! To-morrow morning you shall have a real treat. All the time you're eating your breakfast, I'll repeat 'The Walrus and the Carpenter' to you;* and then you can make believe it's oysters, dear!

"Now, Kitty, let's consider who it was that dreamed it all. This is a serious question, my dear, and you should *not* go on licking your paw like that—as if Dinah hadn't washed you this morning! You see, Kitty, it *must* have been either me or the Red King. He was part of my dream, of course—but then I was part of his dream, too! *Was* it the Red King, Kitty? You were his wife, my dear, so you ought to

know——Oh, Kitty, *do* help to settle it! I'm sure your paw can wait!'
But the provoking kitten only began on the other paw, and pretended
it hadn't heard the question.

Which do *you* think it was?*

A BOAT, beneath a sunny sky,*
Lingering onward dreamily
In an evening of July—*

Children three* that nestle near,
Eager eye and willing ear,
Pleased a simple tale to hear—

Long has paled that sunny sky:
Echoes fade and memories die:
Autumn frosts have slain July.

Still she haunts me, phantomwise,*
Alice* moving under skies
Never seen by waking eyes.

Children yet, the tale to hear,
Eager eye and willing ear,*
Lovingly shall nestle near.

In a Wonderland they lie,
Dreaming as the days go by,
Dreaming as the summers die:

Ever drifting down the stream—
Lingering in the golden gleam—
Life, what is it but a dream?*

THE END

EXPLANATORY NOTES

ABBREVIATIONS

AA   Explanatory notes from M. Gardner (ed.), *The Annotated Alice: The Definitive Edition* (New York: Norton, 1999).

CWLC   *The Complete Works of Lewis Carroll* (London: The Nonesuch Press, 1939).

HoM   M. N. Cohen and A. Gandolfo (eds), *Lewis Carroll and the House of Macmillan* (Cambridge: Cambridge University Press, 1987).

LCD   *Lewis Carroll's Diaries: The Private Journals of Charles Lutwidge Dogson*, ed. E. Wakeling, 10 vols (Luton: Lewis Carroll Society, 1992–2007).

LCHB   S. H. Williams, F. Madan, and R. L. Green, *The Lewis Carroll Handbook* (1931; London: Oxford University Press, 1962).

LCIR   M. N. Cohen (ed.), *Lewis Carroll: Interviews and Recollections* (London: Macmillan, 1989).

Letters   *The Letters of Lewis Carroll*, ed. M. N. Cohen, 2 vols (London: Macmillan, 1979).

LLLC   S. D. Collingwood, *The Life and Letters of Lewis Carroll* (London: Thomas Nelson, 1898).

OED   *Oxford English Dictionary* (online); www.oed.com.

OWC   Explanatory notes from P. Hunt (ed.), *Alice's Adventures in Wonderland and Through the Looking-Glass* (Oxford: Oxford University Press, Oxford World's Classics, 2009).

PA   Explanatory notes from P. Heath (ed.), *The Philosopher's Alice* (London: Academy Editions, 1974).

Penguin   Explanatory notes from H. Haughton (ed.), *Alice's Adventures in Wonderland and Through the Looking-Glass* (1998; London: Penguin, 2003).

TIAB   M. Hancher, *The Tenniel Illustrations to the 'Alice' Books* (2nd edn, Columbus, OH: Ohio State University, 2019).

2 *[Frontispiece]*: the opening image to *Looking-Glass*, which depicts Alice gazing at the White Knight as he rides away from her, was not originally proposed as the frontispiece for the book. Carroll had intended to deploy the picture of the Jabberwock here, but feared it might be too frightening as the initial illustration to the story. Carroll was keen to ensure that the text did not alarm children, which no doubt was both a matter of conscience and one of marketing. There are, however, substantial lasting benefits to his final choice of frontispiece that have little to do with either concern. In the first edition the image appears just before the title page, which is then followed by the prefatory poem. The illustration captures one of the most evocative moments in the text (from Chapter VIII, when

the Knight departs, moments before Alice becomes queen) and brings it into dialogue with the opening poem and its poignant reflection on youth, senescence, and ageing. The alignment of poem and image is thus a more exacting marriage than 'the hideous Jabberwocky' (*LCHB*, 58) which illustrates the ballad. Janis Lull has also observed that 'all the Knight's accessories [. . .] relate in some way to *other* parts of the story': the fire-irons on the saddle resemble those of the first chapter; the wooden sword and rattle recall the battle of the Tweedles in Chapter IV; the bell and wine predicts Alice's entry into the palace and subsequent banquet in Chapter IX (Lull, 'The Appliances of Art: The Carroll-Tenniel Collaboration in *Through the Looking-Glass*', *Lewis Carroll: A Celebration*, ed. E. Guiliano (New York: Clarkson N. Potter, 1982), 101–11, at 105). For Michael Hancher, this 'elaborate kind of referential supplement' makes the *Looking-Glass* frontispiece 'a synopsis of the whole book, a mirror of the looking-glass world' (*TIAB*, 157).

3 *[Title]*: the title of *Through the Looking-Glass, and What Alice Found There* saw several iterations before the final printed edition. In his early musings on the book's production, Carroll referred to it variously as 'a sort of sequel to *Alice*' (*HoM*, 44) and as 'the 2nd volume of *Alice*' (*LCD*, v. 199). Upon finishing the first chapter in January 1869, he confirms an initial title: 'Finished and sent off to Macmillan the 1st chapter of *Behind the Looking-Glass, and what Alice saw there*' (*LCD*, vi. 379). A specimen title page was produced the following year bearing the alternative title of '*Looking-Glass House, and what Alice saw there*'. Carroll continued to revise the title and entertained various possibilities until 1870, engaging in frequent dialogue with his publishers who, as M. N. Cohen and A. Gandolfo have observed, took 'a keen interest in deciding the title of the sequel to *Alice*' (*HoM*, 85). In response to a letter from Carroll (now lost) which must have offered multiple suggestions, Macmillan writes: 'as to the main title, I decidedly prefer the first form of words: "Behind the Looking-Glass." Looking-Glass World is too specific. You answer that there is a *world*. In the first title there is a charming vagueness which I think wholly harmonizes with your peculiar humour' (*HoM*, 85). Lewis Carroll's nephew and first biographer, Stuart Dodgson Collingwood, recalls that it was Lewis Carroll's friend Henry Parry Liddon 'who suggested the name finally adopted' (*LLLC*, 117). The rejection of 'House' and 'World' in the title makes Alice's experience through the glass rather more ethereal and highlights the sense of forward movement that emerges so strongly in the shape of narrative, whilst the preference for 'found' over 'saw' makes Alice's experience that of an active participant rather than mere observer.

4 *[Chess board and moves]*: Carroll deploys contemporary abbreviations for the chess pieces so that, for instance, 'R. Q.' is Red Queen and 'K. B.' is King's Bishop. Carroll here outlines Alice's trajectory (as White Pawn) across the chessboard so as to win in eleven moves. The game is duly set

out, with the movement of each piece/character detailed across a total of twenty-one moves, demonstrating that the story itself is designed around the game. Carroll was known to be a chess player (see *LLLC*, 84) and was an exacting writer and thinker, yet opinion varies as to the technicalities of the game as diagrammed here. Falconer Madan, co-author of the *Lewis Carroll Handbook*, appears exasperated in his declaration that 'the chess framework is full of absurdities and impossibilities, and it is unfortunate that Dodgson did not display his usual dexterity by bringing the game, as a game, up to chess standard. [. . .] Hardly a move has a sane purpose, from the point of view of chess' (*LCHB*, 62). Carroll himself added a comment on the 'problem' of the game for the 1897 edition of the text:

5 *DRAMATIS PERSONÆ*: (Lat.) 'persons of a drama', generally detailing the main characters of a play or dramatic work, but here deployed by Carroll in the context of a novel. The Dramatis Personæ for *Looking-Glass* was included until Carroll's changes in 1896, at which point it was omitted. Such an inclusion reflects the performative and highly structured nature of the narrative and draws attention to the characters' roles as particular chess pieces discernible via their arrangement on the board. Martin Gardner has observed that the bishop pieces, not directly mentioned in the story as such, are aligned with the Sheep, Aged man, Walrus, and Crow 'for no discernable reason' (*AA*, 141). While *Wonderland* does not have a Dramatis Personæ, Carroll saw the potential for both texts to be performed as dramatic works, seeking assistance from his publisher in this endeavour in November 1872: 'Will you kindly, with all reasonable expedition on receipt of this, engage a couple of copying-clerks, and have *all* the speeches in *Alice* and *Looking-Glass* written out, with the names of the speakers, and such directions as "Enter the White Rabbit," "Exit the Red Queen," in the ordinary dramatic form, *and get them registered as two dramas*, with the same names as the books' (*HoM*, 99). Carroll was here attempting to maintain control over any attempts to dramatize either book, although the effort proved to be ineffectual. Carroll was later heavily involved in the production of a stage-play version of the books produced by Henry Savile Clarke entitled *Alice in Wonderland: A Musical Dream play, in Two Acts, for Children and Others*, which opened at the Prince of Wales Theatre on Coventry Street on 23 December 1886.

As the chess-problem [. . .] has puzzled some of my readers, it may be well to explain that it is correctly worked out, so far as the moves are concerned. The alternation of Red and White is perhaps not so strictly observed as it might be, and the 'castling' of the three Queens is merely a way of saying that they entered the palace: but the 'check' of the White King at move 6, the capture of the Red Knight at move 7, and the final 'checkmate' of the Red King, will be found, by any one who will take the trouble to set the pieces and play the moves as directed, to be strictly in accordance with the rules of the game.

Martin Gardner has noted that 'it is true [. . .] that red and white do not alternate moves properly' and 'that both sides play an exceedingly careless game', but concludes that 'Considering the staggering difficulties involved in dovetailing a chess game with an amusing nonsense fantasy, Carroll does a remarkable job' (*AA*, 137–8). Hugh Haughton concurs, arguing that to criticize the game on the basis of plausibility ignores that it is played out in a dream and dramatized from Alice's point of view as a piece on the board, rather than with the bird's-eye view of players or spectators (Penguin, 325). Late in her life, Alice Liddell Hargreaves recalled how 'Much of *Through the Looking-Glass* is made up of them [stories Carroll told the children], particularly the ones to do with chessmen, which are dated by the period when we [the Liddell children] were excitedly learning chess' (*LCIR*, 84). There is a clear sense of playful recollection and story-making in *Looking-Glass*. While the episodic nature of the text is more rigid than the card-play of *Wonderland*, in keeping with the structures of the chessboard, any liberties Carroll takes reflect the whimsical nature of his narrative and his commitment to playing out a story as much as a game. The characters are inflected by the movement limitations and liberties of the pieces they represent, while the stories and events that Carroll recalls affect the play. There is a symbiotic relationship between story and game that make neither fully subservient to the other.

6 *CHILD of the pure unclouded brow*: as with *Wonderland*, *Looking-Glass* begins with a prefatory poem, but one which strikes a darker and more melancholy note than its predecessor, particularly through the coldness of the winter rather than summer palette. It is distinctly reflective verse, recalling a happier past and lamenting the distancing effect of time. It is a poem told through recollection and memory, a nostalgic longing for a period heard only in echo and with a distinct air of regret (by comparison, *Wonderland*'s initial poem is told very much in the present). Carroll made a number of changes to the poem on the 1870 proofs, all of which were included in the first published edition (for details, see *LCHB*, 60).

half a life asunder: at the time of the publication of *Looking-Glass*, Lewis Carroll was 39 years old. Alice Liddell, at 19, was almost exactly half his age.

fairy-tale: there are three references in the opening poem to the story as fairy tale. Lewis Carroll frequently referred to both books as fairy tales, although critics have questioned that designation. Most famously, J. R. R. Tolkien argued that they 'are not fairy-stories' due to 'their dream-frame and dream-transitions' ('On Fairy Stories', *The Monsters and the Critics* (1947; London: HarperCollins, 1997), 109–61, at 117).

I have not seen . . . thy silver laughter: even before the publication of *Wonderland*, the relationship between Carroll and the Liddells had begun to break down; in 1863 there was a period of almost six months in which

Carroll had no contact with any member of the family. The break in the friendship has never been fully explained, although there has been much speculation by biographers regarding the content and context of missing diary pages from June of that year. Alice Liddell, in her adult reflections, recalls how 'my mother tore up all the letters that Mr Dodgson wrote to me when I was a small girl. [. . . I]t is an awful thought to contemplate what may have perished in the Deanery waste-paper basket' (*LCIR*, 87). There were subsequent reunions between Carroll and the Liddells, but these were infrequent, and Carroll's diaries recall his 'aloof' attitude towards them (*LCD*, iv. 264). That said, at the time of publication, Carroll *had* seen Alice relatively recently; in June 1870 he photographed Alice and Lorina in his studio at Badcock's yard. While Carroll recalls the visit as 'a wonderful thing' (*LCD*, vi. 121), the resultant photo of Alice is a stiff and awkward image that is as melancholy in aesthetic as the *Looking-Glass* poem and indeed bears no trace of either 'sunny face' nor 'silver laughter'.

No thought of me. . . hereafter—: Carroll here clearly fears being forgotten by Alice. As it happens, Alice, along with many other child friends, would recall him dearly in later life (see *LCIR*).

rhythm of our rowing—: recalls the famous journey of 4 July 1862 in which Charles Dodgson, Robinson Duckworth, and the three Liddell children rowed up the river Thames to Godstow. The stories told on that journey are the genesis of *Alice's Adventures in Wonderland*.

older children: Carroll displays a flexible view of childhood which could extend long into the life cycle, as he explained in the preface to *The Nursery 'Alice'*:

> I have reason to believe that 'Alice's Adventures in Wonderland' has been read by some hundreds of English Children, aged from Five to Fifteen: also by Children, aged from Fifteen to Twenty-five: yet again by Children, aged from Twenty-five to Thirty-five: and even by Children—for there *are* such— [. . .] Children of a 'certain' age, whose tale of years must be left untold, and buried in respectful silence. (London: Macmillan, 1890, n.p.)

Carroll's views in this regard were shared with his friend and fellow author, George McDonald, who comments that 'I do not write for children, but for the childlike, whether five, or fifty, or seventy-five' (*A Dish of Orts* (1882; London: Sampson Low Marston & Company, 1893), 317). Both writers show a commitment to producing stories 'for children' which have a broad appeal.

bedtime: references to bed and bedtime in this stanza have multiple valances, none of which are particularly subtle. There is an allusion to the marriage bed, and to sexual consent, in the imagery of the summoned 'melancholy maiden', as well as to the inevitability of death. There is, too, a more modest conceit of children simply resisting going to bed.

Without, the frost. . . nest of gladness: the poem gives a clear sense as to the seasonal shift from *Wonderland* to *Looking-Glass*, with the former set in the summer months and the latter in a much cooler winter. The reference to an interior space, complete with firelight, predicts the story's opening setting and contrasts with the exterior, riverbank opening scene in the first book.

6 *'happy summer days'*: the final three words of *Alice's Adventures in Wonderland*.

bale: sorrow.

pleasance: in the proofs of *Looking-Glass* the line read 'pleasures' but Carroll introduced this change before the first printing. Alice Liddell's middle name was Pleasance, making the context of the poem even more overt. As well as evoking delight and joy, the word can also refer to an enclosed or otherwise secluded garden, 'laid out with pleasant walks, trees, garden ornaments, etc.' (*OED*).

9 *[illustration]*: the initial illustration to the first chapter of *Looking-Glass* contrasts distinctly with that of *Wonderland*. While both depict animals, *Wonderland*'s image signals from the opening the queerness of the scene, with Tenniel's illustration making the anthropomorphic nature of the White Rabbit overt (he stands on his hind legs, sports a jacket and waist-coat, carries an umbrella, and consults his pocket-watch). The *Looking-Glass* scene, by contrast, is domestic and distinctly non-fantastic. This image of the black kitten playing with the ball of wool, while charming, is hardly whimsical. The opening of *Looking-Glass*, in both image and text, is a more domestic and rational affair, and it takes Carroll longer to move his heroine into the fantasy landscape than in the first book. All the same, Tenniel's rendering of the kitten's large neck-bow, along with Alice's constant one-way conversations with the animal, points to the strange ways in which pets are frequently anthropomorphized in real as well as fantasy worlds.

One thing was certain: the opening depiction of Alice, sitting by the fire as one of her kittens plays with a ball of worsted wool, appears to be a recollection of, or allusion to, a satirical article in the November 1846 issue of *Blackwood's Magazine* entitled 'Advice to an intending Serialist. A letter to T. Smith, Esq., Scene-Painter and Tragedian at the Amphitheatre'. The piece included a lampoon of Dickens's *The Cricket on the Hearth* (1845), and features a ball of pink worsted, a girl staring into a fire, and a debate over whether a kitten or an old cat is the cause of trouble. Kathleen Tillotson has observed these parallels in 'Lewis Carroll and the Kitten on the Hearth', *English: Journal of the English Association*, 8 (Autumn 1950), 136–8.

white kitten. . . black kitten: this early introduction of motifs of black and white immediately sets up the context of the chess game (played out across black-and-white squares, and usually with black-and-white pieces).

old cat: there are multiple references to the Liddell's tabby cat, Dinah, in *Wonderland*, although she never actually features in the story. Carroll's stress upon her age is in keeping with the general ethos of the book, which emphasizes poignant reflection on time passing, growing up, and ageing. That the cat is engaged in washing her kittens recalls Alice's recollections of her and her siblings' own practices with their cats in the Deanery: 'Every day these kittens were bathed by us in imitation of our own upbringing' (*LCIR*, 83).

worsted: high-quality, firmly-twisted wool yarn.

10 *[illustration]*: Tenniel's image of Alice curled up in her chair is the first visual indication as to Alice's evolution since the previous story. While there are few physical changes (beyond a slight increase to the wave of her hair), the most significant are to her clothing and in particular the introduction of the now iconic striped stockings and hairband. That such curved headbands are now commonly referred to as 'Alice bands' is a product of Tenniel's rendering of the heroine's hairstyle in *Looking-Glass*. For more on the evolution of Alice's dress and influence on fashion, see K. Vaclavik, *Fashioning Alice: The Career of Lewis Carroll's Icon, 1860–1901* (London: Bloomsbury Academic, 2019).

wicked: Alice uses the word in a jocular fashion, to imply mischievousness.

11 *"Do you know . . . the bonfire to-morrow"*: this speech provides some opportunity to date the scene. For most critics, the reference to tomorrow's bonfire suggests Guy Fawkes Night (5 November), an event celebrated at Christ Church with a large bonfire in Peckwater Quadrangle. The dating of 4 November would neatly place the story exactly six months after *Wonderland* (in which Alice reveals the date is 4 May). Alice Liddell's birthday was, hardly coincidentally, 4 May and most critics agree that in *Wonderland* Alice is 7 years old. When through the Looking-Glass, Alice informs the White Queen that she is 'seven and a half exactly' and Humpty Dumpty that she is 'Seven years and six months', so the dates appear to neatly align. Yet some critics have argued for another date. On 10 March 1863 Oxford held a grand celebration for the wedding of the Prince of Wales to Alexandra, Princess of Denmark. The events included a large bonfire and Alice attended the evening festivities in the company of Lewis Carroll, who recalls in his diary entry that 'It was delightful to see the thorough abandonment with which Alice enjoyed the whole thing' (*LCD*, iv. 173). Alice's observation of the preceding evening's preparations at the start of *Looking-Glass* appears rather more voyeuristic and cloistered than excited (particularly as it is the boys who are permitted to be outside), although both the fictional and real Alice initiate plans to visit the bonfire the next day (Alice Liddell, in fact, wrote to Dodgson on 9 March to request that he 'escort her round to see the illuminations tomorrow evening' (*LCD*, iv. 171)). Although Dodgson makes no reference in his diary to the weather, snow was recorded over the period of the marriage festivities, offering further evidence that the scene may recall preparations for the wedding rather than Guy Fawkes Night. For Morton N. Cohen, the celebration of the marriage was so significantly memorable that it served to determine not only the dating of the opening scene to *Looking-Glass* but also the nature of the story itself: 'The royal wedding set the stage for the tale; the chess figures that dominate the story are Alice's own

memory pieces of that exciting celebration' (*Lewis Carroll: A Biography* (1995; London: Macmillan, 2015), 94).

Snowdrop: generally believed so named after Mary MacDonald's pet kitten. Mary was the daughter of George MacDonald, who published *At the Back of the North Wind* in the same year as *Looking-Glass*. The literary allusion in the naming of the kitten is multilayered, as Mary's 'Snowdrop' was in turn named after a fairy tale from *Chamber Dramas for Children* written by her mother, Louisa Powell MacDonald (1870).

11 *punished*: Alice's oscillation between seeking to punish and show warmth to her kitten reflects her self-positioning in a pretend parental role, playing out the possibility of being in a dominant position (as adult) as opposed to a subservient one (as child). Yi-Fu Tuan, in his study on *Dominance and Affection* (New Haven: Yale University Press, 1984), has argued that, for adults, both children and animals function as playthings. Alice's treatment of the kitten reflects this play-acting through assuming that mock position of control, whilst recognizing her innate connection to the kitten through her reflections on her own punishments and what 'they'—i.e. adults—might in turn do to her.

Wednesday week: the Wednesday after next.

'*Go to sleep . . . summer comes again*': Alice's reflections here provide a rather saccharine revision to the sentiments expressed in the melancholy prefatory poem. The symbolic connections between snow, sleep, and death are here overcome by Alice's focus on springtime and resurrection. There is, however, a hint of unease in her follow-up comment: 'I do so *wish* it was true!'

12 *"Well, you can be one . . . I'll be all the rest"*: this problem over who gets to play which parts in a two-man game may foresee the predicament Alice finds herself in during the chess game. Alice gets to be just one piece, while all the rest are controlled by another hand (Carroll's own).

Do let's pretend . . . you're a bone!: Alice's delight in pretence games reaches a rather violent apogee here as her imaginative play becomes predatory. As in her play-punishments of the kitten, this moment reflects Alice's desire for dominance and power (made obvious when she moves through the Looking-Glass and seeks to become a queen), but it is a disturbing and somewhat surprising metamorphic choice. As Alan Benwell points out:

> the zoologically real hyena is an unsublime, queer animal that disturbs and unsettles fundamental categories of nature, politics, gender, and sexuality. With its huge head, massive bone-crunching jaws and teeth, and cold glaring eyes, with its bristling mane and front legs that seem too long for its hind legs, the hyena is frightening and ungainly, as if it were composed of mismatched parts, a kind of animal from Frankenstein's laboratory. More troubling than this ugliness, is a definitional queasiness. ('Hyena Trouble', *Studies in Romanticism*, 53 (Fall 2014), 369–97, at 370)

Carroll's 'Alice' books hardly shy away from depicting predatory or composite creatures (as in the *Looking-Glass* Jabberwock or *Wonderland*'s

Mock Turtle and Gryphon) yet the alignment of the girl with the predator remains uncomfortable. Nevertheless, it echoes Alice's dominant stance on animals across both books, whereby she views them as foodstuffs and regularly asserts her superiority in the food chain. The creatures of *Wonderland* and *Looking-Glass* routinely expose that humans are the most dangerous and threatening force in nature.

all my ideas: a child cousin of Lewis Carroll, also named Alice, claimed to have given him the idea for the mirror motif of *Through the Looking-Glass*. Recalling their relationship in January 1932, Alice Wilson Fox (née Raikes) described a time when she was asked by Carroll to stand before a mirror, holding an orange in her right hand, and report to him in which hand the little girl in the mirror held the fruit. When she informed Carroll that the mirror-child held it in her left, and he sought her explanation for that fact, she reportedly enquired whether if 'I was on the other side of the glass, wouldn't the orange still be in my right hand?' In her memory of the event, Alice claims to have much amused Carroll with this response, and he in turn told her that it was 'The best answer I've had yet' (*LCIR*, 197). Alice's memory suggests that Carroll might have played this game frequently. Carroll did not record a meeting in his diary of this kind with Alice Raikes (indeed, the first reference to meeting her in his diaries was in June 1871, only six months before the text's publication). Another possible source of inspiration for the looking-glass setting is a passage from George MacDonald's *Phantastes* (1858):

> What a strange thing a mirror is! and what a wondrous affinity exists between it and a man's imagination! For this room of mine, as I behold it in the glass, is the same, and yet not the same. It is not the mere representation of the room I live in, but it looks just as if I were reading about it in a story I like. All its commonness has disappeared. [. . .] I should like to live in *that* room if I could only get into it. (London: Smith, Elder and Co., 1858, 154–6)

Like *Looking-Glass*, *Phantastes* deploys a dissolving mirror as a mechanism into fantasy. For more on the influence of George MacDonald on Lewis Carroll, see R. B. Shaberman, 'Lewis Carroll and George MacDonald', *Jabberwocky*, 5/3 (Summer 1976), 67–88.

the wrong way: the idea of things going the wrong way foretells Alice's awkward journey across the Looking-Glass chessboard, which frequently involves travelling in ways that seem bizarre, backwards, and antithetical to progress.

13 *Looking-glass milk*: in an extended explanatory gloss, Martin Gardner links Alice's speculation about the taste of Looking-glass milk to stereo-isomers—molecules which have the same atoms but differ in spatial arrangements (*AA*, 151–3). Several other critics have made similar connections. Joanna Shawn Brigid O'Leary, for example, argues in 'Where "things go the other way": The Stereochemistry of Lewis Carroll's Looking-Glass World' that the extensive mirror-images of *Through the*

Looking-Glass have 'a chemical subtext' (*Victorian Network*, 2 (2010), 70–87, at 72). Although Carroll had an interest in chemistry, not least as a photographer, the allusion seems a little far-fetched.

13 *drawing-room*: room for withdrawing (i.e. after dinner).

Let's pretend. . .into it: while both 'Alice' books are dream narratives, *Looking-Glass* gives Alice more active control over the fantasy landscape. Alice here initiates a game of pretence, whereby readers are told explicitly that she is playfully imagining the glass giving way and allowing her entry into the Looking-glass House. The imaginative, make-believe nature of the fantasy contrasts with her apparent accidental tumble into *Wonderland*.

14 *[illustrations]*: the paired illustrations of Alice travelling through the Looking-Glass are an especially fine example of Carroll's (and Tenniel's) keen awareness as to the page-turning mechanisms of the book-as-object and highlight how the first edition operated as a work of total design. As originally presented, the first of these illustrations appeared on the recto or right-hand page; as the reader turns it over, the second image appears on the verso. The placement of three corresponding lines of text at the foot of each side of the page completes this careful alignment, as it details her through-movement. The experience of manipulating the book has Alice physically move through the mirror in the reader's hand just at the moment of its description; as Michael Hancher puts it 'The leaf, in effect, is the mirror' (*TIAB*, 173). The result is not only especially tactile, but also draws the reader into the detail of the comparative images, so as to observe that, on the Looking-Glass side, subtle changes have taken place to the objects on the chimney-piece (the flower vase and carriage clock now bear amused grotesque faces; the ornament atop the fireplace surround sticks out its tongue). Even the Tenniel monogram is inverted in the Looking-Glass image, although Alice herself is not reversed.

chimney-piece: also known as mantelpiece, referring to the structure above and around a fireplace.

they. . . can't get at me!: the mysterious 'they' implies the adults with whom Alice so desperately seeks to align herself (in terms of her desire for power) and equally seeks to escape. This tension about the desire for (and inevitability of) growing, alongside a melancholy lament upon it, abounds in *Looking-Glass*.

15 *little old man*— Alice's first encounter beyond the glass with an old man—one of many aged characters she will encounter across a text with a melancholy take on ageing. In this instance, at least, the clock is grinning.

[illustration]: Tenniel's image of the chess pieces amongst the cinders depicts them in mirrored pairs, in keeping with Carroll's description of them 'walking about, two and two!'. Tenniel, however, adds the pair of bishops to the gathering, which otherwise go unmentioned across *Looking-Glass*. For most critics, the lack of direct reference to the bishops reflects Carroll's esteem for the clergy. Note, also, the varying states of

anthropomorphism that emerge in Tenniel's picture, as if the chess pieces are here caught just in the act of coming to life.

as if I were invisible—: Alice's invisibility is a strange product of her move through the glass, but continues the motif of dominant play as she now manipulates the chess pieces unseen. As a comparatively gigantic, all-powerful, and now invisible force, Alice's play in this initial scene continues that which she exerted over her kitten on the other side of the glass. Yet her treatment of the pieces—which, of course, in a game of chess are moved about at the player's hand—predicts her own forced movement across the Looking-Glass board once she becomes a pawn and must move square by square with little control over the process or direction.

16 *curiosity*: the first reference in *Looking-Glass* to Alice's celebrated curiosity, made famous in *Wonderland* through her cry of 'Curiouser and curiouser'.

voice of my child: all of the pawns in *Looking-Glass* are aligned with servile or young characters, making childhood equate with low social rank.

My precious Lily!: when Alice decides to become a pawn in the next chapter, the Red Queen instructs her to take the place of Lily (referred to as 'the White Queen's Pawn'), for she is 'too young to play'. Perhaps the distress and confusion of the White Queen throughout the story can be attributed to this child-switch—the character here displays a maternal instinct that is rare in either 'Alice' book. For some critics, Lily is named after George McDonald's eldest daughter, Lilia (see OWC, 276). For others, it is a lampoon of John Ruskin's *Sesame and Lilies* (1865; see L. Mooneyham White, 'Domestic Queen, Queenly Domestic: Queenly Contradictions in Carroll's *Through the Looking-Glass*', *Children's Literature Association Quarterly*, 32 (Summer 2007), 110–28).

fender: metal frame placed in front of a fire to prevent coals escaping.

"Imperial fiddlestick!": the White Queen has previously referred to her pawn as a flower, a child, a kitten, and finally (rather incongruously) a figure of imperial power. The White King finds the final designation absurd—his exclamation of 'fiddlestick' is akin to 'nonsense'.

volcano: the volcano, to Hélène Cixous, is one of many pointed references to heat and fire that abound in the first chapter of *Looking-Glass*. She argues that the bonfire, fireplace, volcano, and flaming eyes of the Jabberwock provide a celebration of fire that helps to drive out 'the coldness of the atmosphere' that precedes the narrative via the dedicatory poem. She also suggests that this battle, between red (fire) and white (snow), sets the stage for the chess match to follow. (See H. Cixous, 'Introduction to Lewis Carroll's *Through the Looking-Glass* and *The Hunting of the Snark*', trans. M. Maclean, *Literary History*, 13 (Winter 1982), 231–51, at 240.)

bar to bar: Martin Gardner suggests that the slow movement of the White King 'from bar to bar' (*AA*, 155) reflects the fact that king pieces in chess can only move one square at a time. Queens, by contrast, can move up to seven squares in a single move, which is reflected in the White Queen's 'rapid journey' by Alice's hand.

17 *[illustration]*: Tenniel's illustration of the White King's panicked ascent makes his vulnerability particularly apparent. There is a clear sense of scale provided by the image, with Alice's hand as large as the King himself. The illustration recalls Tenniel's similar image for Chapter IV of *Wonderland*, as Alice's monstrously oversized hand bears down upon the White Rabbit as he cowers upon the cucumber frame. Play with scale, of course, is an overriding feature of the *Alice* books, and while there are few moments in *Looking-Glass* in which Alice has control over the pieces she encounters, Tenniel here captures the sense of dominance embedded in this instance.

whiskers: by the time of Carroll's writing, 'whiskers' tended to refer to the hair on either side of the face down to the chin, also known as sideburns, rather than to a moustache. Tenniel's depiction of the White King aligns, therefore, with the White Queen's declaration that he has no whiskers even though the illustrator depicts him sporting hair above his lip.

memorandum: written record. Martin Gardner states that the Queen's declaration that the White King should record the event in his memorandum book 'suggests the practice of recording chess moves so that a player won't forget the game' (*AA*, 155). Yet the White Queen goes on to suggest that the King should specifically record his feelings of the event, which are more difficult to recall than the proceedings themselves.

18 *[illustration]*: this first visualization of the White Knight comically has him depicted as half-horse, half-man. The upper half of his body is shaped much like a traditional knight chess piece, although with the addition of arms that curiously end in hooves. His lower body, however, is that of a human knight, complete with armour and spurs. The depiction differs from later illustrations of the Knight, where the horse's head is more obviously a helmet and he regains his hands. Despite Alice's observation as to the Knight's lack of balance, Tenniel has him sitting astride the poker with some poise.

[Reverse printed stanza]: the reverse printing of the first stanza of the 'Jabberwocky' poem is an example of Carroll's commitment to exploring novel textual and illustrative techniques in book design. As early as 1868 Carroll enquired of Macmillan as to whether they had a method 'for printing a page or two, in the next volume of *Alice*, in reverse?' (*HoM*, 59), repeating the request the following year: 'I think I told you that I want to have 2 pages of "reverse" printing in the new volume—such as you must hold up to the looking-glass to read' (*HoM*, 76). Carroll's sense of playful and tactile engagement with the book can clearly be seen in this example of requiring a reader to interact with an actual mirror as part of their reading practice. As it turned out, Carroll soon concluded that this would be 'too troublesome for the reader' (*HoM*, 77) and the final version includes only a single reversed stanza.

19 *JABBERWOCKY*: one of the most famous nonsense poems in English, 'Jabberwocky' started life in 1855 in *Mischmasch*—a family magazine written and edited by Carroll from 1855 to 1862. He included the first four lines under the title 'Stanza of Anglo-Saxon Poetry' as 'a curious fragment',

including 'learned footnotes' and a literal English translation: 'It was evening, and the smooth active badgers were scratching and boring holes in the hill side; all unhappy were the parrots; and the grave turtles squeaked out.' Carroll concluded that the fragment was 'an obscure, but yet deeply-effecting, relic of ancient Poetry'. Its expansion in *Looking-Glass* develops the piece into a quasi-heroic narrative poem detailing a young boy's defeat of a fabulous monster, recalling epic poems such as *Beowulf*. Carroll's commentary on the original stanza in *Mischmasch*—and its replication via the pompous and clueless Humpty Dumpty, who offers his own reading on the expanded version in Chapter VI of *Looking-Glass*—is meant to be humorous and satirical, providing a comedic nod to the dangers of over-interpretation. His English translation makes the 'meaning' of the stanza no clearer, and destroys the grammatical, structural, and audible logic of the piece, all of which provide the foundations to successful nonsense verse. Thus while it is of course tempting in explanatory notes to give a gloss to all unfamiliar words, and many editors have done so, such an act rather plays into Carroll's satirical hands. Many suggestions have been provided as to possible interpretations of individual words, all as unlikely as each other. I therefore refer the reader to the playful glossing of Carroll himself, both via Humpty Dumpty (see pp. 69–71) and in *Mischmasch* (see S. D. Collingwood (ed.), *The Lewis Carroll Picture Book* (London: Collins' Clear-type Press, 1899), 38–9), but attempts at exegesis beyond the poem's sensations, sounds, and sagacity belie its purpose. Given the importance of the sounds of the words, Carroll later gave assistance to the reader about pronunciation. In the preface to *The Hunting of the Snark* (1876), for example, he writes:

> let me take this opportunity of answering a question that has often been asked me, how to pronounce 'slithy toves.' The 'i' in 'slithy' is long, as in 'writhe'; and 'toves' is pronounced so as to rhyme with 'groves.' Again, the first 'o' in 'borogoves' is pronounced like the 'o' in 'borrow.' I have heard people try to give it the sound of the 'o' in 'worry.' Such is Human Perversity. (*CWLC*, 678)

He extended this advice in his 1896 changes for the 6s. Edition of *Through the Looking-Glass*, explaining that

> The new words in the poem 'Jabberwocky' [. . .] have given rise to some differences of opinion as to their pronunciation: so it may be as well to give instructions on *that* point [. . .]. Pronounce 'slithy' as if it were the two words 'sly, the': make the 'g' *hard* in 'gyre' and 'gimble': and pronounce 'rath' to rhyme with 'bath'. (*CWLC*, 126)

In keeping with the form and function of the poem, Carroll took the pronunciation of it far more seriously than he did its literal interpretation.

wabe: in the first edition of *Looking-Glass*, 'wabe' was incorrectly printed as 'wade' in the first stanza of the poem (although, interestingly, it was rendered correctly in the reverse-printed stanza). It provides a particularly easy way to identify the first printing.

19 *Jubjub bird. . . Bandersnatch*: both the Jubjub bird and the Bandersnatch make appearances in *The Hunting of the Snark*. Several of the strange words of the *Looking-Glass* 'Jabberwocky' also reappear in this later poem.

somebody killed something: Alice's struggle in this moment to interpret the poem, although entirely in keeping with the nonsense mode, reduces it to terms that are in keeping with her overall attitude to power across the 'Alice' books (i.e. largely as a predator seeking dominance over the animal kingdom). She positions a person as a 'somebody' and an animal as a 'something', in a mode that gives clear ontological supremacy to the former. That the Tenniel illustration depicts the monstrous hybrid as sporting human clothing perhaps rather undercuts her reading, however, and provides a subtle nod to a continued theme in the 'Alice' books of humans representing significant danger to other creatures. As Peter Heath sees the 'Jabberwocky', it is 'a sorry tale of the destruction of innocent wildlife' (*PA*, 139). The Jabberwock is one of only two animals to die in either 'Alice' book, the other being the innocent and naïve Oysters (who also appear only in a poem) who succumb to the appetites of the Walrus and the Carpenter.

20 *[illustration]*: Michael Hancher traces the lineage of this terrifying illustration to a cartoon entitled 'A Little Christmas Dream' drawn by Tenniel's colleague George Du Maurier for the 26 December 1868 issue of *Punch*. That image shows another terrible composite monster bearing down upon a child figure, but where Du Maurier's child flees from the creature, Tenniel's has the hero(ine) commence battle. The overwhelming difference in size between the child and monster is particularly absorbing, and Hancher notes that Tenniel seems to make the young knight an 'androgynous projection of Alice's own fears' (*TIAB*, 103), rendering him in such a way as to closely resemble Alice herself in her meeting with Humpty Dumpty, who will tutor her as to the poem's meaning (see image on p. 66). That the Jabberwock is an amalgam of many animal parts (overall, something of a dragon, but with a fish-like head, rabbit-teeth, the wings of a bat, and eagle-like talons) recalls the fractured animal parts of the Mock Turtle in *Wonderland*, but the inclusion of a waistcoat adds an additional humanizing layer. For a discussion of the changing placement of the 'Jabberwocky' illustration, see note to Frontispiece.

21 *look at the garden first*: Alice's desire to go straight to the garden when through the Looking-Glass repeats her wishes upon tumbling into Wonderland: 'she decided on going into the garden at once' (*CWLC*, 21).

giddy: a sensation alike to dizziness; a spatially confused state that may cause one to fall.

22 *[Title]*: the reference to these flowers being 'live' is quite particular. All plants are *living* organisms, but the sense of life Carroll alludes to here is that endowed by the flowers' ability to communicate with Alice via direct speech, showing command of language normally reserved for humans. 'Being' here equals a command of language, reflecting long-standing

philosophical arguments that it is language that separates man from the rest of organic life. Carroll's extension of language to all manner of creatures and objects essentially disrupts the power dynamics by which Alice herself 'lives', upending chain-of-being principles that date to Aristotle, and continually forcing Alice into situations where her dominance is not assured.

Tiger-lily: in the original manuscript, the Tiger-lily was a passion flower. Stuart Dodgson Collingwood recalls that Carroll made the change due to his 'reverence for sacred things': 'In his original manuscript the bad-tempered flower was the passion-flower; the sacred origin of the name never struck him, until it was pointed out to him by a friend, when he at once changed it into the tiger-lily' (*LLLC*, 127). The passion flower is symbolically associated with Christ's suffering and sacrifice in Christian theology.

"We can talk": this episode with the flowers is generally considered to be a parody of section 22 of Alfred Lord Tennyson's *Maud* (1855) which includes many of the same talking flowers (lily, rose, violet, larkspur). Over the period of Carroll's writing, England was also experiencing a particular craze for floriography—otherwise known as the language of flowers—whereby particular arrangements of blooms could convey symbolic meaning and thus transfer encoded messages from sender to recipient.

23 *[illustration]*: Tenniel's detailed depiction of the garden gives the sense of a mass of foliage, although he renders in detail only the rose bush and the tiger-lily. Note that although Carroll mentions only one Rose and Tiger-lily in the Dramatis Personæ (both as red pawns), Tenniel depicts several flowers. In the case of the Rose, he also gives the flower human, cherub-like features, whereas the Tiger-lily shows no obvious anthropomorphism. Note the deliberately challenging sense of scale in the image; the fore-grounding of the flowers makes it hard to determine the relative size of Alice in relation to them.

Alice was so astonished: Peter Heath notes that while Alice 'shows surprise at a rational vegetable; the flowers show none at a mobile one'. He ventures that because the flowers know of only one category of organism, they are 'less inhibited by Aristotelian prejudices' (*PA*, 141). This limited knowledge also means that they describe every being in the garden in botanical terms, including the Red Queen and Alice herself.

It isn't manners: the Rose's criticism echoes and inverts that of Alice to her kitten in the opening scene, a sure sign that the power dynamics through the Looking-Glass have shifted.

you're the right colour: this assertion from the Rose begs the question as to what 'colour' Alice is. The Rose is identified in the Dramatis Personæ as a red pawn, but we soon learn that Alice is to start the game as a white pawn (thus as an opponent). Of course, there is often slippage in Carroll's fantasy worlds when it comes to the colour of roses, as depicted through painting white roses red in *Wonderland*.

24 *I'll pick you!*: as is typical of Alice, her first response is to assert her dominance, in this case via a violent threat against the daisies.

pink daisies turned white: a further playful allusion to flowers changing colour at Alice's hand, recalling and inverting painting white roses so they would appear to be red in *Wonderland*. Note that the daisies, unlike the other flowers, are referred in the plural, in keeping with the fact that Carroll lists four daisies as pawns in the Dramatis Personæ (two red, two white).

the Rose. . . a Violet: several critics suggest that the inclusion of the Rose and Violet recall the two youngest Liddell daughters: Rhoda Caroline Anne Liddell and Violet Constance Liddell.

25 *her petals are shorter*: this is probably a reference to hair, which adult women kept up in this period.

you're beginning to fade. . . petals getting a little untidy: in addition to referring to Alice's hair being down, here is a rather unpleasant gendered comment on Alice's ageing, implying that her youth is fading, in keeping with the general lament in *Looking-Glass* on the passage of time. The sense of untidy and loosening petals, with its hints of 'deflowering', also has sexual overtones.

"She's one of the thorny kind": later revised in 1896 so as to read: 'She's one of the kind that has nine spikes, you know.' Several critics suggest that Carroll was motivated to make the change so as to remove an in-joke reference to the Liddell governess 'Miss Prickett' (nicknamed 'Pricks' by the children). Given Carroll's earlier substitution of passion flower for Tiger-lily, so as to remove any religious symbolism, it seems equally likely that this revision reflects a desire to omit any possible allusion to the Crown of Thorns. The change also highlights the illustrative detail of the Queen's crown, which Tenniel rendered with nine points.

footstep: note the singularity. As a chess piece, the Queen has but one 'foot'.

"She's grown a good deal!": this size change continues the theme of metamorphosis from *Wonderland*, but Alice appears to escape the frequent growing and shrinking that characterizes her first adventure. There is no specific detail here as to the Queen's growth, so we only have Alice's word as to who has changed size.

26 *[illustration]*: Tenniel's rendering of Alice, standing before the Red Queen with her hands neatly tucked away while the monarch delivers instructions, speaks to the clear symbiosis between author and illustrator. Following the publication of *Looking-Glass* and subsequent staging of the book in Henry Savile Clarke's 'Dream play', Carroll wrote a piece for *The Theatre* which explained his vision for his various 'puppets'. The Red Queen he depicts as 'cold and calm; [. . .] formal and strict, yet not unkindly; pedantic to the tenth degree, the concentrated essence of all governesses!' ('"Alice" on the Stage', *The Theatre*, 1 April 1887, 182). Tenniel had captured this sense of the Queen exactly, her sharp angles contrasting with his rendering of other royal chess pieces but speaking to

her character. The rigidity of her clothing, compared to that of Alice, shows that the chess pieces are carved. This image particularly emphasizes that the Red Queen is a piece in the game; note the pedestal on which she stands, which is later replaced by human legs and feet.

It succeeded beautifully: Alice succeeds here because her actions are a mirror inversion. As Martin Gardner notes: 'Walk toward a mirror, the image moves in the opposite direction' (*AA*, 170).

face to face with the Red Queen: Alice and the Red Queen are now in adjacent squares (thus 'face to face'), as depicted in the prefatory diagram to the chess moves.

27 *as sensible as a dictionary!*: an amusing reference in the context of a work of nonsense, where dictionary definitions rarely lend sense to words (see, for example, the 'Jabberwocky' poem).

little hill: Peter Hunt suggests that the reference to the hill may recall a trip made by Carroll in April 1863 to visit the Liddell child in the village of Birdlip, Gloucestershire, and a walk over Leckhampton hill (OWC, 283). Carroll recalls in his diary for 4 April that 'the day could hardly have been better for the view' (*LCD*, iv. 186).

[illustration]: this depiction of the Looking-Glass landscape is the only instance in which readers are provided with a clear visual image of the chessboard. From here on, Alice sees only with the restricted view of a pawn until she becomes queen. In Tenniel's preliminary drawing of the image, Alice appeared in the foreground beneath the boughs of the tree. This was likely changed at Carroll's request. Hugh Haughton suggests that the image is 'a parody of Renaissance Perspective, the basis of so many mirror-theories of art' (Penguin, 335).

28 *a great huge game of chess*: the first direct acknowledgement in the story that chess functions as a narrative principle. For a discussion of other works in which 'life itself is compared to an enormous game of chess', see *AA*, 172–3.

I should like to be a Queen, best: in keeping with Alice's aspirations to authority, she immediately seeks to become the most powerful chess piece. The Red Queen's ensuing encouragement of Alice rather belies the point of the game—a white pawn becoming a second queen would put the red player at a significant disadvantage.

Lily's too young to play: as a kitten, Lily is indeed young. But as the Red Queen is also a kitten, the assertion is somewhat suspect.

you're in the Second Square. . .Eighth Square. . .a Queen: as a pawn, Alice begins the game on the second row of the chessboard. If a pawn reaches the final row on the opposite side of the board (the eighth square), it becomes a queen (or, rarely, another piece of the player's choosing).

the Queen went so fast: a further reference to the ability of queen pieces to traverse large portions of the board in a single move. (See note to p. 16.)

28 *[illustration]*: Tenniel's image perfectly captures the doubleness of movement and stasis explained in the text. As an illustration, it can render
a sense of fast movement (here, in particular, through the elevation and
angle of Alice and the Red Queen as they are lifted from the ground and
through the employment of horizontal line-work). Yet, as a fixed image,
Tenniel's pencil also leaves the characters perpetually in one place.

29 *Now . . . same place*: Martin Gardner states that this passage 'has probably
been quoted more often (usually in reference to rapidly changing political
situations) than any other passage in the *Alice* books' (*AA*, 174).

little box. . . "Have a biscuit?": the Red Queen's biscuit box is curiously
predictive of an early piece of *Looking-Glass* merchandise. In the early
1890s, Carroll was involved in a rather vexing and drawn-out licensing
agreement to produce a biscuit tin with Charles Manners (of Messrs
Barringer, Wallis, and Manners, Tin Plate Decorators and Manufacturers
of Decorated Enamelled tin boxes). The final product was sold containing
Jacobs Biscuits and depicted multiple scenes from *Looking-Glass* (colour-
ized versions of the Tenniel illustrations). For an extensive discussion
of Carroll's input into the production of the Looking-Glass tin, see
Z. Jaques and E. Giddens, *Lewis Carroll's Alice books: A Publishing History*
(Aldershot: Ashgate, 2014).

30 *remember who you are!*: as well as predicting an episode in the next chapter,
the Red Queen's warning recalls some of Alice's extensive problems
remembering who she was in *Wonderland*.

she was gone: this sudden disappearance reflects the Red Queen's movement as set out by Carroll in the list of moves (R. Q. to K. R.'s 4th). The
Red Queen thus moves to the fourth rank in the Red King's Rook's file.
Or, put simply, she moves out of the way at the edge of the board. Alice,
whose perspective as a pawn in the game is now limited to the adjacent
squares, can no longer see where she is.

31 *proboscis*: the elongated mouthpart of an insect through which liquids are
collected. Also refers to the trunk of an elephant, predicting Alice's discovery that the bees are elephants.

six little brooks: these represent the horizontal lines of the chessboard that
Alice must cross to reach the eighth square. Each time Alice crosses
a brook into a new square, Carroll indicates the movement with three rows
of stars (of varying numbers, for no obviously discernible reason). Her
jump over the first brook begins Alice's initial move across two squares (as
pawns can do on their first play), through White Queen's third and then
on to White Queen's fourth. Her travel by rail reflects both this increased
speed and that she moves through a square without stopping.

32 *(I hope you understand. . . I don't)*: Carroll here intrudes upon the narrative in one of a handful of occasions across the 'Alice' books where he
breaks the frame and speaks directly to the reader. Such a practice is fairly
common in nineteenth-century children's literature; Charles Kingsley's
The Water-Babies (1863), for example, engages in extensive dialogue with

an implied child reader, often taking the form of bizarre and unrelated musings seemingly for the author's own benefit.

telescope. . . microscope. . . opera-glass: Carroll's quick movement through a series of optical devices reflects the nineteenth-century fascination with technologies of seeing and a general interest in modernization.

very queer carriage-full of passengers: the experience of the Victorian railway carriage could quite reflect this assessment. Michael Hancher writes that 'the lack of privacy to be had in even a first-class railway compartment was the basis for countless *Punch* cartoons during the fifties and sixties' (*TIAB*, 119). By 1870, England sported 16,000 miles of track, and over 400 million passengers travelled by rail. There was also a pervasive view that such travel could cause psychological trauma; cases of erratic behaviour, or 'railway madness', were regularly reported in mid-century newspapers. Thus Alice's sense of her companions being both queer and copious is rather in keeping with the spirit of the day.

33 *[illustration]*: a great deal of attention has been paid to this illustration of the railway carriage, so much so that critical interpretations of the scene tend to prioritize Tenniel's image over Carroll's words. William Empson, writing in *Some Versions of Pastoral* in 1935, declared that the man in the carriage dressed in papers was Benjamin Disraeli (he also suggested that he reappears later as the Unicorn of Chapter VII, see note to p. 82). Martin Gardner concurs, arguing that 'A comparison of the illustration of the man in white paper with Tenniel's political cartoons in *Punch* leaves little doubt that the face under the folded paper hat is Benjamin Disraeli's' (*AA*, 181–2). Yet there is very little in the text to suggest that Carroll had Disraeli in mind. If there is a connection, which seems tenuous, then it is Tenniel's alone. The rendering of Alice in this image is equally a cause for question; it is the first of two occasions in *Looking-Glass* where Alice's movement across a brook causes not only a change in square but also a change to her outfit (here to include a feathered pork-pie hat, muff, coat, bag, and boots). As Kiera Vaclavik notes, there is no textual cue for this radical shift—the haberdashery is entirely Tenniel's (*Fashioning Alice*, 65). There are many possibilities as to why Tenniel made this change—not least that such an outfit would be both appropriate for travel and 'very much up to date' (*TIAB*, 123)—but critics tend to favour the illustrator having modelled the image on a variety of sources (the most frequently cited being Augustus Leopold Egg's *The Travelling Companions* (1862), John Everett Millais's *My First Sermon* (1865), and Walter Crane's *Annie and Jack in London* (1869)).

extremely small voice: Carroll's choice to have this small voice represented by a diminutive typeface reflects not only his exacting standards of book design but also pleasure at communicating in miniature. Morton N. Cohen recalls the details of one of many 'fairy' letters he sent to child friends: 'the entire letter postage-stamp size, the handwriting so miniature as to be almost invisible. He must have written these letters with a fine geographer's pen and meant them to be read with a magnifying glass' (*LCIR*, 195).

33 *'Lass, with care'*: a pun on labelling breakable packages 'Glass, with care'.

got a head on her—: a reference to the Queen's head featuring on stamps (which, of course, Alice seeks to become). Also a quip that recalls another Queen's desire to see her head removed in *Wonderland*.

I wish I could get back there!: as a pawn, Alice cannot move backwards. Her desire to do so reflects her constant dissatisfaction with her present condition, as shown in Chapter I by her wish to escape into the Looking-glass House and subsequent irritation with the house in Chapter II as she sought to view the garden.

34 *Fourth Square*: the train's leap into the air moves Alice into the White Queen's fourth square, as outlined by Carroll 'to Q.'s 4th (*Tweedledum and Tweedledee*)'. Alice does not, however, immediately encounter the next pieces Carroll here lists in the game (the Tweedles as Castles), but is rather delayed by the Gnat (not a piece in the game) and a dalliance with another white pawn (in the form of the Fawn).

Goat's beard: Alice's grasping at the Goat's beard was a suggestion of Tenniel. In the original manuscript, Carroll had her instead grab an old lady's hair, but his illustrator suggested in a letter of 1 June 1890 that 'The jerk would naturally throw them together' (*LLLC*, 125). As well as heeding Tenniel's suggestion, Carroll cut the old lady from the scene entirely.

35 *[illustrations]*: Tenniel's series of three illustrations of the Rocking-horse-fly, Snap-dragon-fly, and Bread-and-butter-fly endow the nonsense insects of Carroll's prose with natural-historical realism. As Rose Lovell Smith has argued in relation to *Wonderland*: 'Tenniel's illustrations pick up on but also extend [a] Darwinist and natural history field of reference in Carroll's text [. . .]; Tenniel's drawings of animals [. . .] produce *Alice* as a kind of natural history by resembling those in the plentiful and lavishly illustrated popular natural histories of the day' ('The Animals of Wonderland: Tenniel as Carroll's Reader', *Criticism*, 45 (Fall 2003), 383–415, at 388). Each of Tenniel's *Looking-Glass* insects is rendered with the type of fine, magnifying detail of an entomological guide, while Alice and the Gnat's accompanying discussion of their features, habits, and diets equally aligns with the function of such texts. It is telling that both Rocking-horse-fly and Snap-dragon-fly are rendered in a bucolic, fecund environment (against large ivy leaves), whereas the wilting Bread-and-butter-fly sags on bare ground, in keeping with Alice's sense that it must struggle to find food. Hancher notes the presence of ivy here as a 'compositional device [that] draws attention to the ivy that flourishes elsewhere' (*TIAB*, 123), such as on the tree behind the Tweedles and on Humpty Dumpty's wall. Tenniel's choice to depict the Rocking-horse-fly with dappled coat recalls the fashions of the day, and may allude to Queen Victoria's 1851 visit to Collinson & Sons Rocking

Horse Manufacturers, during which the monarch expressed a particular preference for the dappled grey coat. From that point on, the firm concentrated on producing this design.

I don't rejoice in insects . . . names of some of them: although Alice appears rather more fearful of insects than interested in them—and is only able to recall a few of their names—entomology was an increasingly popular form of participatory science in the nineteenth century for adults and children alike. A multitude of texts were published in the era that encouraged the study of insect life, many of which drew upon fantasy and the fairy realm as part of their attempt to encourage an early interest in the field. Carroll's extended discussion of Looking-Glass insects, which of course provides the title for the chapter, is in keeping with this Victorian craze. See J. F. McDiarmid Clark, *Bugs and Victorians* (New Haven: Yale University Press, 2009) and M. Keene, *Science in Wonderland* (Oxford: Oxford University Press, 2015).

why do things have names at all?: as shown throughout the 'Alice' books, Alice sees the world only through a limited human perspective. People name animals—a right inscribed to Adam in Genesis—and as such it matters very little if the names are of use to their recipients. Yet understanding the world through words alone also *limits* meaning and knowledge, as Carroll has already shown in the 'Jabberwocky' poem. Alice's insistence that names are useful to people anticipates her paradoxical encounter with the Fawn, in which it is a lack of names that proves essential to communication and companionship.

36 *Rocking-horse-fly*: Hugh Haughton notes that 'Carroll's prose is always studded with hyphenated compounds, but here they come into their own to create new species. Nonsense etymology and nonsense entomology meet' (Penguin, 337).

Snap-dragon-fly: in this period, snapdragon alluded to 'a game or amusement (usually held at Christmas) consisting of snatching raisins out of a bowl or dish of burning brandy or other spirit and eating them whilst alight' (*OED*). Carroll's description of the insect's body continues the Christmassy context.

plum-pudding: a boiled suet pudding (containing raisins, currants, citrus peel, and spices). Also known as figgy pudding or Christmas pudding.

Frumenty: a porridge-like dish of medieval origin made by boiling cracked wheat in milk. The name derives from the Latin word *frumentum*, meaning 'grain', and is sometimes spelt 'furmenty'.

Christmas-box: Stephen Nissenbaum explains that the Christmas box was 'developed in seventeenth-century London [. . .] by young tradesmen's apprentices and other low-level workers, who kept earthen-ware boxes—the ancestor, really, of the piggy bank—into which, during the Christmas season, they asked those who employed their services to put money' (*The Battle for Christmas* (New York: Vintage Books, 1997), 110). Eugene Giddens notes that in real gift-giving 'Christmas boxes are long gone' by the 1840s, but books continued to be called *The Christmas Box* late into the nineteenth century (*Christmas Books for Children* (Cambridge: Cambridge University Press, 2019), 20).

37 *"It always happens"*: a further sorrowful reflection on mortality. The short lifespan of insects gives Carroll the opportunity to make several quips about the inevitable march towards death, as in Alice's reflection upon insects' fondness for flying into candles. That the Gnat later appears to have 'sighed itself away' is in keeping with this melancholy trajectory.

silent for a minute or two, pondering: one of several instances across the 'Alice' books where Carroll makes his heroine pause for thought—usually following the exposition of a philosophical problem or truth—and in doing so implies that the reader should do the same.

call me 'Miss!', as the servants do: a reminder that Alice is envisioned as an upper-middle-class child, for whom having servants would be the norm. Carroll intended that his 'Alice' books be primarily marketed at a middle- and upper-class readership; when exploring the possibility of lowering the price of later editions of *Wonderland*, Carroll explained that 'the present price puts the book entirely out of the reach of many thousands of children of the middle classes, who might, I think, enjoy it (below that I don't think it would be appreciated' (*HoM*, 77).

an ugly one: recalls Alice's fears in *Wonderland* of becoming 'Mabel', although in that case it was the possibility of having to 'live in that poky little house, and have next to no toys to play with' (*CWLC*, 26) that concerned her.

38 *"Dash"*: Alice chooses a particularly regal name for the potential lost dog. The *Oxford Dictionary of National Biography* notes that as a child Queen Victoria owned and doted upon a King Charles Spaniel by the name of Dash, who was to be 'the first in a long line of beloved little dogs'. Dash makes a return appearance in *The Nursery 'Alice'* as the 'dear little puppy' of Chapter VI.

What does it call itself, I wonder?: Alice here forgets her own observation, when conversing with the Gnat, that names are only useful to people.

who am I?: an inversion, of course, of the caterpillar's famous ontological question: 'Who are *you*?' (*CWLC*, 48).

begins with L!: Alice may be recalling the surname of Carroll's muse (Liddell) or the name of her piece in the game (Lily) or the title she was given on the train (Lass).

a Fawn came wandering by: the Fawn, who represents another white pawn, must now be in the adjacent square. Note the rhyming pun of the names (fawn/pawn).

39 *[illustration]*: Tenniel's depiction of Alice and the Fawn traversing together through the wood with no names is the most comforting visualization of human–animal relations in either of the 'Alice' books. Tenniel seems to particularly labour the emotional intensity and bucolic nature of the image to support Carroll's emphasis on the subsequent dissolution of species unity captured in this moment.

"I'm a Fawn. . .you're a human child". . .Alice stood. . .some comfort: this encounter brings to a heady conclusion the chapter's focus on the limitation of naming. Unburdened by their names, Alice and the Fawn can exist comfortably together. Yet as soon as the Fawn recalls its name, it also recalls Alice's humanity (and thus, naturally, it flees). Alice quickly redirects her immediate grief, to take comfort in the recovery of her name, but fails to properly recognize that it is naming itself that causes such melancholy fracturing. Carroll makes clear that names separate humanity from other species, in a way that predicts Jacques Derrida's case in his famous talk on 'The Animal that Therefore I am (more to follow)'. Derrida himself took inspiration from the 'Alice' books: 'Although time prevents it, I would of course have liked to inscribe my whole talk within a reading of Lewis Carroll' (trans. D. Wills, *Critical Inquiry*, 28 (2002), 369–418, at 376). Of course, the Fawn's flight also represents this second white pawn moving to another square.

"I'll settle it". . .did not seem likely to happen: Alice here assumes a power that, as a pawn, she does not have. She experiences the illusion of choice in this moment, but her path in the game is predetermined.

40 *two fat little men*: Frankie Morris suggests that while 'two fat little men' are 'hardly the heroes of a medieval romance', the chapter that follows seems nevertheless to suggest they are indeed knights and to be a parody of the 'Knightes Tale' from Chaucer's *Canterbury Tales*, 'specifically the meeting in the grove' (*Artist of Wonderland: The Life, Political Cartoons, and Illustrations of Tenniel* (Charlottesville: University of Virginia Press, 2005), 200). It is telling, however, that Carroll did not choose to select the knight chess pieces for these characters, making them instead white rooks.

must be: note that the chapter concludes with an unfinished sentence. As Virginie Iché notes, 'The deliberate omission of a period at the end of the sentence, along with the blank space at the bottom of the page, encourages the reader to guess who these "two fat little men" might be before turning the page to have access to the next chapter and to the solution to that riddle-like sentence' (Iché, 'Submission and Agency, or the Role of the Reader in the First Editions of Lewis Carroll's *Alice's Adventures in Wonderland* (1865) and *Through the Looking-Glass* (1871)', *Cahiers victoriens et édouardiens*, 16 (2016), 1–13, at 8). Such playfulness continues to demonstrate Carroll's care and consideration as to the formal qualities of a book, and his utilization of its form in his narrative design. The 1897 edition introduced a full stop in error, spoiling the effect, but it was later corrected.

41 *[illustration]*: as with several of the illustrations, the initial image of the Tweedles demonstrates the careful page layout of the first edition. Carroll had the text on the verso (the left-hand side of the double-page spread) conclude with 'she was startled by a voice coming from the one marked "DUM" '. The Tenniel illustration appeared at the top of the recto, and has Alice duly surprised, as shown by what Hancher notes is her 'awkward, startled posture' (*TIAB*, 166). The necessary eye movement

between text and image might be said to create this act of startling, as readers encounter the two mirror-imaged twins. They are an exact reflection of each other, the only discernible distinction being the inscriptions 'DEE' and 'DUM' upon their collars (one of which—Tweedledum's—curls up on one side).

41 *[Title]*: the *OED* notes that the stem 'tweedle' is 'employed in combination with other elements to denote the action of the verb, or a high-pitched musical sound; chiefly in the humorous phrase tweedledum and tweedledee'. The earliest example the *OED* records refers to the rivalry between two musicians (Handel and Bononcini) as recorded in an epigram by John Byrom in *Miscellaneous Poems* (1773): 'Strange all this Difference should be | 'Twixt Tweedle-dum and Tweedle-dee!' (*OED*).

standing under a tree: having spent some time in the fourth square, Alice now encounters the white castles in the form of the Tweedles. These pieces cannot occupy the same space at once, although the Red Queen has already informed Alice that the fourth square 'belongs to the Tweedles'. The Castles start the game in the far corners of the board, so the Tweedles would actually 'belong' elsewhere. This is one of the many liberties that the narrative form must take with the actual game.

Wax-works. . . for nothing: the original purpose of waxwork figures had little to do with monetary gain but rather with funerals and death rites, particularly with respect to royalty of whom full-sized waxwork effigies were often created (such as, for example, the model of Henry III made for his funeral in 1272). Carroll, however, was no doubt referring to the increased popularity of wax museums or waxworks, one of the most famous and notable of which is Madame Tussauds, established in London in 1835. Tweedledum is correct, therefore, in his assertion that these commercial waxworks 'weren't made to be looked at for nothing', although the earlier history of the waxwork effigy also resonates with the text's investment in highlighting, sometimes in macabre ways, the proximity of life and death.

Nohow!: a largely defunct word meaning 'by no course of action, method, or agency; in no way, by no means, not at all' (*OED*).

42 *old song*: Iona and Peter Opie note in the *Oxford Dictionary of Nursery Rhymes* (1951) that the first written version of the poem Alice here recalls appears in *Original Ditties for the Nursery* (*c*.1805, printed for J. Harris). Yet its prognosticating function, rather than its heritage, matters most to *Looking-Glass*. Via her recollection of the song, Alice shapes (or at the very least predicts) the events of the chapter. This is a rare instance of a pawn shaping play.

That's logic: it is axiomatic to state that *Alice* teems with logical puzzles and wordplay, although here is the first explicit, direct reference to logic in either book. Carroll wrote several texts and papers on logic, in keeping with both his academic work as a mathematician and his lifelong fascination with logic play. His most notable works in this regard are *The Game of Logic* (1886) and *Symbolic Logic* (1896), the first of which opens with a prefatory poem 'To my Child-friend' and uses an accompanying board game with nine counters to explore various kinds of logical statement. Falconer Madden notes that 'The game is, as a game for children of ordinary capacity, a failure' (*LCHB*, 131). *Looking-Glass*, certainly, is more successful at engaging logical puzzling.

"First Boy!": referring to the first-ranked student in a class academically, although neither Tweedle seems a likely candidate.

"You've begun wrong!": another example of the strange denizens of *Looking-Glass* schooling Alice in manners and etiquette, reversing the power dynamics she establishes over her kitten at the start of the book.

43 *'Here we go round the mulberry bush'*: James Orchard Halliwell-Phillipps in *Popular Rhymes and Nursery Tales* (London: John Russell Smith, 1849, 217), records two versions of this song, both accompanied by a dance in which children join hands and move in a ring. In one version, which it seems Alice recalls, the children dance around a 'mulberry-bush' on a 'sunshiny morning'; in the other, it is a 'bramble-bush' on a 'cold and frosty morning'. The difference, no doubt, aligns with when the plants bear fruit, although given that *Looking-Glass* is replete with wintery allusions, the latter would seem more in keeping. In most modern versions of the song, the mulberry bush and the wintery morning appear together—both brambles and sunshine have disappeared.

"You like poetry?". . .*doubtfully*: note that Alice, older in *Through the Looking-Glass*, shows more resistance to poetry and verse than she had in *Wonderland*. Here, however, she tends to be forced to listen to it rather than to recite; she still seems perfectly content to spontaneously recall poetry as it occurs to her.

'The Walrus and the Carpenter': Hugh Haughton notes that this is 'A rare instance of a nonsense poem in the Alice books which is not a parody' (Penguin, 339). The narrative poem is entirely of Carroll's own invention (like 'Jabberwocky'), and offers a rather savage and strangely out-of-keeping warning as to the dangers of the very curiosity Alice is famous for, as well as a critical eye to gluttony and the destruction of natural resources. The rationale for the choice of the particular participants involved is rather unclear. Peter Hunt, drawing on Roger Lancelyn Green, suggests that the Walrus 'was probably suggested by a stuffed walrus in the Sunderland Museum, which Dodgson had known since childhood' (OWC, 285). Carroll recalled that Tenniel found the combination of the Walrus and the Carpenter 'hopeless' and requested that the Carpenter be abolished; Carroll instead offered him the option of Baronet or Butterfly, but it seems Tenniel relented to the idea of penning the Carpenter (see M. N. Cohen and E. Wakeling, *Lewis Carroll and His Illustrators* (New York: Cornell University Press, 2003), 170–1). Such an instance of Tenniel querying and indeed changing Carroll's narrative was not uncommon; see, for example, the goat's beard from the railway carriage (see note to p. 34) and the excised wasp in the wig episode (Introduction, pp. xiii–xiv). The choice

to make the Oysters the subject of the predators' greed, however, is more obvious; as Rebecca Stott notes, 'Since the Romans oysters have been associated with gluttony and acts of gluttonous bravado' (*Oyster* (London: Reaktion, 2004), 83). Positioning them as innocents aligns with the fact that they have no defence system once their shells are penetrated and are consumed alive. Lewis Carroll granted William Boyd the rights to set to music any of the verses of *Through the Looking-Glass*, and 'The Walrus and the Carpenter' setting was published quickly after the book's initial publication, appearing in *Aunt Judy's Magazine* in March 1872.

43 *billows*: swells of the ocean, as occasioned by the wind.

Shining with all his might . . . she thought: note the gendering of the sun as male and moon as female, in keeping with much poetic usage which deploys French or Romance language gendering as opposed to Germanic grammatical genders.

44–47 *[illustrations]*: Tenniel depicts the Walrus and the Carpenter across this trio of images as differently stylized Victorian males. The Walrus is a dapper gentleman in jacket and waistcoat who maintains a stiff bearing throughout (note Tenniel taking full advantage of the potential to exaggerate the walrus whisker to imply a heavy moustache). The Carpenter is dressed in attire more appropriate to a tradesman, including tool bag and folded paper hat (an early example of disposable headwear necessary in dusty environments), and Tenniel rather unkindly has him sport a gormless expression and oversized features. Michael Hancher notes a number of antecedent *Punch* drawings that Tenniel leant upon when devising these pictures, although some of the connections seem fairly tenuous (see *TIAB*, 19–21). Most convincing is his observation that the final image of the gluttonous Walrus and Carpenter, amidst a littered array of oyster shells, mirrors that of an earlier Tenniel cartoon entitled 'Law and Lunacy' (*Punch*, 25 January 1862). The carpenter 'strikes a pose almost identical to that of an oyster-eating lawyer in Tenniel's cartoon' (*TIAB*, 24). Such connections give some insight into the work and process of Carroll's illustrator, although do little to illuminate *Looking-Glass* itself. Frankie Morris, however, usefully notes the importance of the placement of these images, which he argues are one of a series of 'sets' in the 'Alice' books. Continuing the theme of real precision in the making of *Alice*, Morris observes that

> The Walrus and seated Carpenter pictures, both on verso sheets, have the same background. If the reader looks fixedly at the first cut, with its eager little Oysters, and then flips quickly to the second sheet, the two cronies may seem to shift and the Oysters turn to piles of shells. (*Artist of Wonderland*, 179)

Subsequent editions have tended not to maintain the positioning of these images, and so the effect is lost.

44 *walking close at hand*: in another request from Tenniel, seemingly motivated by his sense of the visuals of the scene, Carroll changed his original line from 'walking hand-in-hand' to 'walking close at hand'. Such a change,

however, also aligns more effectively with the design of the chess game; Carroll has the Walrus and Carpenter in the roles of Red Bishop and Red Knight respectively. As such, they begin on the board side by side or, put another way, 'close at hand'.

45 *briny*: salty.

four young Oysters: note that Carroll has four Oysters feature in his chess game, all as pawns, two red and two white. Presumably the white Oysters get 'consumed/taken' by the Red Bishop and Red Knight, although the fate of the other two is unclear (at least in the game).

hadn't any feet: continues the playfulness around feet and chess pieces found throughout *Looking-Glass*, particularly in Tenniel's illustrations. Here, of course, Tenniel does furnish all the fated Oysters with the spindly legs and shoes that will carry them to their deaths.

46 *The time has come. . .pigs have wings*: Michael Hancher notes that the Walrus's proposed conversations 'make up one of the most celebrated agendas in the history of nonsense literature as well of one of the most memorable lists in poetry' (Penguin, 340). The list details increasingly whimsical topics (from the mundane shoes—particularly irrelevant to Oysters without feet—through to the possibility of pigs flying). As with most of Carroll's nonsense, it is the sound and ordering of the words that matter here, rather than their literal meanings or allusions. Note, however, that the (im)possibility of pigs flying also concerns the Duchess in *Wonderland* (*CWLC*, 89), while queries over the heat of the sea (in a poem concerned with the plundering of the Earth's natural resources) are curiously predictive of global warming's impact on oceanic temperatures.

A loaf of bread. . .good indeed: it is no doubt the choice of bread, pepper, and vinegar as accompaniments that finally alerts the Oysters as to who is on the menu. Note George Augustus's recollection of their consumption in *Twice Around the Clock, or The Hours of Day and Night in London* (London: Houlston and Wright, 1859), 326:

> I will abide by the Haymarket oyster-shop, rude, simple, primitive as it is, with its peaceful concourse of customers taking perpendicular refreshment at the counter, plying the unpretending pepper-castor, and the vinegar-cruet with the perforated cork, calling cheerfully for crusty bread and pats of butter

48 *But answer came there none. . .every one*: Carroll frequently permits anthropomorphic creatures and foodstuffs the opportunity to critically respond to those who might eat them (i.e. the Pigeon fearful for her eggs or the composite Mock Turtle of *Wonderland*, and the talking Mutton in *Looking-Glass*). It is unusual, therefore, for characters to be silenced in the manner of the Oysters' deaths. Carroll himself seemed to reverse his position on leaving the Oysters without further voice, proposing to Henry Savile Clarke a new ending for the stage-play version following its opening. In the extended poem the ghosts of the Oysters rise-up in vengeance against their wanton consumers. Tweedledum and Tweedledee introduce the moment of punishment thus:

DUM: The Carpenter he ceased to sob;
The Walrus ceased to weep;
They'd finished all the Oysters,
and they laid them down to sleep—

DEE: And of their craft and cruelty
The punishment to reap.

The ghost of the second Oyster then sings:

2nd OYS: O woeful, weeping Walrus, your tears are all a sham!
You're greedier for Oysters than children are for jam.
You'd like to have an Oyster to give the meal a zest—
Excuse me, wicked Walrus, for stamping on your chest!
For stamping on your chest!
For stamping on your chest!
For stamping on your chest!
Excuse me, wicked Walrus, for stamping on your chest!
(Cited in C. Lovett, *Alice on the Stage* (Westport: Meckler, 1978), 66)

Savile Clarke approved of the recriminatory revision and it was included in later productions, although Carroll never chose to revise *Looking-Glass* accordingly.

48 *[illustration]*: this depiction of the Red King is the only illustration of the piece throughout *Looking-Glass*. Tenniel makes his isolation quite clear (although, in terms of Carroll's game, he is in the Red King's fifth square so is rather exposed on the board). Despite the fact that the King is the most crucial chess piece (in that checkmate wins the game), it is also relatively weak. Kings generally spend much of the game protected and unmoving (here creatively interpreted by Carroll as asleep). Tenniel perhaps picks up on this weakness, along with Tweedledum's coddling comment about him being a '*lovely* sight', by depicting him curled up small in the foetal position, almost like a baby or young child. There is a sense of vulnerability and weakness to the image, which reflects the properties of the piece itself.

They were both very unpleasant characters—: Alice here struggles with a philosophical puzzle—does she judge based on actions or intentions? She quickly concludes that they are both 'very unpleasant', although she dwells on the ethics rather fleetingly before moving on.

49 *you're only a sort of thing in his dream!*: while both *Wonderland* and *Looking-Glass* are dream narratives, the second adventure makes that framing far more overt and, in the process, philosophically challenging. Tweedledum's contemptuous suggestion that Alice has no existence outside the Red King's dream presents her (albeit briefly) with an ontological crisis. The circularity of the enquiry has something of the looking-glass to it in itself, resembling the effect of someone holding a mirror up in front of another mirror, and thus creating an endless replication of reality and reflection that cannot be easily separated.

Martin Gardner notes that this discussion puts Berkeleyan metaphysical ideas about being existing only in the mind against what he terms more 'common-sense' positions (*AA*, 198). Carroll returns to the topic of dreams and being in his work on *Symbolic Logic*.

"you'd go out . . . like a candle!": Carroll again ties death to the flame of a candle; this image of Alice recalls the insects who fly into candles of Chapter III, and more overtly her fear when shrinking in *Wonderland* that she might be 'going out altogether, like a candle' (*CWLC*, 21).

what are you, I should like to know?: Alice inverts the famous *Wonderland* question 'who are *you?*' into 'what are *you?*' In doing so, she reasserts her sense of dominance and authority, relegating the Tweedles to the status of 'whats' (things) rather that 'whos' (persons).

"I am real!": continuing the dream thread, this query about the relative 'realness' of Alice—and the wider cast of characters—has been crucial to interpretations of the *Alice* books since their initial publication. Much ink has been spent of the case for separating, or aligning, the 'real' Alice Liddell with the fictional version, alongside a keen critical interest in puzzling out the 'who's who' of *Wonderland* and *Looking-Glass* (the Dodo and White Knight aligned with Carroll himself, the Red Queen with the Liddell governess, etc.). For more on the suggested 'real people' behind *Alice,* see J. E. Jones and J. F. Gladstone, *The Red King's Dream, or Lewis Carroll in Wonderland* (London: Pimlico, 1995).

50 *large umbrella*: comically enough, Alice Liddell would later have the opportunity to own an umbrella handle designed in the very shape of the Tweedles. Carroll wrote to Alice (now Alice Hargreaves) in January 1892, to tell her of a friend in the ivory-carving business who had carved a selection of umbrella and parasol handles based on the Alice characters:

> I have just inspected a number: and, though nearly all are unsuited for use, by reason of having slender projections (hands, etc.) which would be quite sure to get chipped off, thus spoiling the artistic effect, yet I found one ('Tweedledum and Tweedledee') which might safely be used as a parasol handle, without wearing out the life of the owner with constant anxiety. (*Letters*, ii. 883)

[illustration]: the second illustration of the Tweedles is notable in its break with the mirroring of the first. While the initial image of the Tweedles emphasizes their likeness in image, form, and pose (appearing, indeed, as if waxworks), the second presents a moment of disconnect, and thus the cause of the ensuing battle, as Tweedledum rages and Tweedledee hides from impending rain beneath his umbrella so that only his feet can be seen. Also visible in the image is the source of the unhappiness—the broken rattle lies on the ground in the lower left of the image. Tenniel's interpretation of the rattle did not align with Carroll's own; as Martin Gardner has pointed out, Carroll later wrote to Savile Clarke regarding what he saw as Tenniel's error (no doubt attempting to ensure that the dramatist did not continue the theme in the stage play): 'Mr Tenniel has

introduced a false "reading" in his picture of the quarrel [. . .]. I am certain that "my nice new rattle" meant, in the old nursery-song, a child's
rattle not a watchman's rattle as he has drawn' (cited in *AA*, 200). It seems
likely that Carroll was right in his interpretation of the song, although
Tenniel's rendering of the Tweedles as identical schoolboys (of nearly equal
height to Alice) makes neither a baby's rattle nor a watchman's rattle well
suited. Michael Hancher suggests that Tweedledum appears in this scene to
be modelled on Tenniel's earlier *Punch* illustrations of John Bull (a fictional
personification of England, who made appearances in cartoons and caricatures from the mid-seventeenth through mid-twentieth centuries). He cites
in particular an illustration of 'Master Bull and His Dentist' from 27 April
1861 which shows a young version of the figure 'almost as distressed as
Tweedledum' (*TIAB*, 6) and sporting near identical costume.

51 *bolsters*: long cushions to support the head in bed.

   "to keep his head from being cut off": a further quip about life and death,
   framed around the pervasive thread of beheading that pervades both 'Alice'
   books.

52 *[illustration]*: Hancher has highlighted the connections between the array
   of mock-battle equipment which Tweedledum and Tweedledee sport in
   this image and multiple mid-century *Punch* cartoons which render the
   'supposed mock-heroics of the Chartist movement' (*TIAB*, 9–10). Tenniel
   takes care in the image to suggest the items which the Tweedles (strangely)
   find in the wood, all of which were generally common to Victorian house-
   holds. A quantity of tablecloths or blankets, a coal-scuttle, saucepan,
   hearth rug, and bolster can clearly be seen, while Tenniel also seems to
   have added the dish itself as breastplate for Tweedledum, perhaps to com-
   pensate for Tweedledee having the dish-cover serve the same purpose.
   Note that across this series of illustrations in this chapter, Alice finds herself increasingly part of events; having initially been startled by the
   appearance of the little men, she then attempts to calm Tweedledum and
   finally relents to 'clothe' them for a pretend battle. Tenniel and Carroll
   together position Alice in a distinctly matriarchal role here, and Alice's
   need to act responsibly with respect to the beings and creatures of *Looking-
   Glass* increases from this point in the narrative.

53 *monstrous crow*: the Crow has a shaky presence in the story, existing first in
   the old song and then through the hazy impression of its wings stirring up
   windy weather as the chapter concludes. It is never directly seen. Carroll
   positions it as a red bishop in the chess game, but we are given little detail
   as to its movements; that said, the sense of threat it poses, and its hasty
   arrival, aligns the Bishop's ability to quickly traverse on the diagonal with
   the facility to take any piece that is in its bounds of movement. As Alice
   and both Tweedles are white pieces, their alarm at the arrival of the Crow/
   Red Bishop is to be expected.

54 *White Queen. . . with the shawl*: as detailed in Carroll's list of chess moves,
   the White Queen arrives in this moment in the Queen's Bishop's fourth

square, and is thus adjacent to Alice (still in Queen's fourth). Her wild running, like previous descriptions of the Red Queen's fast movements, reflects the ability of queens to traverse multiple squares in a single move. Several critics have pointed out that the White Queen's move here highlights the sloppy nature of the game, as she misses the opportunity to checkmate the Red King. Of course, such carelessness is in keeping with the White Queen's character, and is in any case necessary if the game is to continue so that Alice can become a queen herself. More strange, perhaps, is that Carroll lists Alice meeting her with the shawl as one of her eleven 'moves' in his opening list, although she stays in the same square, merely changing orientation so as to 'meet' the Queen.

"Bread-and-butter, bread-and-butter": the Queen's repetition of 'bread-and-butter' echoes Carroll's; while the 'Alice' books are replete with food references, bread and butter is a particular staple. In *Wonderland*, Alice helps herself to bread and butter at the Mad Tea-Party, and the Hatter brings some along with him to the trial (complaining there that his poverty has led to the bread and butter getting thin). In *Looking-Glass*, Alice has already encountered a Bread-and-butter-fly (its wings made of 'thin slices') and listened to the tale of the Walrus and the Carpenter (the latter of whom finds the butter *'spread too thick'*). Soon she will re-encounter the Hatter (now Hatta), still clasping a piece of bread and butter, and then be required to work out a riddle of the Red Queen where the answer will be 'Bread-and-butter, of course'. The food stuff crops up as frequently in the books as in the Victorian diet.

55 *[illustration]*: this visual image of the White Queen captures the feel of Carroll's textual descriptions and echoes how he would later describe her in his 1887 article for *The Theatre*: 'the White Queen seemed, to my dreaming fancy, gentle, stupid, fat and pale; helpless as an infant; and with a slow, maundering, bewildered air about her just suggesting imbecility, but never quite passing into it' (' "Alice" on the Stage', 182). There is a softness to this image that belies both the rigidity of the chess piece (so much more obvious in Tenniel's illustrations of the sharply angular Red Queen) and the fashions of the day, as the White Queen's restrictive crinoline pokes out awkwardly from the bottom of her skirt and she wraps herself in the softer folds of the shawl. Note, too, the softness of the expression on Alice's face as she attempts to assist the untidy Queen. Tenniel's depiction of the pair is the second in quick succession to show Alice tending to an incompetent, childlike character and continues the theme of dressing.

lady's-maid: female servant who assists wealthy women with their dress and personal needs.

"The rule is . . . never jam to-day": Carroll here originates an expression which has since become a proverb, largely for promises that will never be met. Martin Gardner notes that the use of 'jam' is likely a pun on the Latin *iam*, which means 'now' but only in the past and future tense (*AA*, 206); *iam*,

therefore, can never be in the present (tense). Of course, jam also aligns with the Queen's repeated mutterings about bread and butter.

56 *large piece of plaster*: dressing used to cover a superficial wound.

next Wednesday: Carroll seems to have a particular penchant for aligning law and order with Wednesdays—in Chapter I, Alice instructs her kitten that she is saving up all its punishments for Wednesday week.

[*illustration*]: Tenniel's image gives readers prior knowledge as to an over-lap between *Looking-Glass* and *Wonderland*—Alice is yet unaware that the Hatter has slipped beyond the glass. The King's Messenger is clearly rendered as the mad *Wonderland* denizen; down on his luck, he has lost his patchwork waistcoat, trousers, and spotted bow-tie, but has retained his famous headgear (even if he is not permitted to wear it). He is not, in fact, even permitted to look at it; in a proof version of this image (which shows him in profile rather than portrait), the prisoner stares glumly at his hat as it hangs on the wall whereas in the final version his downcast eyes look only to the floor. The approved version, in fact, is altogether more austere than in proof. In the initial design, Tenniel allows him access to bread and a cup of tea and grants him the freedom to move about; in the published version, the Hatter has just a jug (presumably of water) and finds himself firmly shackled by the ankle to the wall. The revised version, although more severe, fits with the White King's later explanation in Chapter VII that the prisoner 'hadn't finished his tea when he was sent in'. Such a downcast image of punishment before the crime serves to heighten the nature of the debate at hand between Alice and the White Queen. As Mary Liston has pointed out, in both 'Alice' books 'public law rules emerge spontaneously, apply retroactively, and communicate irrational or unreasonable content' ('Rule of Law through the Looking Glass', *Law and Literature*, 2 (2009), 42–77, at 54). The extemporaneous appearance of the Hatter (only recognized as such through the illustration), miserably interred prophylactic-ally and, to Alice at least, irrationally, reflects such a mirror-imaged rule of law.

57 *I soon shall*: that the White Queen's memory 'works both ways' permits her to experience events which haven't happened yet. While Alice struggles to understand such prophetic abilities, she herself has experienced something similar (if differently orientated) in the previous chapter, when she urges the monstrous crow to arrive, recalling her knowledge of how events will play out via the lyrics of the old song that kept ringing in her head.

58 *seven and a half exactly*: Alice is six months older than she was in *Wonderland* (see note to p. 11).

'exactually': a conflation of 'exactly' and 'actually'.

I've believed . . . before breakfast: one of the most famous quotations from *Looking-Glass*, used generally to encourage positive and creative thinking. In Carroll's original, however, the alignment with the mirror-imaged world and a character he imagined as 'suggesting imbecility' makes the idea rather more nuanced and not so directly emboldening as when taken out of context. Despite the fact that Carroll is generally considered to be one of the founding fathers of make-believe, many critics have pointed out that he also encouraged his young friends to exercise caution. As he advised Mary Macdonald: 'If you set to work to believe everything, you will tire out the believing-muscles of your mind, and then you'll be so weak you won't be able to believe the simplest true things' (*Letters*, i. 64).

flying after it: in the classic quick style of the queens, the White Queen moves to the Queen's Bishop's fifth square.

crossed the little brook: Alice now advances into the White Queen's fifth square, thus staying adjacent to the White Queen who has just moved.

so like a sheep: as listed in the opening chess moves, the White Queen's move transforms her into a sheep. This is a strange metamorphosis in terms of the game; the move implies that the Sheep and the White Queen are one and the same, but Carroll lists the Sheep separately as the White Queen's Bishop in the Dramatis Personæ. Certainly the Queen is in the Bishop's file, but that does little to explain this awkward doubling. This oddity is one of the more pronounced liberties Carroll takes with the game.

wrapped herself up in wool: the transformation of the White Queen into a sheep operates as an extension of the behaviours she has shown thus far in the chapter: her helpless mutterings being not unlike bleating and her sudden wrapping 'herself up in wool' akin to all her larks with the shawl. There is an overlap here with the sobbing/grunting baby-pig of *Wonderland* and a sense that the Queen might make a better sheep than she does monarch, much like Alice's earlier observations: 'it would have made a dreadfully ugly child: but it makes rather a handsome pig, I think' (*CWLC*, 64).

59 *[illustration]*: modelled on what was then a grocery at 83 St Aldate's Street in Oxford, Tenniel's rendering of the interior of the shop ensured that it would quickly become colloquially known as 'Alice's shop' and is now officially styled as such (selling a range of *Alice* merchandise). In keeping with *Looking-Glass* reversals, Tenniel's illustration switches the positions of the doors and windows from the original building so as to create a mirror image. Tenniel captures the enclosed nature of the space—truly 'a little dark shop', as Carroll writes—and conveys a wonderful sense of busyness, with a cacophony of unrelated 'things' on display that are hard to make out. It is one of his more detailed illustrations in terms of background.

60 *a large bright thing*: in the context of the dark shop, Alice's attention is immediately arrested by a vivid but unidentifiable 'thing', that resists a knowable form and expected behaviour, including even being properly *seen*. Carroll's rendering of this moment can be read as something of a prototype for Bill Brown's much later work on 'Thing Theory'. As he writes: 'we only catch a glimpse of things. [. . .] We begin to encounter the thingness of objects when they stop working for us [. . .]. The story of objects asserting themselves as things, then, is the story of a changed relation

to the human subject' ('Thing Theory', *Critical Enquiry*, 28 (Autumn 2001), 1–22, at 4). Both the shop where 'things flow about', and Alice's broader encounters with other strangely enlivened, resistant, and unknowable beings, can be read as a story of just such changed relations.

60 *teetotum*: small spinning toy with letters and numbers on the sides which reference actions in the game and a spindle to the middle that allows it to be twirled.

Feather!: a rowing term referring to positioning the oar spoon above and parallel to the water during the recovery section of a stroke. Lewis Carroll was a frequent and knowledgeable rower, and had taught the Liddell children how to do so during their trips on the river. Alice Liddell recalled in a memoir of her childhood that it was 'a proud day when we could "feather our oars" properly' (*LCIR*, 86). Clearly Alice Liddell had a better handle on the practice than her namesake.

catching a crab: rowing error in which the oar becomes caught in the water just as the rower attempts to extract it, so that the handle strikes the rower. As well as slowing the boat, 'catching a crab' can unseat the rower (as Alice experiences in a few strokes' time). As with the command to 'feather', Alice takes the expression quite literally.

61 *"you're a little goose"*: although used affectionately, 'goose' here means silly (which explains Alice's mild offence).

So the boat. . . darling scented rushes: the later part of this chapter—taking place in the recognizable Oxford shop and recalling much memorialized boating trips with the Liddell children—might be said to skim closer to the 'surface' than at any other point in the fantasy. This moment in particular appears to break the frame. It offers a bucolic but unusually descriptive image of Alice (recalling Pre-Raphaelite painting in description), and is more heavily romanticized than the rest of the book (outside the interlude with the White Knight and the poems which bookend the story). The moment is somewhat in keeping with the tonality of those verses, in its reflective affect, although the melancholia is tempered somewhat. It is as voyeuristic as it is enchanting.

"The prettiest are always further!": as Hugh Haughton notes, the phrase 'recalls such proverbial expressions as "the grass is always greener on the other side" and "distance lends enchantment to the view"' (Penguin, 343). In the context of Carroll's poignant reflections on distant days, Alice's remark also seems to apply to memory and experiences that recede with age.

What mattered. . . to think about: continuing the nostalgic theme of this scene, Carroll's comments here about Alice's lack of care and notice can be read as a reflection on the distance that had developed between the real Alice Liddell and Charles Dodgson by the time of the publication of *Looking-Glass*. Dream rushes here act like memories of childhood pleasures, and Carroll implies that Alice has discarded them as she has grown-up in favour of the 'many other curious things to think about'. Whereas in Chapter II the Rose, rather unkindly, suggests that it is Alice who is 'beginning to fade' (i.e. age), here it is 'the happy summer days' of *Wonderland* (*CWLC*, 120) that have lost 'all their scent and beauty' (in direct contraction to Carroll's hopes as inscribed in the concluding lines of that novel). Another, more uncomfortable reading, might suggest that the depiction of a beauty that fades the moment it has been 'picked' (or plucked) has sexual overtones.

62 *she wasn't a bit hurt*: Carroll takes particular care to reassure readers on this matter—even following her far longer fall into *Wonderland*, he similarly comforts that 'Alice was not a bit hurt' (*CWLC*, 18).

[illustration]: while Carroll claims that 'the oars, and the boat, and the river, had vanished all in a moment', Tenniel is able to capture the exact fleeting instant of metamorphosis. The image shows Alice as if rowing directly into the hazily reappearing shop, although her attention appears to be directed elsewhere. The image overlays with the previous illustration of the scene—the counter, door, windows, and 'things' of the shop appear unchanged—although their placement does not take advantage of the page-turning mechanisms of the book shown elsewhere.

63 *farthing*: English coin of the period worth one-quarter of a penny.

Then I'll have one. . . .you know: Martin Gardner suggests that Alice's resistance to doubling up on eggs is a reference to the fact that students at Christ Church in Carroll's day 'insisted that if you ordered one boiled egg for breakfast you usually received two, one good and one bad' (*AA*, 216).

she went off: Carroll here signals the White Queen's next move to King's Bishop's eighth.

here's a little brook!: Alice's walk through the queer shop leads her to the edge of the square, and her crossing of the brook takes her to White Queen's sixth.

64 *HUMPTY DUMPTY himself*: unlike her previous encounters through the Looking-Glass, Alice recognizes the humanoid egg at once. His fame has a fairly sketchy history. The *OED* ties the first recorded use of the name to a seventeenth-century 'drink made with ale boiled with brandy' and later to 'a short, dumpy, hump-shouldered person'. Iona and Peter Opie recall in the *Oxford Dictionary of Nursery Rhymes* (215) that his first appearance 'in the nursery sense [. . .] does not occur before 1785', noting that it 'does not appear in early riddle books, but this may be because it was already too well-known'. His usual visual depiction as an egg serves as an embodiment of the answer to the rhyme-riddle (i.e. an egg cannot be restored from a fall no matter what resources are used). The fall of Humpty Dumpty is often tied to historical events—such as the death of Richard III at the Battle of Bosworth Field in 1485 or the fall of Colchester in 1648 during the English Civil War—although these links are fairly tenuous. The sense of something that shatters and cannot be repaired does, of course, serve as a metaphor for Carroll's long lament on childhood, ageing, and loss throughout *Looking-Glass*.

64 *on the top of a high wall*: no doubt Humpty Dumpty's poetic history of
sitting on a wall informed Carroll's decision to designate him a castle
piece. That Carroll chooses, specifically, a high wall not only increases the
sense of precariousness but also continues the overlap with castles.

softly repeated: Alice's repetition of the Humpty Dumpty verse is also
a repetition of a previous encounter. Her time with the Tweedles in
Chapter IV largely mirrors the structure of meeting Humpty Dumpty in
Chapter VI: the initial discovery of the character(s) prompts the memory
of a verse, the events of which subsequently play out across the chapter
but not before Alice has been told a new poem in turn.

65 *last line*: the final line of the poem differs in Alice's recollection to most
familiar versions, which generally conclude 'Couldn't put Humpty
together again'. Alice objects to the line as 'much too long for the poetry'
and certainly her version adds the awkwardness of two extra syllables to
what would otherwise be pentameter.

"Must a name mean something?": Alice fails to notice the hypocrisy of her
assertion, when compared to her conversation with the Gnat in Chapter III.
There she insists that names mean a great deal to humans because they are
useful in creating human-dominated order (particularly as applied to
other creatures). When here questioned by a talking egg (pre-animal in
designation, no less), she is resistant to the idea that a being of another
order entirely could give names their own meanings and thus impose their
own linguistic structures on the world.

the shape I am—and a good handsome shape it is, too: the extensive connections between the name Humpty Dumpty and the visual image of an egg
means that shape and word are indeed now synonymous. One doubts,
however, that Carroll's proud character would enjoy the *OED* definition
of his shape as detailed above and he is certainly resistant to being called
an egg.

a History of England: Humpty Dumpty may be referring to *A Child's
History of England* by Charles Dickens, which was first published in serial
form from 1851 to 1853 in *Household Words*. There are, of course, many
other such histories that could be contenders, although the reference
could equally merely allude to Humpty Dumpty's general pomposity and
obsession with his regal connection. Hugh Haughton notes that 'Humpty
snobbishly prefers history to nursery rhymes and dwells on his associ-
ations with kings rather than vulnerable children and eggs' (Penguin, 344).

I'm not proud: quite contrary to Humpty Dumpty's assertion here, the
entire framing of his vanity and pretension in this chapter serves as a playful extended example of pride coming before a fall.

66 *[illustration]*: Tenniel's illustration does a particularly impressive job of
capturing the precarious nature of Humpty Dumpty's position even if it
takes licence with Carroll's text by ignoring the suggestion that he 'was
sitting with his legs crossed' and preventing the reader from observing
Alice's anxiousness by having her back to the viewer (for similarities with

the young knight of the Jabberwock illustration, see note to p. 20). The humanoid egg is balanced upon a very narrowly pointed wall, the right-angled section disclosing its width and shape. While some critics have suggested that the illustration makes Humpty Dumpty appear childlike, there is a clear sense of age to his facial expression, with lines to his eyes and forehead. The L-design of the image served in the first edition to neatly enclose the section of text where he and Alice grasp hands, so that image and text directly reflect one another. Such careful placement has generally been lost in subsequent editions.

67 *Leave off at seven. . . left off at seven*: yet another passage that criticizes Alice's growth beyond the idealized age of 7. Carroll makes several direct and more oblique references to the fact that Alice is now 7½, but here it takes a rather nasty turn. Humpty Dumpty's initial lament that 'it's too late now' echoes the broader sense of Alice's unavoidable 'fading' with age (such as in the discussion of dream rushes in the previous chapter and untidy petals in Chapter II). Yet the egg's comments have a more sinister edge—his advice to 'leave off at seven' suggesting that it would have been better if she had died as a child, at the idealized age of 7, than to have lived on into adulthood (while Alice may have only aged six months in the narrative, Alice Liddell was 19 by the time *Looking-Glass* was published). When Alice responds that 'one can't help getting older', Humpty Dumpty's comment that '*two* can' implies that murder, in fact, would have been preferable. Of course, Carroll himself is one of the implied twosome here, and part of his comment seems to be a lament at his own decision to allow Alice to 'live on' into a second book. Had Carroll not sent Alice through the Looking-Glass, on a headlong march across the board to power, then she would indeed have stayed 7 forever in *Wonderland*. Another way of reading Carroll's comment on 'two' rather than 'one' being able to stop ageing is to see it as an allusion to reproduction, wherein the ageing process can be halted by extending one's genetic line through offspring. Given that the character in question is a child, this slant on the passage does little to make it more palatable.

un-birthday present: this famously amusing mirror inversion is particularly playful given Carroll's own stance on birthdays. Although he was a profuse giver of gifts, he rarely did so for birthdays. As he explained to Mary Mallalieu: '*I never give birthday presents*. You see, if once I began, *all* my little friends would expect a present every year, and my life would be spent in packing parcels' (*Letters*, i. 927).

68 *worked the sum for him*: while Humpty Dumpty is knowledgeable in matters of linguistics, his difficulty processing the sum suggests he may not have a mathematical mind. Of course, the author's dual personas harnessed skills in both areas—as Lewis Carroll the *author* and Charles Dodgson the *mathematician*.

'glory' doesn't mean 'a nice knock-down argument': as a pair, these terms continue the undercurrent of pride leading to a fall; as the *OED* has it,

glory may refer to a 'boastful spirit' and Humpty Dumpty will soon find himself knocked down from the wall.

68 *When I use a word...that's all*: this exchange between Alice and Humpty Dumpty captures the linguistic playfulness around words and their meanings that pervades both 'Alice' books. Alice repeatedly encounters characters who use words in ways that counter what she sees as their established definitions—as inscribed by a human, right-side-of-the-glass logic. Humpty Dumpty, as a non-human, declares himself able to use language (and to master it) in whatever way he sees fit. The result is a cross-species dialogue in which Alice must continually give the power to the other side, having to repeatedly enquire as to what things mean to make any sense of the Looking-Glass world. Authority shifts here, as human powers of language are put to question. The case that words have no fixed meanings, of course, would become a founding principal of deconstruction. Humpty Dumpty's pompous and riddling sense that he can instruct words to have meaning finds its modern equivalent in Donald Trump's now infamous 'covfefe' tweet, where he set the task of finding the 'true meaning' of what was actually a mistyped word.

69 *They've a temper... I can manage the whole lot of them!*: Humpty Dumpty's personification of adjectives and verbs predicts a later educational imitation of the 'Alice' books. Audrey Mayhew Allen's *Gladys in Grammarland* (1897) includes encounters with all sorts of humanized parts of speech—from King Proper Noun to Prime Minister Personal Pronoun—as part of an educative drive to tutor in proper usage.

the meaning of the poem called 'Jabberwocky'?: having been primed by Humpty Dumpty that he can make words mean whatever he wants them to, Alice sees this as an opportunity to get some answers to the linguistic confusion of the verses that she read in the Looking-glass House. In keeping with his conceited over-intellectualizing, Humpty Dumpty proceeds to give a reading of the first stanza that concurs in most (although not all) points to those set out in the original 'glossary' of the *Mischmasch* 'Stanza of Anglo-Saxon Poetry'. As outlined with regard to 'Jabberwocky' (see note to p. 19), the whole exercise functions as a spirited commentary on the limits of interpretation and, as nonsense verse, attempts to 'explain' it through linguistic glossing that makes the 'meaning' of the poem entirely evasive.

70 *portmanteau... two meanings packed up into one word*: as Humpty Dumpty describes, a portmanteau brings two words (and thus two meanings) together into one. This use of the word originates in *Looking-Glass*—a portmanteau is also 'a case or bag for carrying clothing and other belongings when travelling' (*OED*), and the sense of one word being inside another itself reflects this dual use. Carroll provides further explanation in his Preface to *The Hunting of the Snark*:

> take the two words 'fuming' and 'furious.' Make up your mind that you will say both words, but leave it unsettled which you will say first. Now

open your mouth and speak. If your thoughts incline ever so little towards 'fuming', you will say 'fuming-furious'; if they turn, by even a hair's breadth, towards 'furious', you will say 'furious-fuming'; but if you have the rarest of gifts, a perfectly balanced mind, you will say 'frumious.' (*CWLC* , 678)

[illustration]: as a verbatim visualization of an overly literal translation, Tenniel's illustration is very much in on the 'Jabberwocky' joke. Of course, in the context of a nonsense fantasy where most images of the Looking-Glass world feature some degree of impossibility, inversion, or invention the depiction does not jar as much as it might. What emerges in particular, however, is that Tenniel's visual assemblage of all the translated aspects of the poem makes its nonsensical nature all the more apparent, so much so that the image appears overcrowded with 'visualized meanings' all vying for the reader's attention.

71 *gyroscope*: an instrument in the form of a freely rotating wheel or disc which is positioned on an axle that allows for free movement in any direction—used to measure orientation and acceleration.

gimblet: i.e. gimlet, a hand tool used to bore holes into (primarily wooden) surfaces.

hoping to keep him from beginning: a further instance of Alice's increasing irritation with the distractions of poetry, although here (as elsewhere in *Looking-Glass*) her attempts to stave off the recitation prove futile.

In winter, when the fields are white: Hugh Haughton suggests that this poem is an 'instance of a Carrollian lyric without a known parodic model or source' (Penguin, 346) although Martin Gardner has noted a possible allusion to 'Summer Days' by Wathen Mark Wilks Call (*AA*, 228). Humpty Dumpty's choice to begin the poem with the wintery stanza reflects the seasonal feel of *Looking-Glass* although it is jarring as a procession through the seasons, for one might expect a beginning to occur in spring. The initial four stanzas move through a series of instructions as to how the poem (and perhaps the poetic tradition in general) is to be received: first with delight (in winter), then with exposition (in spring), followed by understanding (in summer), and finally with inscription (in autumn). This initial set of instructions provides something of a preface for the poem to follow—which Alice, despite such heavy-handed guidance, fails to understand or delight in. She is hardly alone in this reaction; Richard Kelly has suggested that it is the weakest of the book's verses, arguing that 'The language is flat and prosaic, the frustrated story line is without interest, the couplets are uninspired and fail to surprise or to delight, and there are almost no true elements of nonsense present, other than in the unstated wish of the narrator and the lack of a conclusion to the work' (*Lewis Carroll* (New York: Twayne, 1977), 71). Certainly this poem has not been celebrated or remembered in the manner of 'Jabberwocky' or 'The Walrus and the Carpenter'. Angela Zirker, however, has argued that critical derision of this poem fails to read it as the riddle Carroll was intending. She suggests that the poem is one of a trio—flanked by the Walrus and the Carpenter from Chapter IV and the White Queen's riddle from Chapter IX—and that 'by having readers go both forward and backward in arriving at a meaning of the song, Lewis Carroll makes them adopt the double movement characteristic of the world in which Alice progresses but in which there is also a notion of "living backwards" '. Zirker suggests that 'if one reads the "fishes" as oysters, the poem suddenly makes sense' (' "All about fishes"? The Riddle of Humpty Dumpty's Song and Recursive Understanding in Lewis Carroll's *Through the Looking-Glass and What Alice Found There*', *Victorian Poetry*, 56 (Spring 2018), 81–102, at 95).

73 *[illustration]*: Michael Hancher has pointed out that the image of Humpty Dumpty and the Messenger is 'one of the simpler reflections in the 'Alice' books of Tenniel's work for *Punch*' (*TIAB*, 12). The image of Humpty Dumpty is notably similar to Tenniel's rendering of 'The Gigantic Gooseberry' from the 15 July 1871 issue of *Punch*, in terms not only of size and shape but also of facial feature. In the *Looking-Glass* version, comedy is lent to Humpty Dumpty's precarious balance, as he here switches up tottering on a wall for standing tiptoe on a stool, as well as to the contradictory bodily shapes of the two characters (the short and round Humpty next to the tall and lean Messenger recalling the Jack Spratt nursery rhyme).

the messenger: in Carroll's Dramatis Personæ, the Messenger is identified as a red pawn.

74 *"Is that all?"*: Alice here responds to the unsatisfactory ending of Humpty Dumpty's poem in exactly the same terms as she did to the disappointing advice of the Caterpillar in *Wonderland*.

giving her one of his fingers to shake: this recalls a Victorian aristocratic practice of offering only two fingers when shaking hands with those of socially inferior status. The pompous Humpty Dumpty inches things up a notch by extending only one.

She never finished the sentence: the third in a quick trio of unsatisfactory endings—first the incomplete poem, then the sudden goodbye, and finally Alice's interrupted sentence. Such a conclusion of thwarted communications provides a fitting summary for the entire exchange between Alice and Humpty Dumpty.

75 *memorandum-book*: the White King here reappears exactly as he was last encountered in Chapter I, still taking notes in his memorandum-book.

Four thousand two hundred and seven: Martin Gardner notes that the White King's exacting record is likely an allusion to Carroll's fascination with the number 42, suggesting that the tally reflects that 'seven is a factor of forty-two' (*AA*, 125).

two of them are wanted in the game: a comment on the fact that two of the horses must be retained for the white knight chess pieces. In fact, only one is needed, for the Unicorn (already equine) serves as one of the white knights according to the Dramatis Personæ.

the two Messengers: both white pawns in the game.

76 *[illustration]*: Hugh Haughton suggests that Tenniel's image of the heaps of soldiers 'evokes Uccello's *Battle of San Romano* in the National Gallery, London' (Penguin, 346). If so, it offers an appropriate mirror inversion of the first in Uccello's triptych of paintings. But while Tenniel's image certainly has the feel of battle to it, and gives a strong sense as to a vast army, the illustrator is also careful to depict entirely unidirectional movement; all the soldiers and horses march and tumble in a linear fashion, from right to left, with no sense of an approaching army. The image appears to more directly recall Tenniel's own depiction of the mess of chess pieces amongst the cinders in Chapter I—certainly the bearing of the marching soldiers in this image mimics that of the castles in the fireplace. Notably, Tenniel chooses to render the soldiers in sixteenth-century battle array; while the general tenor of the chapter is Anglo-Saxon in interest, Tenniel likely had little idea what soldiers from the period would have worn and thus chooses a design that merely suggests historical distance.

Anglo-Saxon attitudes: the chapter's playful interest in the Anglo-Saxons extends what Carroll started with the 'Jabberwocky' poem, which was first styled as a 'Stanza of Anglo-Saxon Poetry' (see note to p. 19). Carroll here continues to demonstrate a fondness for medieval pastiche, lampooning the scholarly interest in the Anglo-Saxon period that was fashionable at the time of his writing. Carroll's alignment of 'attitudes' with the exaggerated physical movements of the Messenger continues the historical jest.

Haigha: a punning pseudo–Anglo-Saxon spelling of 'Hare', which is mirrored by its pronunciation to rhyme with 'mayor'.

"I love my love with an H": a common Victorian parlour alphabet game in which players fit words to letters in sequence. Mrs Lydia Maria Child described it as follows:

> This game may be played by any number, each taking a letter as it comes to her run. Any mistake or hesitation incurs the penalty of a forfeit. She that begins may say: A. I love my love with an A because he is Artless. I hate him with an A, because he is Avaricious. He took me to the sign of the Anchor, and treated me to Apples and Almonds. His name is Abraham, and he comes from Alnwick. (*The Girl's Own Book*, 1833)

An exemplar appears in J. O. Halliwell's *The Nursery Rhymes of England* (1848) in the class of 'scholastic' rhymes.

77 *Hatta*: a punning pseudo–Anglo-Saxon spelling of 'Hatter'.

I must have two: the White King's insistence on pairs extends throughout the chapter—from the paired knights through to the battling duo of the Lion and the Unicorn. Jan Susina has suggested that the paired 'Anglo-Saxon messengers function very much in the manner of Hugin (Thought) and Munin (Memory), Odin's two ravens, in providing the White King with information' (' "Why is a Raven like a Writing-Desk?": The Play of

Letters in Lewis Carroll's *Alice* Books', *Children's Literature Association Quarterly*, 26 (2001), 15–21, at 18).

77 *great eyes rolled wildly from side to side*: this continued play with performative physical 'Anglo-Saxon attitudes' also extends the connection to the 'Jabberwocky' poem. The reference to Haigha's great and wild eyes—along with his 'fearful faces', strange 'wriggling' movements, and being 'too much out of breath to say a word'—rather recalls the 'eyes of flame' of the Jabberwock, who came 'whiffling through the tulgey wood, | And burbled as it came'. Alice herself will later in this scene become known as 'the monster'.

ham sandwich. . . Hay, then: as elsewhere in *Looking-Glass*, Alice herself has dictated or predicted the order of events, as both the ham sandwich and hay are the foodstuffs she cites in her alphabet game.

throwing cold water over you: Alice responds here in a similar manner to Chapter I, where the White King's fainting episode led her to find a bottle of ink to throw over him.

sal-volatile: smelling salts, used to revive someone who has fainted.

78 *[illustration]*: were readers not to have made the connection already from the linguistic cues, Tenniel's illustration makes clear that Haigha should be understood as the March Hare of *Wonderland*. He has lost his Tea-Party attire, however, and now sports an outfit as reminiscent of a medieval jester as it is of a messenger. Note that here, as in *Wonderland*, Tenniel has the Hare replete with human hands (no doubt making it all the easier for him to pull the sandwich from the bag). Tenniel expands Carroll's sense that Alice is amused by the whole episode, by having her cover her mouth (presumably so as to hide her laughter from the White King). What doesn't emerge, in either text or illustrations, is the sense that Alice recognizes the Hare or the Hatter from her younger adventures.

have you buttered!: a strange punishment, perhaps punning on beaten or battered, but in keeping with the Tea-Party allusion of the Hare, who in *Wonderland* himself butters a pocket-watch. The idea of buttering a person generally recalls fortune over penalty; the *OED* notes that having one's bread buttered indicates being well provided for.

79 *the Lion and the Unicorn*: heraldic symbols of the United Kingdom. The Lion represents England and the Unicorn Scotland. They appear on the royal coat of arms, flanking shield and crown. In the context of Carroll's game, the Unicorn features as one of the white knights while the Lion is a red castle.

the words of the old song: Alice is once again prompted to recall an old verse. In *The Oxford Dictionary of Nursery Rhymes* (269), Iona and Peter Opie suggest that 'the rhyme tells the story of the amalgamation of the Royal Arms of Scotland with those of England when James VI of Scotland was crowned James I of England'. They note that in the new coat of arms, the lion is rendered as sporting a crown, whereas the unicorn is merely armed, creating an impression of a conflict over a union. A song about fighting over a crown is rather fitting in the context of a chess game, in which the two sides fight to defeat the other's king.

Bandersnatch: a further connective allusion in this chapter to the 'Jabberwocky' poem.

just out of prison. . . oyster-shells: in Chapter V the White Queen explains that the King's Messenger is in prison for a crime he is yet to commit. Based on her explanation of the order of events, Hatta appears to have been released before his trial (which, the Queen recalls 'doesn't even begin till next Wednesday'). The reference to the prisoner not having finished his tea before his incarceration accords with Tenniel's melancholy illustration of the scene (see note to p. 56). The oyster shells provide a further connecting strand between chapters and characters—perhaps Hatta (a lowly white pawn) has been offered the remnants of the Walrus (a red bishop) and the Carpenter's (a red knight) gluttonous meal.

80 *it was very dry*: as with the Red Queen's biscuits in Chapter II, Alice finds Looking-Glass sustenance too dry to consume.

[illustration]: Tenniel gives an impressive image of the general fray in this scene, as the two combatants appear hazily sketched in the cloud of dust, the Unicorn (as Alice herself mentions) distinguishable by his horn. It is Hatta who takes centre stage, his infamous hat quelling any doubt as to his identity even as he is otherwise clad in mock-Anglo-Saxon weeds so as to match his fellow Messenger. Tenniel is also carefully attuned to the landscape of the scene, switching up the woodland background common to most of his illustrations to make the battle overtly urban and thus to reflect the setting of the song.

81 *There's the White Queen. . .enemy after her*: Carroll records this move as White Queen to Queen's Bishop's eighth. The enemy the King refers to is the Red Knight, which Carroll has the White Queen 'flying from'. As several critics have pointed out, there is no need by the rules of the game for the White Queen to feel threatened by the Red Knight's position (she, in fact, could take the knight piece). Yet her panicked flight is in keeping with Carroll's caricature of her as stupid and bewildered.

It's large as life, and twice as natural!: a Carrollian linguistic substitution of the phrase 'Large as life and *quite* as natural' (normally referring to artistic representation). Carroll's version has become the more common usage.

"I always thought they were fabulous monsters!": a particularly charming Looking-Glass inversion, whereby a legendary fantastical beast perceives a human child in the same terms. It also begins an ontological challenge to Alice's identity, as both Lion and Unicorn struggle to classify her.

"Is it alive?": the Unicorn's question reduces Alice to an 'it'. Rather uncharacteristically, Alice takes this questioning of her humanity with surprisingly little by way of indignation. The sense of querying what counts as 'alive' circulates throughout *Looking-Glass*—from the garden of 'live' flowers through to the vivification of inanimate chessmen.

81 *"if you'll believe... Is that a bargain?"*: while Alice seems perfectly happy to allow the Unicorn to dictate the terms of her existence here, Peter Heath has pointed out that the covenant is a poor one from Alice's point of view: 'Having survived her identity crisis, and recovered from Tweedledum's aspersions on her claim to reality, she ought by now to have acquired a solidly Cartesian conviction on her own existence' (*PA*, 206). Of course, much of Alice's journey through the Looking-Glass can be read as an exercise in loosening her sense of entitled dominance over the rest of the world, a hierarchical and distinctly human conviction generally borne out of Cartesian principles.

82 *[illustration]*: the detail of Tenniel's illustration of the Lion and the Unicorn in this scene has prompted a number of commentators to see the characters as allegories of Benjamin Disraeli and William Ewart Gladstone, both of whom served as British prime ministers and were renowned rivals engaged in a continual tussle for power in the latter half of the nineteenth century. Michael Hancher, in his exploration of the development of this critical conviction, suggests that such identity claims have come through a comparison of 'typical Tenniel caricatures of the two prime minsters' (*TIAB*, 117) in *Punch*. Yet he concludes that there is 'nothing peculiarly Disraeliesque about the Unicorn', beyond the inclusion of a goatee also common in many heraldic images of unicorns, and that 'the case for Gladstone is no better', with little connection between the *Punch* and *Looking-Glass* illustrations beyond the fact that the Lion is 'as dour as the Gladstone figures' (118). Although Carroll was a keen supporter of Disraeli as 'quite the greatest statesman of our time' (*Letters*, i. 423), there is little in the text of *Looking-Glass* itself to make a connection between this scene and either politician, beyond the rivalry of the 'old song' that predates them. As Hancher has it: 'To allegorize the Lion and the Unicorn into Gladstone and Disraeli is a pleasant idea, but it was not Tenniel's or Carroll's' (*TIAB*, 118). Note that Tenniel, as so often the case in his illustration of Carroll's text, has creative licence to imagine characters that receive little by way of visual description from their author. Tenniel here has the Lion sport glasses (although Carroll makes no reference to his eyesight) but gives him no further attire. The Unicorn, by contrast, continues the mock sixteenth-century wear of the other soldiers (albeit more courtly in function), recalling that he serves as one of the white knights on the board.

like the tolling of a great bell: a likely allusion to Big Ben, which at the time was the largest bell in the United Kingdom. The clock and its tower were completed in 1859.

"Are you animal—or vegetable—or mineral?": echoing Alice's earlier play, the Lion initiates another parlour game, this time a variant of 'Twenty Questions' in which players try to determine the selected object or being through 'yes' or 'no' answers, first querying if it is animal, then vegetable, then mineral. Alice plays the game more obliquely in *Wonderland* with the Duchess (Chapter IX). Yet as the question is here directed at Alice herself,

it continues the ongoing challenge to her identity and security as a human, with both animal and fantastical beast here able to challenge her classification. The period of Carroll's writing—in the wake of Darwin's publication of *The Origin of Species* (1859) and contemporaneous to his later *Descent of Man* (1871)—had seen the straightforward taxonomical divisions of earlier periods put to question in ways which troubled the edges of humanity and, by association, human uniqueness and superiority. Throughout both *Alice* books, Carroll's heroine is questioned not only as to *who* she is, but also as to *what* she is.

"It's a fabulous monster!": despite Alice's comfort with the term, being a monster is a particularly vulnerable classification in the Looking-Glass world. If Alice were to reflect upon her earlier reading, she might recall the story of the monstrous Jabberwock, brought to an untimely end by a young knight. Given the dual Anglo-Saxon framing of both episodes, and the fact that the Unicorn is himself styled as a knight, Alice perhaps has rather more to be concerned about than she seems aware.

83 *you chicken!*: although the insult has a modern feel, it is early modern in attribution. The *OED* cites Shakespeare's *Cymbeline* (1623) as an early use of the term to mean 'a faint-hearted person; a coward'.

"The Monster has given the Lion twice as much as me!": a literalization of the idiom of 'the lion's share', meaning the majority portion of something. The phrase derives from Aesop's *Fables* and offers comment of the dangers of partnership between unequal ranks. In most versions, the Lion goes hunting with three weaker animals (cow, goat, and sheep) and on dividing the spoils makes a claim to all four quarters: the first due to his rank as king, the second due to his strength, the third due to his bravery, and the last due to his willingness to kill any 'partner' who quibbles his claim.

sprang across the little brook in her terror: Alice advances to the White Queen's seventh square. Hugh Haughton notes that this move, like the previous brook crossings of Chapters IV and VI, are 'shadowed by violent forces' (Penguin, 348). In this instance, it is the 'terror' of the deafening drums which spark her movement.

84 *[illustration]*: Tenniel's illustration to this moment is disquieting, in keeping with the sense of terror Carroll inscribes on to the scene. Tenniel has Alice not only dropped to her knees, as in Carroll's text, but also awkwardly hunched as if in pain. The overwhelming nature of the aural is cleverly rendered into visual form; he dissolves the scene entirely but for empty plate and knife (Tenniel here looks ahead to the next chapter, where these items will feature), so that Alice appears in relief against a background of seemingly never-ending drums. That the instruments are beaten by a series of disembodied human hands adds to the eerie terror of the moment.

85 *Only I do hope. . .see what happens!*: Alice briefly returns to conscious reflection on the dream frame of the 'Alice' books. The shift in square

leads her to recall Tweedledum's accusation in Chapter IV that Alice is 'only a sort of thing' in the Red King's dream. Alice is here keen to take possession of the dream as uniquely her own, seemingly at any cost—she claims that she is tempted to wake the Red King to 'see what happens' despite Tweedledum's deathly warning that she would then 'go out—bang!—just like a candle!' These risky reflections are, however, quickly interrupted by the arrival of the appropriately risk-averse White Knight, who plans to see her safely across the square. Alice's dissatisfaction with the idea of 'belonging to another person's dream' sets up a conflict between the wistful tone of the chapter (the author's own) and the resistant subject determined to progress (Alice herself). These reflections provide a subtle but notable introduction to the chapter's primary tensions.

85　*a Knight, dressed in crimson armour*: the Red Knight here advances to the Red King's second square, so is now adjacent to Alice. His move is a powerful one, in that he hereby does (as he exclaims) check the White King and also threatens the White Queen. His incongruent shouts of 'Ahoy' introduce a series of watery references that continue throughout the chapter.

　　"You're my prisoner!": the Red Knight's claim here to have captured Alice is false—she is safe from his advances (from the standpoint of the chess game, at least).

　　a White Knight: the White Knight's arrival mimics that of the Red but, in keeping with the bumbling nature of most of the white pieces, his claims to check are false (he would only have checked his own King by the move). The White Knight has attracted substantial critical commentary as to his symbolic function. He has been read in all manner of allegorical modes; as Judith Bloomingdale précises: 'As absurd hero of his age, the White Knight is at once Christ, St. George, the Knight of the Grail, Lancelot, Don Quixote, and finally modern man' ('Alice as Anima: The Image of Woman in Carroll's Classic', in R. Phillips (ed.), *Aspects of Alice* (London: Victor Gollancz, 1972), 378–90, at 388). Most substantively, the White Knight is widely thought to align with Lewis Carroll (or rather Charles Dodgson) himself. The physical description to follow, along with his fascination for invention, support the sense that the White Knight is a self-portrait, although more compelling still is the tender (but equally tense) relationship between the White Knight and Alice, with the whole chapter assuming something of the mood of the prefatory poem that Carroll suggested 'May tremble through the story'. More concrete evidence as to Carroll's identity as the knight is offered by Jeffrey Stern in his discussion of a hand-drawn board game by Carroll, which he inscribed to 'Olive Butler, from the White Knight. Nov. 21, 1892' ('Carroll Identifies Himself at Last', *Jabberwocky*, 74 (1990), 18–20).

　　some bewilderment: Alice's confusion is entirely sound, for neither Red nor White Knight have any control over the square she is in.

86　*Rules of Battle*: the absurdity of the moment is underscored by the demand that the rules be observed (which Alice goes on to lampoon). The rules of the battle at hand (i.e. of the game of chess being played) are such that there is no need to fight—the arrival of the White Knight in the same square as the Red means he has already won. The scene recalls something of the childish battle theatrics of Tweedledum and Tweedledee.

Punch and Judy: a slapstick puppet show, dating in England from the 1660s and popular throughout the Victorian and into the modern period. In making this connection, Alice aligns one comical scene of mock battle with another, for Punch and Judy shows are infamous for their casual violence and dark humour.

how quiet the horses are!: appropriate for military equines. War horses are normally drawn from breeds known for gentle temperament as well as strength and endurance.

[illustration]: whilst previous battle scenes are only obliquely shown (as in the Lion and the Unicorn) or fail to actually occur (as in the Tweedles), Tenniel here puts the combat between the knights centre stage. Alice's peeping position behind the tree offers her the perfect spot to commentate, and Tenniel is careful to render some of the 'rules' she highlights. The White Knight can be seen awkwardly clasping his club across his chest, using his arms rather than his hands to wield the weapon, and the Red Knight—having just been struck—appears ready to tumble off the near side of his horse, his left foot loose from the stirrup. Tenniel's visualization of the horse helmets that both knights sport replicates the common shape of a chess knight. Yet by also riding horses, a strange doubleness occurs, creating the sense of all four knight pieces being present in the moment rather than just two.

87 *a glorious victory*: hardly glorious, in the obvious sense, in that the battle was won before it commenced. It does, however, recall Humpty Dumpty's definition of 'glory' as 'a nice knock-down argument'. The victory completes the White Knight's move in Carroll's playlist ('W. Kt. takes R. Kt.').

So you will. . . end of my move: the White Knight here highlights that Alice is but one square away from becoming a queen (as she is about to reach the eighth square). He nods to the shift in their positions that will occur at the moment of transition. The White Knight is here to see her 'safely', but with an air of bitter regret, into adulthood. The metaphor is clear: when she crosses the threshold, he (Carroll, or rather Dodgson) must retreat for it will be the end of his 'move' (time in Alice's Liddell's life). It is a poignant and thin veneer, which begins a nostalgic but uncomfortable interlude. Although the scene between Alice and the Knight is painfully brief when read through the lens of Carroll's real-life relationship with Alice Liddell, it is telling that the author presents it in the longest chapter in the book, stretching out the moment for as long as possible.

"May I help you off with your helmet?": although the White Knight purports to be there to see Alice safely to the next square, Alice spots the ruse immediately. In terms of both narrative and metaphor, it is the Knight not the child who is in need of assistance.

87 *deal box*: box made of fir or pine wood.

my own invention: Lewis Carroll was a keen inventor of all manner of objects, some of which were merchandise associated with *Alice*. His comments on his 'Wonderland Postage-Stamp Case'—designed to hold multiple stamps of differing values and benefiting from what Carroll called 'two Pictorial Surprises' to the cover—can be seen to reflect his playful stance on the practice:

> What made me invent it was the constantly wanting Stamps of other values, for foreign Letters, Parcel Post, &c., and finding it very bothersome to get at the kind I wanted in a hurry. Since I have possessed a 'Wonderland Stamp-Case', life has been bright and peaceful, and I have used no other. I believe the Queen's laundress uses no other. ('Eight or Nine Wise Words about Letter-Writing' (Oxford: Emberlin and Son, 1890), 6–7)

Other inventions included a device called a nyctograph and an associated substitution cipher, which allowed him to capture notes on waking at night without the bother of rising from his bed to light a candle, a large quantity of games and word puzzles, and various means of measurement. Much like the White Knight, his inventions were largely of limited note, excepting—of course—for that of the Wonderland and Looking-Glass worlds themselves.

88 *We'd better take it . . . plum-cake*: Gillian Beer notes that the White Knight's decision to take the empty dish encapsulates his belief that 'Receptacle precedes principal' (*Alice in Space* (Chicago: Chicago University Press, 2016), 114). The White Knight is no risk-taker, and seizes every opportunity he can to act prophylactically, regardless of the likeliness of the event, possessing such items as a mousetrap for his horse's back and anti-shark anklets for its legs. Carroll here appears to lightly admonish himself in his desire to guard against the inevitable (i.e. the onset of time) through the possession of objects that protect him only from the most dubious and far-fetched events.

89 *not a good rider*: this should not particularly surprise Alice, for she has observed in Chapter I that the knight 'balances very badly' when sliding down the poker. Alice Liddell refers to her own bad fall from a pony in her recollections of Lewis Carroll (*LCIR*, 84).

Otherwise he kept on pretty well: a playful contradiction—if he falls whenever the horse stops, and again whenever it starts, he is not able to stay on at all. Carroll allows this inconsistency to exist without comment.

[illustration]: Tenniel provides a substantial number of visual interpretations of the White Knight, with four in-chapter illustrations plus one that became the frontispiece (see note to frontispiece). This image—capturing the knight as he is about to tumble over his horse's head—offers the most detail, beside that which prefaces the book, as to the knight's features and vast array of belongings. As discussed above, the horse is loaded with

objects which assimilate events from across the *Looking-Glass* narrative in a manner which Janis Lull notes makes the White Knight 'a sort of propertymaster, whose furniture both recapitulates what has gone before and anticipates what will come' (Lull, 'The Appliances of Art: The Carroll-Tenniel Collaboration in *Through the Looking-Glass*', *Lewis Carroll: A Celebration*, ed. E. Guiliano (New York: Clarkson N. Potter, 1982), 101–11, at 110). The whole chapter, in fact, can be read as a melting pot of references to the entirety of the story, all roads as it were leading to Alice's encounter with the White Knight, which Tenniel renders carefully in his visualization. Yet Tenniel's vision of the White Knight differed aesthetically to that of Carroll's; Collingwood recalls that Carroll instructed Tenniel that 'The White Knight must not have whiskers; he must not be made to look old' (*LLLC*, 111), yet the final version retains the trappings of age (albeit with a heavy moustache and noticeable bald patch rather than whiskers, see note to p. 17). Given the overall thrust of the chapter, and indeed the spirit of the opening poem, Carroll's resistance to the White Knight appearing old is rather incongruent, excepting of course that Carroll himself was only 39 at the time of publication. That the final image of the White Knight does not visually recall Lewis Carroll has led several critics to conclude that, just as Carroll styled the textual White Knight as a self-portrait, so too did Tenniel make the visual version in his own image. There is a pleasing doubleness, or mirror image, to the idea that both of Alice's creators—author and illustrator alike—drew themselves in the portraiture of the White Knight. Other candidates for models for the White Knight have also been put forward—Michael Hancher discusses, for example, the suggestion that Tenniel's friend and colleague, Horace 'Ponny' Mayhew, might have been the model in mind (*TIAB*, 87–92).

90 *"Does that kind go smoothly?"*: Alice's playful suggestion that the White Knight choose a wooden horse rather than a live one plays comically with the idea of the inert chess horse. That both knights continually topple from their mounts is a droll allusion to the jerky L-shaped movement of their pieces. Her suggestion that he ride a toy horse more appropriate to the nursery than battlefield further emasculates a knight whose cavalry attire includes bunches of carrots and an umbrella.

91 *sugar-loaf*: block of refined sugar moulded in the shape of a cone, common until the end of the nineteenth century.

92 *[illustration]*: Michael Hancher notes that this image is one of several illustrations 'shown to best advantage in [its] original setting', for the 'immediately relevant passage of text is strategically placed as a caption' (*TIAB*, 267). Tenniel's decision to depict the White Knight upturned in the ditch visually emphasizes his contradictory chivalric role. It is Alice who here must rescue the knight, any pretension as to hierarchy undone by the sheer farce of the armoured legs and feet sticking up from the ground. It is rather ironic, given their reversed roles, that a pair of disembodied legs disappearing into the earth (albeit generally clad in stripes) has come to be synonymous with Alice herself—a universal signifier for

her original tumble into Wonderland via the rabbit hole. Note that the knight's horse is not an especially loyal mount. Many romantic visualizations of the horses of chivalric knights show them forlornly gazing at their fallen rider; that Tenniel has the horse quietly cropping grass and entirely unperturbed lampoons the chivalric mode still further. Interestingly, when mounted, the horse is visually depicted as highly capable and well trained (despite the incompetence of the rider). The frontispiece image has the grey elegantly perform a passage movement (an elevated, powerful trot), with a well-developed top-line and rounded neck (albeit somewhat overbent). The knight, by contrast, sits awkwardly with uneven weight and hands too high.

93 *"Is it very long?"*: a continuation of Alice's increasing resistance to being forced to listen to poetry (see note to p. 43).

The name of the song... what it's called, you know!: an extended jest on metalanguage through differentiating what something is 'named', 'called', or really 'is'. As Peter Heath has it: 'Since anything can be given a name, including a name itself, and since the name of a thing is not necessarily the same as what it is called, the White Knight has a perfect right to the distinctions here enumerated, though it is not obvious what reasons he has for making them' (*PA*, 218). The answer seems likely to be simply Carroll's own delight in playing with the meaning of names and naming, and sense as to the arbitrariness of signifiers, as shown throughout *Looking-Glass*. For a detailed unpacking of what Roger W. Holmes calls this 'most complex discussion of the function of words' in the 'Alice' books, see his 'The Philosopher's *Alice in Wonderland*', *Antioch Review*, 19 (1959), 133–49, at 137).

94 *Of all the strange things... melancholy music of the song*: entirely out of keeping with the rest of the story (although akin to the prefatory *Looking-Glass* poem and the conclusion of *Wonderland*), Carroll initiates a jarring shift in tone in this paragraph so as to have Alice memorialize the moment in memory, capturing it 'like a picture' in a particularly sentimental episode. Carroll is generally light on visual description, but here he draws out details that are meant to encode the scene with a sense of nostalgia and loss. The White Knight's features—mild blue eyes and kindly smile—recall descriptions of Carroll made by child friends (see, for example, Isa Bowman's recollections in *LCIR*, 90). The whole scene assumes an air of poignant romance, with Alice herself unusually willing to linger and assume a passive, reflective stance as she merely watches and listens. It is curious that Tenniel chose not to picture the scene quite as Carroll imagined it. The closest illustration is that of the frontispiece as the Knight departs—the shadows of the forest throwing him into relief—but it lacks that dazzling sense of Carroll's description. Alice neither shields her eyes nor leans upon a tree, and the idyllic reference to the horse quietly cropping grass is cut and repurposed in an earlier image (see note to p. 92). The scene is as fleeting as it is strange, and the very next lines (even before the song itself has been sung) shatter the illusion by introducing a bitter

edge of resentment onto the picturesque scene as the author struggles to reconcile the variety of emotions entangled in this final parting.

'I give thee all, I can no more': the opening line of Thomas Moore's 'My Heart and Lute' which was set to music by Sir Henry Rowley Bishop. Alice's quick observation that the White Knight had not invented the tune is a jarring return to her usual impatience and tendency to critique.

no tears came into her eyes: Alice's lack of emotion at the impending parting conflicts with the overt sentimentality of the preceding description. Carroll here both highlights and mocks his own fears and self-pity in a rather exposing expression of vulnerability.

I'll tell thee everything I can: like 'Jabberwocky', the White Knight's song is an extension and revision of an earlier poem by Carroll, in this case 'Upon the Lonely Moor' which he published anonymously in *The Train* in 1856. Both versions are parodies of Wordsworth's lyric poem 'Resolution and Independence' (1807), which describes the narrator's meeting with an elderly leech-collector and muses on ageing, moving from idyllic imagery to melancholia in a manner not dissimilar to Carroll's own. Writing to his uncle, Hassard Dodgson, in May 1872, Carroll explained his rationale for parodying the poem in *Looking-Glass*:

> 'Sitting on a Gate' *is* a parody, though not as to style or metre—but its plot is borrowed from Wordsworth's 'Resolution and Independence,' a poem that has always amused me a good deal (although it is by no means a comic poem) by the absurd way in which the poet goes on questioning the poor old leech-gatherer, making him tell his history over and over again, and never attending to what he says. Wordsworth ends with a moral—an example I have *not* followed. (*Letters*, i. 177)

Although not loaded with the sentimentalism of a moral turn, the entire of the White Knight's chapter centres on navigating issues of resolution and independence (as Carroll resolves to adjust to Alice's shift into the independence of adulthood) in a manner less comic and far more romantic (in the Wordsworthian sense) than Carroll here implies. As U. C. Knoepflmacher observes: 'It is hardly coincidental that Carroll should invoke Wordsworth just before Alice moves onward to the eighth square. The Knight vainly tries to detain the resolute girl; she, in turn, just as vainly, expects to find her progression to be crowned by power and maturity' ('Revisiting Wordsworth: Lewis Carroll's "The White Knight's Song"', in L. M. Shires (ed.), *Victorians Reading the Romantics* (Columbus, OH: Ohio University Press, 2016), 144–61, at 145).

aged aged man: according to Carroll's Dramatis Personæ, the 'Aged man' is a white bishop in the game. Such explains how the White Knight might encounter him, as they commence play in adjacent squares.

mountain-rill: shallow and narrow channel in the earth, here on a mountainside.

Rowland's Macassar Oil: a hair oil, produced by London barber Alexander Rowland from the late eighteenth century but popular into the early 1900s.

95 *I shook him well*: the speaker's violent shaking of the Aged man predicts that of Alice with the Red Queen/black kitten on waking from her dream.

[illustration]: Tenniel's image makes it clear that the narrator of the poem is the White Knight himself. Several critics have suggested that Carroll saw himself in the Aged man, a projection of his future that recalls the musing of the Wordsworth poem he parodies. He referred to himself as the Aged Aged Man some years later, when he was 58 (abbreviated to A.A.M.; see M. Bakewell, *Lewis Carroll: A Biography* (London: Heinemann, 1996), 287). As noted above, Carroll was keen that the White Knight illustration should not make him appear old, no doubt so that he might contrast with the more aged projection. The illustration of the Aged man is noticeably indistinct. His face is mostly hidden by the White Knight's arm, but there are subtle hints of connection to the Knight; his shaggy hair sticks out in mirror image and his precarious position balanced upon a gate recalls the White Knight's earlier discussion of his invention for a new way of getting over a gate. While the Aged man's attire is clearly visualized as a rural counterpart to the White Knight's courtly armour, both Tenniel and Carroll have laden the Knight elsewhere with obvious connections to nature, from his invention of a rustic wooden box that can function as a beehive through to the loading of bunches of carrots on to his saddle.

set limed twigs for crabs: a nonsense inversion of the practice of smearing a sticky substance on to twigs so as to catch birds.

96 *Hansom-cabs*: two-wheeled, covered horse-drawn carriages, patented in 1834 and used as taxicabs during the Victorian era.

Menai bridge: a suspension bridge completed in 1836. It was designed by Thomas Telford and connects the island of Anglesey with mainland Wales.

97 *But you'll stay . . . you see*: the White Knight's offer to support Alice is here refracted back, as he seeks her encouragement and romantically envisions her as a medieval maiden waving her handkerchief as a token of her favour. The parody continues Carroll's self-mockery.

you didn't cry so much: Alice has not cried at all. The comment is a further Carrollian jest, with a hint of resentment, at Alice's differing response to their parting.

he reached the turn . . . out of sight: the White Knight moves to King's Bishop's fifth square. The turn Carroll mentions refers to the L-shape of the Knight's movement.

edge of the brook: the Wasp in the Wig episode was excised at this point, on Tenniel's recommendation, for he could not 'see [his] way to a picture' (see Introduction, pp. xiii–xiv). Galley-proofs indicate that rather than concluding with a full stop, the word 'brook' would have been followed by a comma and the phrase 'and she was just going to spring over, when she heard a deep sigh, which seemed to come from the wood behind her'. The interlude with the Wasp—styled, in keeping with the broader interests of the chapter, as a sulky, peevish elderly gentleman—is one which several critics have observed shows Alice in rather a better light than much of the rest of the narrative. As Martin Gardner has it, 'there is no episode in the book in which she treats a disagreeable creature with such remarkable patience' (*AA*, 302). While such kindness, perhaps, might befit one about to rise to the ranks of royalty, it would also have extended the already lengthiest chapter. The narrative reads all the better for the crossing into adulthood occurring without any further delay and directly after the poignant separation of Alice from her authorial White Knight.

she bounded across: Alice moves into the eighth square. Carroll recalls it in his list of moves as 'coronation'.

a tone of dismay: this is the first border crossing that Alice has made of her own accord, without impetus from a disturbing exterior force (see note to p. 83). Yet her final arrival at her destination is nevertheless marked with 'dismay'. In suddenly reaching the threshold of adult power, Alice becomes immediately troubled and apprehensive.

98 *[illustration]*: mimicking Carroll's 'tone of dismay', Tenniel renders Alice as somewhat uneasy at this point of transition: she grips the tight, cumbersome crown, her eyes wide in surprise. Tenniel also chooses to adapt Alice's dress for the occasion; although it will become clearer in subsequent illustrations, it can already be seen that the collared neck of Alice's dress has been replaced with three strands of beads and an elaborate waistband has been added to a flounced overskirt. Carroll himself makes no reference to any such changes in attire, beyond the acquisition of the crown. Tenniel's visualization of the crown is distinctly that of a chess piece, styled exactly as for the White Queen (the Red Queen's coronet benefits from inlayed jewels not afforded to the White).

99 *Queens have to be dignified*: Alice's experience of both *Looking-Glass* and *Wonderland* Queens to date rather belies this expectation.

one on each side: the Red Queen has moved to the King's first square, so that Alice is now flanked by Queens (the White Queen being in Queen's Bishop's eighth). The Red Queen thus puts the White King in check, although no one appears to notice.

proper examination: Hugh Haughton suggests that the Red Queen's desire to submit Alice to examination may be a comment on the education of women. He notes that the 'first college for women, significantly called Queen's College, was founded in 1848' (Penguin, 352). In 1896, Carroll wrote in opposition to the notion of admitting female students to Oxford, suggesting instead that there should be a charter for a Women's University, a ' "New Oxford" ' from which eventually 'Women-Lecturers and Women-Professors would arise, fully as good as any that the older Universities have ever produced' (*CWLC*, 1070).

100 *lessons in manners*: Carroll's sense that the Red Queen is styled as a governess remerges (see note to p. 26).

Substraction: this spelling, which occurs twice, is sometimes perceived by editors as an error and corrected. The slip, however, is intentional—it serves as a mispronunciation that underscores the confused and bumbling nature of the White Queen (the Red Queen, by contrast, pronounces it correctly). The *OED* also has substraction as a rare expression for 'the withdrawal or withholding of something beneficial or useful, to which another person is entitled'. As the white pieces of *Looking-Glass* are generally more courteous than the red, that both White Queen and Alice fail at substraction is in keeping with their natures.

101–106 [*illustrations*]: Tenniel's three illustrations of Alice as queen in this chapter can be read as something of a series; they mark her ascent to royalty by signalling a shift from anxiety to autocracy. In the first illustration, Tenniel has Alice appear humbled by the presence of two powerful sovereigns who press in on her with unrelenting questions—her feet are pushed together, her body hunched, and her eyes are cast downwards in a manner that conveys uncertainty. By the second image, Alice begins to show a shift in status; there is still anxiety in her brow and askance glance, but she is now elevated above the snoozing Queens who lull beside her, and she clasps her sceptre with more conviction. These first two images are quite obviously paired for comparison; in addition to their compositional similarities, in the first edition they are both positioned on the verso or left-hand page, five spreads apart, roughly centred and of equal size. The third image, however, is quite different; it is larger in size, appears on the recto or right-hand page, and depicts Alice's new-found assurance in her role as sovereign at the moment in which she spies her rule writ large above the doorway. Alice now wields her sceptre high, stands upright and assured in a position meant to convey her sense of dignity, and sports a scornful expression directed at the lowly, rustic subject of the frog. Tenniel is careful across these images to depict the subtleties of her physical ascent and attitudinal shift, as Alice navigates the transition she has so long sought. In an earlier version of the illustrations, Tenniel also had Alice more directly connected to the other Queens through the manner of her dress; preparatory drawings of Alice for this chapter show her with a skirt far more akin in design to those of the other chess royals, with 'the general shape of the carved skirts worn by the Red Queen and the White Queen, though [. . .] more obviously made of soft fabric, real clothing for a real person' (*TIAB*, 135). Critics generally agree that Carroll's known dislike of crinoline necessitated that the images be redrawn for the sanctioned version. The final image is also notable for its detailed background, relatively uncommon in Tenniel's *Looking-Glass* illustrations, which depicts a Romanesque doorway that Hancher argues is 'virtually the same door' as one used for a *Punch* illustration from 1st July 1853 and demonstrates 'how nearly equivalent *Punch* and *Alice* were for Tenniel' (*TIAB*, 31).

101 *its temper would remain!*: compare to *Wonderland*, where it is the Cheshire Cat's grin which remains 'after the rest of it had gone' (*CWLC*, 67).

102 *"Can you answer useful questions?"*: Peter Hunt notes that the Red Queen's questioning of Alice serves as 'a parody of the "instructive" question-and-answer sessions often introduced into nineteenth-century children's novels'

(OWC, 294). Charles Kingsley's fantasy *The Water-Babies* includes a particularly lengthy interlude of mock-authorial questioning of an implied child reader, although it is more earnest in interest than Carroll's. Fanny Ward's *The Child's Guide to Knowledge* (1825) is an example of the sort of dull, instructional narrative Carroll here lampoons.

fiddle-de-dee: meaning 'nonsense' when used as an interjection, and 'an absurdity' when used as a noun (*OED*).

"It's too late to correct it": in chess, once a move is made, it cannot be undone or corrected.

103 *rich . . . clever*: note that the Red Queen positions rich and clever as opposites, like warm and cold.

a riddle with no answer!: recalls the Hatter's Riddle of *Wonderland*. Carroll later provided an answer, in the preface to the 1897 edition, but confessed that it was 'merely an afterthought: the Riddle, as originally invented, had no answer at all'.

"he wanted to punish the fish, because——": that Alice's sentence is incomplete recalls the end of Humpty Dumpty's song, which ends with '*I tried to turn the handle, but——*'

I couldn't remember my own name. . . poor Queen's feelings: the White Queen's terror seems to have caused her to forget that her memory works both ways. Peter Heath points out that Alice is rather insensitive here, given her own fears about losing her name and identity (*PA*, 239). That she does not verbally articulate her utilitarian stance on names does show a degree of character growth.

Your Majesty: the Red Queen's magisterial address to Alice signals that she has become a queen, according to Carroll's opening list of moves. It is intriguing that Carroll chose to separate as two moves Alice's 'coronation' (occurring when she crosses the brook into the eighth square and receives a crown) from her becoming a queen. From the point of view of the game, the White Pawn ceases to be a pawn on arrival in the eighth square, although a player cannot exercise the new-found power of the piece until his or her next move.

104 *putting her hair in papers*: the practice of rolling hair around papers and pinning so as to promote curling.

Hush-a-by lady, in Alice's lap!: a parody of the famous nursery rhyme 'Rock-a-bye-Baby', which first appeared in printed form in *Mother Goose's Melody* (*c.*1765). Its use to lull the Red and White Queens to sleep is rather infantilizing, in the context of Alice's sense that queens must be dignified.

105 *History of England*: Alice assumes some of the pomp of Humpty Dumpty now she has become queen and makes a similar reference (see note to p. 65).

suddenly vanished: the Queens have 'castled'; in a normal chess game, this move would only be possible for a king, but as Carroll later explained in the preface to the 1897 edition, castling here 'is merely a way of saying that [the Queens] entered the palace'.

105 *which bell must I ring?*: Alice's confusion misses the point—the joke here is that there are multiple bells for a single entrance. Carroll exposes and conflates social stratification by reducing the separate entrances of visitors and servants to one threshold but gives them separate bells. Alice wants to add a further layer to this social hierarchy, with a bell marked 'Queen' (note singular), so that her regal status might be recognized as distinctive.

"No admittance till the week after next!": another reference to the White Queen's multidirectional memory, for she explains in Chapter V that she is best equipped to remember things that happen the week after next.

a very old Frog: Alice had previously encountered a frog on a doorstep in *Wonderland*, although the *Looking-Glass* version is decidedly more rustic. The Frog functions as a white pawn in the game.

106 *Wexes it*: vexes it. Carroll has the Frog speak in a cockney accent, pronouncing the V as a W. A cockney is a Londoner, 'esp. a working-class person from the East End; . . . (traditionally) a person born within earshot of the sound of Bow Bells (the bells of Mary-le-Bow church in Cheapside in the City of London) (*OED*).

"To the Looking-Glass world it was Alice that said": a parody of Sir Walter Scott's Bonnie Dundee from his play *The Doom of Devorgoil* (1830). Hugh Haughton notes that 'the echo of Scott's poem conjures up an earlier fight for the crown in "The History of English"' and thus connects to the 'old song' of the Lion and the Unicorn and battling Tweedles (Penguin, 353). Note that the 'shrill voice' sings verses that imply Alice herself has issued the invitation to the Looking-Glass creatures, echoing her sense earlier in the chapter that she 'ought to invite the guests'.

107 *mice in the tea*: recalls the dormouse of *Wonderland*, which the Hatter and March Hare try to put into a teapot.

in she went: Alice's entry into the palace corresponds with the 'Alice castles (*feast*)' move Carroll includes in his initial list of moves.

"I'm glad . . . right people to invite": Peter Heath wryly notes that Alice presents a 'naively egocentric view of the habits and functions of royalty' in this moment: 'If Alice supposes that such personages ever have the remotest idea of who most of the guests at a state banquet are, she certainly has much to learn about her station and its duties' (*PA*, 233).

[illustration]: Tenniel's rendering of the Mutton's graceful bow makes uncomfortable viewing, despite its comedic form—a demonstration of Tenniel's skill in grotesque. Like Humpty Dumpty, the joint's human facial features dominate its form, while the addition of comparatively undersized legs and arms (which appear clothed) create a disturbing connection to the human within the context of an animalized frame. Both beings are, of course, talking foodstuffs who resist Alice's right to claim any sense of dominion—a claim that reaches its apogee in the human consumption of other animals (note that, in *Wonderland*, Alice engages in a lengthy debate with a pigeon on her right to eat eggs). By virtue of it

being a joint, Tenniel is here depicting a dead animal brought back to life at the moment it is due to be consumed. The awkward affixing of human features to its meaty form makes for a disturbing juxtaposition, as does the combination of its genteel bow whilst stood upon a serving platter. Carroll, of course, does not allow Alice so much as a bite.

108 *it isn't etiquette to cut anyone you've been introduced to*: Martin Gardner notes that 'to cut' implies to ignore someone you know, arguing that 'No Victorian reader would miss the pun' (*AA*, 276).

as an experiment. . . cut a slice out of you, you creature!: Alice's entire exchange with the Mutton joint, and in particular her 'experiment' in slicing him, is a comment on vivisection practices. In 1875 Carroll wrote on the subject in *Some Popular Fallacies about Vivisection*, drawing connections between human and animal life through linguistic play on contemporary ideas about evolution:

> O my brother-man, you who claim for yourself and for me so proud an ancestry—tracing our pedigree through the anthropomorphoid ape up to the primeval zoöphyte—what potent charm have *you* in store to win exemption from the common doom? (*CWLC*, 1081)

Those willing to inflict pain of animals, Carroll quite simply argues, might easily do so to humans. His rhetorical appeal here resonates strongly with that of the Mutton, who also places emphasis upon the word '*you*' and makes a call for kinship by terming Alice a 'creature'. Although Alice may have ascended to the top of all human–appointed hierarchies by becoming queen, Carroll continues to deny her sovereignty over animal bodies.

109 *every poem was about fishes in some way*: certainly a strange and unexplained connection. 'The Walrus and the Carpenter' is about oysters, Humpty Dumpty's poem concerns fish, and the name of the White Knight's song is called 'Haddocks' Eyes'. Neither the 'Jabberwocky' poem, nor either of the old songs played out by the Tweedles or the Lion and the Unicorn involve fish, but these are also not 'repeated' to Alice (rather she recalls them herself).

Un-dish-cover the fish, or dishcover the riddle?: Peter Heath argues that this is 'the most deplorable pun in the entire book' (*PA*, 234). The answer is, appropriately, 'an oyster'. Alice, although encouraged to guess, never answers.

extinguishers: conical in shape and used to snuff the flame of a candle.

110 *disappeared into the soup*: the White Queen moves to Queen's Rook's Sixth.

111 *[illustration]*: Tenniel here impressively captures the sense of pandemonium which finally leads Alice to break the dream frame. The illustration is L-shaped so as to wrap the text of the first edition, which serves as a caption, as Alice seizes at the tablecloth and declares she can no longer stand the disorder of the Looking-Glass world. Tenniel makes the image an overwhelming visual assault, as bottle-birds (which look like chess pawns) assume composite forms and take flight, candles shoot wildly into the air, and a hazy rabble of vaguely sketched guests hustle and tumble in all

directions (including the previously non-pictured suety pudding, which can be seen—feet aloft—in the bottom left-hand corner). Although the Red Queen had previously demanded that both Mutton and Pudding be removed, Tenniel has them return for the final crescendo. Alice herself, shown only from behind and stiff in form, looks more like a chess piece than in any other illustration.

111 *"I can't stand this any longer!"*: Alice's exasperated declaration echoes her exit from *Wonderland*, with a cry of 'You're nothing but a pack of cards!' As with the disillusion of the banquet, her courtroom declaration results in uproar, as 'the whole pack rose up in the air, and came flying down upon her' (*CWLC*, 117).

cause of all the mischief: note that Alice's assessment here echoes the opening of the book, where we are told it was 'the black kitten's fault entirely'.

112 *merrily running round and round after her own shawl*: in keeping with Alice's move, which will see the Red Queen taken, Carroll has the Red Queen's power loss represented by both physical diminishment and through aligning her with the behaviours of the infantilized White Queen, who spent much of Chapter V chasing her shawl. Of course, he also foreshadows her transformation into a kitten, by having the shawl serve as a tail.

113–114 *[illustrations]*: Tenniel's dual illustrations are separated in the first edition by a single leaf, appearing on the recto and verso of their respective pages, so that the transformation from Queen to kitten occurs quite spectacularly as the reader turns the page. Tenniel succeeds in capturing the infantilization Carroll describes, as the Red Queen's eyes grow larger and she appears physically reduced, while the position of her arms, legs, and shawl offer a perfect 'dissolving' effect between the two images. Note that Alice's hands, firmly gripping the Red Queen throughout her metamorphosis, provide a sense of scale.

113 *She took her off the table*: Alice quite literally takes the Red Queen piece. Her move results in a checkmate of the (still sleeping) Red King. Alice thus wins the game.

114 *and it really was a kitten, after all*: an emphatic and jarring return to the right side of the glass and an intriguing textual decision, with Carroll making a single (incomplete) sentence function as an entire chapter.

115 *addressing the kitten*: in keeping with the fact that she is just waking up, Carroll has Alice's speech in this moment charmingly muddled, as she confuses the black kitten with her 'Red Majesty' and addresses it both respectfully (as she generally attempted with the Queens) and with severity (as with her scolding approach to her kittens in the opening chapter).

the kitten only purred: having spent time surrounded by creatures who speak and respond in her own language, Alice's return to real-world negotiations with animals are marked by her Cartesian sense that they fail to reply and are impossible to understand. Alice's swift acceptance of the hierarchies of being promoted by humanism is the most disappointing element of her return to reality.

116 *[illustration]*: in Tenniel's final illustration to *Looking-Glass*, the return to the domestic is clear—the story ends where it began. It is the only illustration to include an obviously inert chess piece, all sense of fantastical life evaporated as Alice seeks a return to order. There is little by way of hint in the image as to any change to Alice as a result of her passage through the glass, although her expression—far from reflecting the merry laugh of Carroll's text—retains the rather haughty air Tenniel gave her on entering the palace.

I'll repeat 'The Walrus and the Carpenter' to you: Alice seems to have overcome her earlier struggles with the ethics of this poem, encouraging her kitten to act in the gluttonous manner of its protagonists.

117 *Which do* you *think it was?*: in a rare direct address, Carroll here hands the close of the story—and this 'serious question'—over to the implied child reader. In his redirection of what becomes the book's central question, we see a glimpse of Carroll's erstwhile commitment to valuing a child's-eye view and his genuine care for the perspectives of children.

118 *A boat, beneath a sunny sky*: Carroll's closing acrostic verse firmly dedicates the narrative to his child muse, Alice Pleasance Liddell, with the initial letter of each line spelling out her name. He recalls in a diary entry for 13 March 1863 an attempt to produce a poem 'in which I mean to embody something about Alice' (*LCD*, iv. 173–4), although it is not until the publication of *Looking-Glass* that he realized something of that desire. In content, however, the poem shifts from the particularity of his relationship with Alice, and the pain of its loss, through to recognition that her adventures in *Wonderland* and through the *Looking-Glass* retain the power to delight and entertain the many children yet to hear them. The poem, whilst emotive and personal, also speaks to the memorializing power of the page. As such, the verse is more hopeful and accepting than its prefatory partner, although still bearing hints of that same melancholia, as images of death, cold, and ghostly visions of the past compete with those of life, warmth, and futurity. With its opening reference to a rowing trip, and concluding reflection on the dream-like qualities of life, many critics have suggested that Carroll shapes his final poem to echo the light-hearted nursery lyrics of 'Row, row row your boat | Gently down the stream, | Merrily, merrily, merrily, merrily, | Life is but a dream.'

In an evening of July: Carroll here specifically ties the memory to the 4 July 1862 rowing trip (see note to p. 6) and links this poem with that which opens *Wonderland*. In that verse, however, Carroll refers to the 'golden afternoon' whereas the tone of this final poem has moved things on to the dwindling hours of the evening.

Children three: Lorina, Alice, and Edith Liddell, all of whom were present for the rowing trip.

Still she haunts me, phantomwise: an emotive and intense confession, that bears hint of an obsession that would last a lifetime. Hugh Haughton notes that echoes of this haunting can be found throughout Carroll's diaries and letters, as he struggled in later years to reconcile the real existence of an adult Alice with his memory of a child forever preserved at 7 years old (Penguin, 354–5). Of course, his publication of the *Alice* books has perpetuated that memorializing presence of his child muse.

118 *Alice*: note that this direct reference to Alice's name appears on the eleventh line of the poem—thus at its very centre—in keeping with her central place in Carroll's life.

Eager eye and willing ear: Carroll's future-orientated vision of children still delighting in his stories recalls the conclusion of *Wonderland*, where he prophesied that Alice would as a grown woman 'gather about her other little children, and make *their* eyes bright and eager with many a strange tale, perhaps even with the dream of Wonderland of long ago'.

Life, what is it but a dream? Carroll concludes his final poem with a question, just as he had concluded the narrative itself. There he poses his question directly to child readers; here he implies that it is the dreamy state of childhood itself that provides an answer.

American Literature

British and Irish Literature

Children's Literature

Classics and Ancient Literature

Colonial Literature

Eastern Literature

European Literature

Gothic Literature

History

Medieval Literature

Oxford English Drama

Philosophy

Poetry

Politics

Religion

The Oxford Shakespeare

A complete list of Oxford World's Classics, including Authors in Context, Oxford English Drama, and the Oxford Shakespeare, is available in the UK from the Marketing Services Department, Oxford University Press, Great Clarendon Street, Oxford OX2 6DP, or visit the website at www.oup.com/uk/worldsclassics.

In the USA, visit www.oup.com/us/owc for a complete title list.

Oxford World's Classics are available from all good bookshops. In case of difficulty, customers in the UK should contact Oxford University Press Bookshop, 116 High Street, Oxford OX1 4BR.

ANTHONY TROLLOPE

The American Senator
An Autobiography
Barchester Towers
Can You Forgive Her?
Cousin Henry
Doctor Thorne
The Duke's Children
The Eustace Diamonds
Framley Parsonage
He Knew He Was Right
Lady Anna
The Last Chronicle of Barset
Orley Farm
Phineas Finn
Phineas Redux
The Prime Minister
Rachel Ray
The Small House at Allington
The Warden
The Way We Live Now